THE MAN WHO SHOT THOMAS EDISON

THOMAS EDISON

BY
MARTIN T. INGHAM

www.martinus.us

To my two younger daughters, Kathryn and Lois.
May your lives be truly magical!

The Man Who Shot Thomas Edison

CHAPTER 1:
THE INNOVATORS

The stagecoach was packed. The deluxe carriage wasn't all that spacious, and a dozen passengers with all of their luggage was enough to reach its maximum capacity. It was only about ten miles from the Yucca Junction train station to Selwood, so the ride was tolerable for those determined to make the trip.

Clarence Davison was used to cramped accommodations. The past years had seen him traveling in all sorts of tight spaces. Steamboat cabins, railcar sleeper compartments, and various holes in the wall had been his home on many occasions. Such was the life of a circuit preacher, spreading the good word to the populace.

This latest trip was a break from that hectic life, as he came to see an old friend.

It had been many years since Clarence had seen his mentor, the right and moral pastor, Matthew Jameson, and he was hoping for a warm homecoming. The man was as close to a father as Clarence had in this world, and he hoped to make him proud. Though, that might prove difficult on some fronts. Doctrine was a tricky thing, and biblical interpretations had made many a good man split from friends and family.

Clarence hoped it would not be an issue. There was no

need for his mentor to know he held differing views. So long as he kept his mouth shut and didn't make any rash moves, the old man need never know of his views on magic.

Looking around inside the coach, Clarence examined the faces of his fellow passengers. They were a well-groomed bunch, though they all had the scent of their own humanity upon them. Most of them had been traveling for days, no doubt, and trains weren't noted for their baths. Clarence wouldn't have noticed the smell, had he not spent the night at Yucca Junction's Nexus Hotel, which provided fine cleaning services. A good scrubbing and a freshly laundered suit took away the stink off his own body, and let him sense the scent of others.

However, the sandy-haired fellow sitting beside him wasn't stinking up the place at all, and there was something strangely familiar about him. The stern-faced man didn't seem the kind to crack a smile all that often. He looked about thirty, with smooth hands and a quality suit that identified him as a businessman or educated professional of some sort, which could explain his attention to hygiene.

Clarence let his curiosity get the better of him, and he felt the urge to introduce himself. With a slight adjustment of his body, he managed to present a hand for the other man to shake. The clean-cut man shook the offered appendage silently with a strong grip.

"So, what brings you out to Selwood?" Clarence asked, hoping to get some information out of the silent man.

"Business, and an old friend," the man said.

"What a coincidence. It just so happens I'm traveling to see an old friend, myself," Clarence said.

"Really?" the man said, disinterested.

"Well, more than a friend, actually. The man practically raised me after my father died. It'll be good to be back."

"Not your first trip to Selwood, then," the man mentioned.

"No, I've been here a few times," Clarence replied. "Though, I mostly grew up in Kansas. We didn't move out to Nevada until seventy-six. I only spent a year in Selwood before going back east to college, and haven't been there since."

"College? You wouldn't happen to be wrangling for a job

offer, would you?" the man asked suspiciously.

"No," Clarence said. "Why ever would you think that?"

A mustached man sitting across from Clarence cleared his throat and caught the young man's attention. "Hey, buddy, don't you know who this guy is?"

"No," Clarence said, adding a questioning look to his reply.

"That's Thomas Edison."

The name didn't escape Clarence, though at first he thought it must be some sort of joke. What would one of the world's foremost inventors be doing out here, riding the stagecoach to a town like Selwood? It might be the Nye County Seat, but it was still something of a backwater. Famous folks didn't spend weeks on trains and coaches just for a casual visit.

"It must be some friend you're visiting," Clarence remarked.

"You could say that," Edison said. "You really had no idea who I was?"

"No, Sir," Clarence replied, hiding his embarrassment.

"Then you're the odd sort of fellow who likes to chat-up strangers," Edison said, looking at him funny. "There aren't many types of businesses where that comes as a prerequisite."

"I guess not, but mine does," Clarence mentioned, regaining a carefree expression. "I'm a country preacher, spreading the good word."

Edison stiffened his lips and shook his head. "I'm sorry," he replied.

"For what?" Clarence asked, feeling the man's disdain like a palpable substance drifting through the air.

"Sorry that you've chosen to throw your life away on such nonsense," Edison said, turning his face to the window.

The words slapped Clarence like ice water, and they seemed to have a similar effect on a few of the other passengers. Though none of the others said a word about it, their sour expressions spoke volumes.

"Spreading the truth of God is never a waste," Clarence said, unwilling to let the comment go unchallenged.

Edison sighed and turned his gaze back from the passing

scenery, to study his sudden antagonist. "The days of biblical superstition are nearing an end. No educated man can deny the truth of science."

"You profess that both are equally exclusive, but they're not," Clarence added quickly. "Yes, I am an educated man, and thereby I recognize the truth; science is every bit the creation of God. It is divine will that we seek to further understand His creation through the physical arts, for it serves to bring us closer to Him."

"Nonsense," Edison said unwilling to budge. "How can a rational mind truly believe that a being massive enough to forge this world of ours would in any way resemble our limited human existence, or care about us in the least?"

"You say God doesn't love us?"

"I say that we are less than ants compared to such an entity, and to think *it* cares for us more than that is childish fantasy, at best."

It was not something Clarence had expected to hear, though he'd run into a few such unbelievers over the years. There were always men who thought more of themselves, or less of God, to suit their own beliefs. The philosophies of Marx and Darwin were setting unholy trends within educated circles... but to hear it from someone as bright and progressive as Thomas Edison? It was enough to shake anyone's faith in mankind.

There was no sense arguing any further. A man of Edison's stature was not likely to bend to the brief pontifications of a young preacher. Still, Clarence wasn't going to lay down in defeat. He was a soldier of Christ, and felt called to action.

"I'm sorry," Clarence said.

"For what?" Edison asked.

"That your genius has led you to such an empty existence," Clarence replied.

A few of the spectators in the coach smirked at the slight, as Edison glared over at the young man seated next to him. Clarence maintained a cold, calculating look, feeling this wasn't a time to crack. This was a test, for certain, and one the Lord most certainly wouldn't let him fail.

After studying Clarence's face for a long period of silence,

Edison smiled. He seemed on the verge of laughter, but he never got that far. Eventually, after grinning and fighting back chuckles, he said, "My life is anything but empty. I have a wife and children, a company that is on the cutting edge of societal evolution. I am advancing and improving human civilization unlike anyone else before me, and I really want for nothing. How can that be called empty?"

Clarence ignored the boastful retort and continued to pursue a purchase in the man's soul. "Material wealth is meaningless without spiritual salvation. As it says in Matthew, *'what is a man profited, if he shall gain the whole world, and lose his own soul?'* You can't take it with you."

"That's assuming I'm going anywhere," Edison rebutted. "But, even assuming that wild improbability, what does the hereafter matter now, to those of us who are stuck in the here and now? I see it as a much better thing to improve the lives of the living than concern myself with the affairs of the dead. That is my most prevalent concern, and no amount of preaching will turn me away from the ways of progress."

Following his lecturing reply, Edison relaxed and stared straight ahead, seeming satisfied with himself. The conversation came to an end as abruptly as it had begun, leaving the many passengers of the stagecoach in varying degrees of discomfort and annoyance. When it became apparent that the debate was truly over, the people regained their usual, dispassionate expressions, as they waited to arrive at their destination.

Clarence felt he had done all he could for the man, and didn't regret the exchange. Uncomfortable as it may have been, he knew he'd sowed his seeds this day—if not in Edison, then in the other passengers in the cramped confines. It felt good to witness, in any circumstance.

Despite the heated exchange, Clarence still felt a hint of admiration for Thomas Edison, knowing the man was doing God's work, whether he knew it or not. Truly, the advancement of science and knowledge was the greatest purpose any man could hope to have, and the chosen vessels for such discovery held many faces. Edison was truly a man of innovation, worthy of respect above and beyond his flawed humanity.

* * *

Blood was running down his shirt. It was no surprise. That's what happens when you have a six inch knife stuck into your shoulder and twisted sideways. It didn't hurt much, just a cold sting. The damp shirt was more annoying than the injury itself to the unlikely deputy, Jesse Woodson James.

The drover who'd stabbed Jesse was gawking, shocked to see the man with a badge taking the wound so calmly. From the look on the former outlaw's face, you might think he'd been spit on, rather than stuck three inches above the heart. The surprise was fleeting, morphing into annoyance.

"That was mighty uncivilized of you," Jesse said, drawing his revolver. The unmistakable clicking sound of the hammer cocking echoed inside the still barroom.

The drover put up his hands and stumbled backwards, looking unprepared for the consequences of his actions. His gun remained in the holster at his side, and he knew it was too late to draw. Jesse had him dead to rights.

Jesse felt giddy, both from the blood he was losing and the thrill of having a man at his mercy. He wanted to put a bullet in the idiot, teach him a lesson for daring to be so unpleasant. Killing wasn't just easy for the outlaw-turned-lawman, but entertainment! Yet, fate was making him change his criminal ways, and it wouldn't serve to shoot a defenseless man with his hands in the air.

If he wanted to shoot someone, he'd have to do it right.

Uncocking his gun and putting it back in the holster, Jesse stepped back. "Go ahead and draw," he invited.

The drover shook his head and kept his hands in the air, clearly unwilling to test his nerves in a legitimate gunfight.

"Draw!" Jesse shouted.

The drover lowered his hands and started to shiver, looking eager to run away. His hands didn't reach for the gun as Jesse wanted, which only made things worse.

"Yankee coward!" Jesse shouted, drawing his gun and putting a hole in the floor between the drover's feet. "Draw, damn it!"

"That's enough, James," a commanding voice said.

Jesse turned around and saw the tall figure of Sheriff Doliber walking into the saloon. The long leather coat swayed with each step as the lawman marched over to the shaking drover. With practiced speed, he slapped a set of cuffs on the panicked cattleman and shoved him into a chair.

"Now, what's the story here?" Doliber asked.

"The coward stabbed me, so I offered him a fair fight," Jesse replied.

"Fair's got nothing to do with it," Doliber answered, clearly upset over the deputy's actions. "You know damn well nothing's fair when it comes to you and a gunfight."

"Yes, I am that good," Jesse boasted, looking pleased.

"You know what I mean," Doliber chided. "Even if you get shot, you're already dead, so you can't lose. That shadow body of yours will regenerate in hours, but if your opponent dies, he'll stay dead."

"The fight's fair," Jesse protested. "Since when does it matter how long you'll be dead?"

Another voice answered from the bar counter on the other side of the room. "Since you provoked the man by spitting on his shoes and suggesting he fornicates with his mother."

Jesse looked over at the elvish barkeeper, the prim and proper proprietor with a grin on his slim lips. "Stay outta this, Solen. Don't need your pointy words muddying things up."

Doliber frowned and folded his arms. "Damn it, James, I thought we had an arrangement. You stay out of trouble, and I help you stay out of Hell."

It was then that Jesse felt the effects of blood loss, and his giddiness sent him into delirium. He may have simply been a shadow—a soul trapped within a mystically-contrived body—but it still mimicked the form and limitations of genuine flesh. Lose enough blood, and he would die, if only for a time.

Having leaked more than a normal body could handle, Jesse felt the cold grip of unconsciousness sweeping over him yet again. When he woke up, perhaps he'd feel more interested in having a reasonable conversation.

With his deputy dead on the floor, Doliber dragged the drover onto his feet. "Come along, you," he grumbled.

"Aw, jeez, Sheriff, I'm really sorry about this, but he shouldn't uh talked 'bout my momma like that."

"Tell it to the judge," Doliber said, pushing the man forward.

"But he's gonna wake up, right? I ain't kilt nobody. Why you arrestin' me?"

"You did stab a man, with malicious intent," Doliber said. "Last I looked, that was still a crime in the State of Nevada."

The drover shut up and accepted his fate, glancing down at the limp body of Jesse James as he passed it.

As Doliber reached the door, he heard Solen's nagging voice behind him. "I suppose you expect me to clean up the mess?"

"He'll clean himself up in a few hours," Doliber replied. "If anything else is broken, you can sue this guy for the damages." He concluded by pushing the drover squarely between the shoulders, forcing him to stumble off the narrow porch and out into the street.

Once they were moving, the drover asked, "How'd you get here so fast?"

"Solen called me," Doliber said. "Sheriff's Office is down the street about two blocks."

"Called? You mean he's got one of them new fangled home telegraphophones?"

"Telephone," Doliber corrected. "No, he hasn't, but he does have a mystic call orb. Most of the businesses in Nye County have one, so they can call me in case there's trouble."

"Mystic? Y'all got some magician working for you, too?" the drover asked.

"I'm a journeyman warlock," Doliber clarified.

"Really? That must sure come in handy," the drover remarked.

"Yes," Doliber replied, sick of the conversation. He dealt with enough miscreants on a regular basis that he couldn't count the number of times he'd explained his powers. So many ranch hands and miners had passed through his jail cells over the last two years he was growing sick of it all. It was rarely anything major, just rough men being themselves in most cases, but there was something dissatisfying about policing the populace. He was capable of so much more, if only he had the wherewithal to pursue it.

There was no denying the service he provided for the people of Nye County, and he'd always been satisfied with his profession, knowing he was doing the right thing and bringing order to the west. Yet, now it was losing its appeal. The mundane aspects of the job were only half the problem, as he continued to question his own abilities and limitations.

When it came down to it, he wasn't sure if he was too good for the job, or not good enough.

Walking down the street was a calming luxury for Sheriff Doliber. It would have been a simple thing to teleport his prisoner to the prison, but he wasn't interested in taking such a leap today. He appreciated a decent walk through town, escorting his prisoner on foot, seeing the citizens watching him with looks of admiration and respect—for the most part. Never mind the few miscreants who shot him dirty looks.

The Sheriff's Office was an ordinary-looking building, with a barbershop across the street and a lawyer's house next door. Three short steps led up to the small deck in front of the door, and a quick turn of the knob granted access to the front room.

The office wasn't much to look at, twenty feet on either side, with a weathered desk in the right-hand corner and a gun rack behind that. A set of steps followed the wall to the left, leading to the second story living quarters, and an archway in the center of the back wall led to the jail cells. This humble facility had been Doliber's home for nearly two years, and it could be his for another two, at least, so long as he didn't decide to leave it.

Pushing his prisoner forward, Doliber caught the attention of the deputy currently occupying the desk. The attractive lady elf was a most unlikely upholder of the law, even more absurd than having a dead outlaw on the job. She had come as a package deal some time ago with a gunslinging dwarf who served as the sheriff's right-hand man.

Doliber had to admit, Joella Talus had proven herself to be as capable as any man, and she was a sight prettier to look at.

"What have you got?" Joella asked, standing up and stretching. She'd been sitting in that seat for hours, and felt her limbs stiffening up.

"Somebody who doesn't know how to take an insult," Doliber said, escorting the man to the nearest cell beyond the archway. After opening the barred door, he unlocked the cuffs and tossed the man into prison without ceremony. A quick mystic trick locked the cell, and he walked out into the office to see his lady deputy.

"Solen wasn't overreacting, then?" Joella added, moving out from behind the desk to give Doliber access to his regular seat.

"No," Doliber said, sitting down and reaching for a box of cigars. He stopped himself before opening the lid, remembering that he was trying to quit. "Jesse goaded the guy into a fight, got himself stabbed pretty bad."

"You knew he'd be trouble," Joella said, finding another chair. The seat in front of the desk wasn't as comfortable, but it served its purpose.

"I know, but it's not like I had a choice," Doliber said, tapping his fingers on the desk, nervously fighting his craving for tobacco. "I needed his help at the time."

"And you feel responsible for him now," Joella added with a smile. "That's admirable. Don't doubt it."

Doliber stared at her and studied the neutral expression on her face. A month back, she'd saved his life in a harrowing act of heroism, and shortly thereafter confessed a growing attraction. Well, not so much confessed as planted a kiss on his lips and walked off in silence. They hadn't spoken about it since, though recently she'd been working on him. Her desires were clear enough, though restrained.

"So, where's Ron?" Doliber asked, realizing his dwarven deputy had disappeared during his short absence from the office.

"He headed down to Carter's livery stable," Joella replied. "Albert Silcox just rode into town."

* * *

Ron wasn't the sort to jump when rich men called. The idea that any man was superior to him because of their monetary means was an insult, something that his country upbringing would not allow. As far as he was concerned, he was the match of any other American in rights and privileges, no matter his alleged social status. Money was just an object, handy to have but in no way indicative of a man's character. Having worked a wide assortment of jobs with a diverse cross-section of citizens over the years, he was not one who was easily impressed.

Albert Silcox was an exception at this point, being someone that Ron could respect despite his wealth. Silcox was a crafty businessman who owned a huge spread up on the Yucca Flat, a ranching enterprise made possible by magically engineered cattle and other ecological mysticism. Recently, he'd grown a keen fascination with Ron, and that left Ron more than a bit prideful, though also a tad suspicious of the man's motives.

Carter's Livery was one of three commercial stables in town, and it was certainly the largest. Owned by one of Selwood's founding families, the place was run at a substantial profit, and there were always offers to buy the place from different cattlemen. The teenage brothers who worked the place would have gladly sold it, if not for their invalid mother who held the deed, and the nagging little sisters who wanted their share when they grew up. Therefore, the place remained a goldmine for all the heirs of Virgil Carter, rather than a quick payday for the sons.

Stepping over a clump of horse droppings, Ron approached the burly man in front of the first stall. "I'm looking for Albert Silcox," Ron said to the man's back. "Got word he was down here asking for me."

The fellow turned around and glared down at the dwarf. The large fellow was young, and had a pale, brown mustache that failed to give his face distinction. Anyone in town could identify the guy as Elwood, oldest son of the family. He was barely seventeen, but many a working man was well into adulthood at that age in the west.

Hooking a thumb to the side and making a peculiar snickering sound with his mouth, Elwood told Ron all he needed to know, and then went back to fiddling with the horse.

Ron continued down into the stable, seeing occupied

stalls all along the left side. The multitude of horses was a common sight, and they were very much the life of modern America. Without a decent horse, a man couldn't get very far on his own. That might be all well and good for some city dweller, or for those who rode the rails, but every regular working man needed a ride. A healthy steed and a good rifle were prerequisites to life, as far as Ron was concerned.

At the back of the stable sat a large, black carriage with a broken wheel. A couple of men were in the process of jacking the vehicle up to fix the damage as Ron approached, but they didn't pay him any mind. He repaid the favor and kept his eyes peeled for Albert Silcox. He finally spotted him by the rear stall, tending to his pair of trotters.

"Ah, Deputy Grimes, good to see you again," Silcox greeted as Ron neared.

"Likewise," Ron said politely, reaching up to shake the old man's hand. "What can I do for you?"

"What, I can't just say hello to a friend?" Silcox asked.

Ron didn't say anything, feeling it best to keep silent. He didn't really consider himself a *friend* of Silcox, though it wasn't polite to say otherwise. The old man had taken a shine to Ron, and that commanded a modicum of manners in return.

"All right, you caught me," Silcox said, sounding happy. "I *do* have an ulterior motive in mind."

"You're not here to strong arm me into the sheriff's job again, are you?" Ron asked. "Doliber hasn't resigned, and I don't expect him to."

"Oh, no, this is nothing of the sort," Silcox replied. "I have some important business dealings to handle at the moment, and I was hoping you would be so kind as to entertain my granddaughter for a few hours. I trust the sheriff can live without you at the moment?"

It wasn't the sort of assignment Ron was used to receiving, but it seemed harmless enough. What would it take to keep this granddaughter occupied? That would all depend on her age and temperament, of course. Either way, the task seemed harmless enough, so Ron accepted.

With Ron's agreement, Silcox walked over to the carriage,

which the men had just put up on blocks. Tapping on the door, the old man beckoned his granddaughter to come out, which surprised Ron. What was she doing in the carriage as it was being jacked up? Hiding?

The door to the carriage swung open, and Silcox reached inside. "Allow me to introduce my oldest granddaughter, Fiora May Silcox," he said, helping the little lady out of the carriage with both hands. As he set her down on the ground, her diminished height was instantly apparent. At first, Ron suspected she was still a child, but as she walked over, he quickly realized the age on her face. This was no little girl, but a young woman two inches shorter than him.

"Fiora, this is Deputy Boron Grimes," Silcox said as the short woman extended a hand for Ron to take.

Caught off guard, Ron cleared his throat and shook Fiora's hand. "Uh, pleasure, ma'am," he said awkwardly.

Fiora smiled at his demeanor.

"I trust you will enjoy yourselves on this fine day," Silcox said, pulling a gold watch out of his pocket to check the time. "Now, if you'll excuse me, I have to meet a man about a herd."

With a spring in his step that defied his many years, Albert Silcox made his way out of the stable, leaving his granddaughter in Ron's capable hands.

Retaining the amused smile, Fiora studied Ron and asked, "So, Deputy Grimes, what ever shall we do together?"

* * *

A small crowd was gathered at the Grayson Stage Company on the northern edge of Selwood. Three coaches were arriving from Yucca Junction, and the welcoming committee was as diverse as the passengers. A few wives were around to greet their husbands, and a number of businessmen were there to shake hands with their traveling colleagues. Besides the people with legitimate reasons for being there, a small enclave of onlookers had shown up to lay eyes on a most noted man of merit.

Thomas Edison stepped out of the stagecoach and avoided eye contact with the pack of greeters. He was getting used to the celebrity, as word of his technological wonders continued to spread. There wasn't a town in America that didn't know his name, and he appreciated the fame. It was good for business.

Meeting the masses wasn't his initial goal on this visit, however. That could wait a few hours. What he really wanted—after stretching his legs—was to find the man who had brought him out west to begin with.

Scanning the crowd, Edison spotted the man he'd come to see. The slim, unassuming fellow with thinning hair and a pair of spectacles raised a hand in greeting as the famed inventor approached.

"Henry!" Edison shouted, shaking hands with Selwood's senior telegraph operator. "Henry Currant, it's been too long."

"I suppose so, Mr. Edison," Henry replied as the handshake ended.

"Is that any way to greet an old friend? Do me the courtesy of calling me by my first name, at least."

"Of course, Thomas," Henry said, feeling a sight intimidated.

"What's the matter?" Edison asked. "Aren't you glad to see me?"

"I suppose," Henry said. "It's been a while, and a lot has changed over the years."

"Things may have changed, but not between us," Edison said, straightening up. "Let's go somewhere more private. We have a lot of catching up to do."

Henry escorted Edison away from the pack and over to the telegraph office a block away. It was pretty quiet there, with only the assistant operator in residence, waiting at the wire.

"So, what brings you to Selwood?" Henry asked, sitting down in a spare seat behind the junior telegrapher. The young man listening at the wire gave him something of a look, clearly bothered by the intrusion—as if a casual conversation might disturb him.

"A few things," Edison replied. "I'm doing something of a tour across the country, showing off a few of my more popular inventions, seeing if I can round up a few new customers. But the reason I'm here, of all places, is you, Henry."

"Me?" Henry asked, sounding pleasantly surprised.

"Yes, a most curious news story came across my desk

about a month ago, about an old coworker of mine who was running for mayor of a prominent Nevada city. I never realized you had it in you."

"Oh, that," Henry said. "No, I'm not really running. Our last mayor died suddenly, and a few folks around town figured I ought to take over, being the respectable sort and all."

"But your name is on the ballot, correct?" Edison said.

"Well, I haven't seen a ballot, so I can't say if they've put it there or not. Either way, I don't expect to win. Like I said, I'm not really running."

"Then don't," Edison suggested. "If you don't want the job, tell these people you have no interest in becoming their figurehead and excuse yourself of any responsibility in the matter."

"It's not that simple," Henry replied, getting sheepish again. "It's not that I wouldn't like to be mayor. I just haven't decided if I want to waste my time on a race I'll probably lose anyway."

"You were never one to take chances," Edison added.

"And you were never satisfied unless you were working on some grand design," Henry said. "Always pushing the boundaries of technology, looking for that new flash of genius. Never afraid to try and fail."

"Time was, you could have followed the same path," Edison mentioned. "I remember that ambitious, young telegrapher who worked with me all those years ago. We made a good team back then. Remember the stock ticker?"

"Hey, now, I only helped you test it," Henry said modestly.

"Yes, and your careful observation and poignant notes helped me to perfect the design. I really couldn't have done it without you."

Henry almost rolled his eyes at the high praise, clearly disbelieving his own importance in the affair. "All right, what do you want, Thomas?"

"You know me too well," Edison said, maintaining his cool, businessman poise.

"I know you're never one to give anyone else credit unless

it'll get you something in return."

Edison gave Henry a dirty look, which let the telegrapher know how insulting the comment had been. The truth often was.

After the tension of the moment faded, Edison replied. "I came here to offer you a job, Henry. I want you to come work for me at Menlo Park."

It was hard for Henry to believe, that a man like Thomas Edison would come all this way for something so trivial. If he wanted to send a job offer to an old friend, that's what the telegraph was for. The fact that they hadn't seen each other in over five years made Henry wonder if there wasn't a sentimental streak in the great inventor.

"You came all the way out here just to offer me a job?" Henry asked.

"Not entirely," Edison replied. "I have other business in mind, but seeing you seemed like a good excuse to visit Selwood. Who knows, this town of yours might go for electricity."

"Perhaps someday," Henry said.

Standing up, Edison straightened his suit jacket and gave Henry a reassuring smile. "Consider my offer. It would be good to have you on board."

"What's the pay?" Henry asked out of sheer curiosity.

"Eighteen dollars a week, to start," Edison replied, "and you'd be accomplishing a lot more for society than you could ever hope to as the mayor of this town."

"I'll consider it," Henry agreed, albeit reluctantly. Though the pay sounded promising, he knew the sort of businessman he'd be working for, and he didn't want to end up losing a friend in the process.

Deciding their conversation had reached its end, Edison chose to see himself out, leaving Henry sitting in silent contemplation. Before closing the door to the telegraph office, Edison said, "I'll be setting up a demonstration in front of your city hall this evening. I trust you'll be in attendance."

"Of course," Henry said.

Edison nodded and left.

Hearing about the exposition gave Henry a slight respite from the hard decisions he had placed before him. The chance to see some of Edison's inventions for himself was exciting, to say the least. Despite the magic he'd witnessed in his lifetime, the idea of an electrically powered light or a talking machine was quite a thrill to consider.

The age of technology was nipping at the heels of mysticism, and it was a growing debate about which power would dominate the future.

CHAPTER 2:
THE GRAND STAGE

The building looked as old as the hills, its clapboard siding weathered and gray. Though, Clarence recalled how it had all come to be built, this humble house at the end of the lane. It was the "left over" land, the extra parcel that had come with the church. Pastor Matthew Jameson had spent his entire life savings on the relocation to Selwood, yet a house had been the last thing on his mind. Coming to town, he'd accepted the hospitality of strangers, as he waited for his new flock and accompanying followers to build him a place of his own.

Clarence remembered the many nails he had personally hammered during the construction. It had only been six years, but time had a habit of wearing upon the world. So much had changed in those few years, and many people had come and gone from the young preacher's life.

He wondered, could he truly return here, to this home he had barely known, and the man who had given his life meaning?

The path leading up to the door was lined by sprigs of grass, yet it was never so green as it should've been. The arid land kept it tan, which disturbed Clarence even now. Things had more color to them in the Midwest, where he'd taken his first steps and first felt the calling of his Holy Savior. Though, he understood why Pastor Jameson had relocated his ministry. Wherever people settled, men of faith had to follow, and Selwood was such a place in need of spiritual guidance.

Yet, did things have to remain so naturally bleak?

Kneeling down toward a clump of dying grass, Clarence reached out his hand and gently brushed the blades, feeling the parched strands scraping his soft skin. It was a simple kind of life, and plants were easy to heal. Tapping into the tiniest fraction of his mystical powers, he sent a faint spark of light into the grass, and in seconds the energy went to work, revitalizing the grass that had rarely seen comfort. Ripples of color flowed up from the roots until each blade shined with natural beauty. A single clump among thousands stood as a minor miracle amidst the wastes.

Clarence stood and admired his work for a moment, feeling a twinge of apprehension as he realized what he had done. The use of magic was becoming second-nature to him, yet he knew what Jameson would say. Magic was the work of Lucifer, a false trickery that abused the natural laws of God. No matter if that power was used for good or evil, it was all wrong in the eyes of the good pastor. Though, it was a doctrine Clarence could no longer share.

It would have been safer for Clarence to stay away, he knew—to perform healings and use his power for the glory of God where it was appreciated—but he couldn't stay away. An inexplicable compunction drew him back to this place, to an old mentor who was more right than he was wrong. A single difference in ideology threatened their oneness of thought, though it was a big difference, and one he wished to remedy.

After all, through God anything was possible.

There was a need to return, Clarence knew. In his own ministry as an itinerant preacher, he had felt the spirit of God working through him. He knew his powers were sourced from the creator, and *that* knowledge left him longing to return home and share the truth with those he cared about. It would be a delicate process, but somehow he would manage it, and sow the seeds of understanding amidst those who would listen. At the very least, he would show his fellow believers what he'd made of himself, and gain the respect of his peers.

Yet, when it came down to it, there were only two people he really needed to please, his heavenly father and his adopted one on Earth. How to go about doing that remained in question as Clarence stepped up to the door and rapped his knuckles upon its whitewashed surface. He waited nervously until his summons was answered.

The door creaked open, revealing the aged figure of Matthew Jameson. The old pastor looked straight ahead into the face of the young man at his doorstep. He appeared just as Clarence remembered him, even wearing the same black suit he'd been wearing when last they'd met. His stance showed no weakness, as the years had been kind to his body, even if his thinned, white hair and wrinkled skin expressed his age.

"Welcome," Jameson simply said, sounding pleased. He stepped aside and invited Clarence into the house.

The interior hadn't changed in the least; a neatly-ordered domicile without much in the way of decoration. This was the home of a true man of God, with little in the way of worldly possessions, despite his lucrative position. The tithes of the flock could have supplied Pastor Jameson with garish luxury, but the old man would have none of it. What he didn't need for his basic needs and limited reading habit went to further the ministry and spread the good word. Clarence tried to follow in those footsteps in so many ways.

"It's good that you've come," Pastor Jameson said, leading the way through the small parlor and into the kitchen. "I was starting to worry. Before last week's telegram, foretelling of your return, I had not heard from you in months."

"My travels took me away from standard mail routes, I'm afraid," Clarence replied, though he knew it was a hollow excuse. Truthfully, he'd stopped writing because he feared what his old mentor would think, were he to reveal what he'd truly been doing recently. Sending letters had become difficult, as omitting the truth of his mystic ministry became more onerous and deceitful.

"Well, you're here now, so I hope we'll have plenty of time to catch up," Jameson said, ushering them both into the Spartan living room. It was a chamber with a few chairs, a reading desk, and a large rack of shelves filled with books. The large space could have easily accommodated three times the furniture, and not a single decoration could be seen; even the twin side windows remained plain and bare with simple gray sheets for curtains.

Taking his seat behind the reading desk, Jameson waved Clarence toward the only other chair, directly across from him. The young man found the padded seat comfortable, like an old pair of shoes that you hadn't worn in years but couldn't deny were pattered to your feet. This was the same chair he'd spent his childhood in, reading before his mentor and learning the wisdom of the ages. Funny, how something that simple could be so comforting; it almost made him forget about the philosophical schism that loomed before him.

"I must say," Jameson started as Clarence got settled in, "when I first heard that you were leaving school to pursue the path of a traveling minister, I had mixed emotions."

"How so?" Clarence asked.

"Oh, it was no surprise. You were always destined to follow the path—of that I had no doubt—and you have always been a sight impulsive. Yet, while I was proud that you were eager to accept the calling, part of me wondered if you were truly ready."

"It wasn't a brash decision," Clarence defended. "I spent eighteen months beforehand listening to professors and scholars of divinity, and I found that little of it was new to me. The important matters of faith I'd already learned from you, and my own meditations told me it was time to move on. I had works to perform."

Pastor Jameson nodded his head knowingly. "I see that now. Your early letters, explaining your ministry in the wild hill country, revealed the truth to me. Hearing of the people you were saving, the souls you were bringing to Christ, it put my early doubts to rest. I'm proud of you, Clarence, truly proud."

The tone of voice and subtle smile were further comfort to Clarence, and he began to wonder if he could shatter his mentor's pride by explaining his current talents. They were on such good terms at the moment, it seemed an utter shame to shatter the illusion. Yet, if his non-magical works could bring his mentor such joy, perhaps Jameson would see that his new path of healing the sick and feeding the hungry with mystical ministrations was righteous. He knew it was a longshot, at best.

"There is something else," Clarence began, preparing to test the waters. "At college, there was a professor, Alvin Bennett, teaching a class called The Divine Ministrations of Mysticism."

"At my Alma Mater?" Jameson said, eyebrows raised in surprise.

"Yes, the course is highly popular, especially among the religious philosophy majors. I... attended the class, myself," Clarence dared to admit.

"I hope you saw it as the blasphemy that it is." Jameson shook his head and hissed through his teeth. "To think, my beloved university would admit such a charlatan to the faculty. I suppose this Bennett practices some form of sorcery, himself?"

"He's a certified Warlock," Clarence admitted.

"Disgraceful," Jameson said. "I tell you, in my youth no Methodist would deign to consider the dark arts as spiritually valid curriculum, let alone the Board of a highly-respected Methodist University."

Clarence felt his hopes dashed, as he saw his old mentor was as rigid as ever when it came to the practice of magic. He had been expecting too much, and knew it would be an insurmountable task to convince Jameson of the righteousness of the mystic arts. Still, he had to press the issue, hope that God could make up the difference.

"I can't say it was wrong to attend the class," Clarence said. "It gave me the impetus to leave school and pursue my ministry abroad."

"Ah," Jameson said, thinking he understood. "I would have done the same. Preaching the truth is far nobler than learning lies."

"That isn't exactly what I meant," Clarence continued.

"What did you mean?" Jameson asked, restoring a reserved composure.

"Besides speaking of the divinity involved with magic, Professor Bennett prompted us to pursue works, to utilize our innate gifts to further the Lord's cause, and better the world around us. It was this prompting that convinced me that I was ready for more than a classroom. I could help people and make a difference in their lives, just as I'd always wanted to. Further schooling could wait."

Jameson nodded approvingly. "I respect that. Yet, I remain skeptical of any advice given by a practitioner of the dark arts."

Hearing the contempt in his mentor's voice, Clarence felt a stinging rebuke. Even though Jameson didn't know that his protégé was one of those "practitioners," it didn't make the insult any gentler.

"Please, don't take this the wrong way," Clarence started, fighting back the nervous lump in the pit of his stomach, "but I can't say I share your convictions that all magic is a dark art."

Jameson was at a loss for words, but his stare spoke volumes. It was his turn to be insulted.

"I have seen the good that magic can do," Clarence persisted. "I've seen it heal the sick and lame. It provides bountiful harvests to feed the hungry. How is that evil?"

"If Judas Iscariot had used his thirty pieces of silver to help the poor and needy, would that have assuaged his guilt for betraying Christ? I tell you no!" Jameson slammed a fist against his desk. "Magic is derived from the devil, the source of all evil, and no amount of superficial good in this world can justify its use. The price is ultimately too high. Can you not see that?"

Clarence did not. Yet, there was no way he would change his pastor's mind—not today, anyway.

After a lengthy and uncomfortable silence, Pastor Jameson let his stern demeanor fade, and he stood up from behind his desk. "I can see that college has filled your head with some curious notions, but let us forget them. There are more pertinent matters to attend at the moment. There is a political debate due to start outside the Town Hall. If you are up for a lively exchange, I feel that that one would be more constructive."

Clarence nodded and smiled, glad for the momentary reprieve.

* * *

The primary debate in the Selwood mayoral race was scheduled for the first Saturday afternoon in August. Workmen had put together a sturdy platform in front of the town hall for the event, and it was destined to be a main attraction for the community. A crowd had been gathering since noon, and half the attendees were women and children—even though they couldn't vote. The civic-minded citizens were eager to hear what the different candidates had to say, and it served as a pleasant diversion from the mundane activities of daily life.

After escorting Fiora Silcox around town, Ron found himself gravitating toward the show. There wasn't much else to do. The young lady seemed fairly satisfied with their unremarkable walk, and she hadn't complained about the slop they'd been served at a local family eatery. She seemed easy enough to please, which was a relief. The offspring of wealthy parents often had a disagreeable streak in them.

Pushing through the crowd, Ron and Fiora made their way to the front of the crowd without too much hassle. When anyone complained about his trespass, Ron flashed his badge and claimed authority. It was a good ploy to get good seating, but also a logical one. As a deputy, he ought to be up front, to keep a close eye on things. Anywhere a large group of people congregated, the threat of trouble lingered.

There were some benches up front, and Ron used his station to procure a seat from a young couple who obliged reluctantly. The pair took a place behind the dwarves and leaned against each other in a most intimate fashion, leaving Ron to wonder what it might be like to fall in love. He'd never had that spark of romance, never known a serious relationship. It hadn't bothered him in his youth, but as he got older the thought of family was starting to weigh on him.

Oddly enough, he hadn't stopped to consider the young woman sitting beside him—not for a moment.

Two men came through the crowd and climbed the steps to the stage. The suits they wore denoted them as the more affluent types, though Ron couldn't place their names. No doubt, he'd remember after today.

The two men sat down in a couple of chairs toward the

back of the stage and waited in silence. A few people in the crowd mumbled questions, and others mumbled answers. There were more candidates due to appear on stage, which accounted for the delay.

Just then, a small commotion arose toward the back of the crowd, as a few people cheered and clapped. A small corridor was made, as a few happy individuals escorted Henry Currant along. The telegrapher gave some halfhearted waves to the people as he passed, appearing uncomfortable with the attention. He made his way up the stairs and took the third seat in-between the two polished gentlemen.

As the crowd once again mumbled amongst themselves, a fourth man climbed the steps, and Ron instantly identified him as Albert Silcox. The aging cattle baron walked over to the podium at center stage and shouted for everyone's attention.

"Citizens of Selwood, it is my pleasure to stand in as moderator for this important forum," Silcox announced, looking pleased with himself.

"What's this?" Ron whispered to Fiora.

"I don't know, but I like it." Standing up, Fiora whistled and waved at her father.

"Hi there, Fiora," Silcox acknowledged, then continued. "While not a citizen of your fair town, the election committee felt it would be appropriate for me to serve in this role, as an impartial observer. Of course, it would have been nice if they'd given me some warning ahead of time. I might have stayed home," he added with a smile.

The crowd laughed a little at his offhanded attempt at humor.

Glancing back at the seated candidates, Silcox continued. "Well, as it appears everyone is ready, I believe we can get started."

"Not so fast, boyo," a voice shouted from the crowd. The distinct, Irish accent was familiar to Ron, and he was suddenly put on edge.

A flash of light appeared on the stage beside Silcox, and a thin dwarf in a bowler hat materialized. He held a rolled up piece of paper in his right hand, and he lifted it above his head.

Before the Irishman could speak, Ron got to his feet and drew his Remington revolver. "Flaherty!" he shouted, recalling his last encounter with the magically skilled fellow.

Flaherty cocked his head and stared back at Ron. "Ah, Deputy Grimes, how nice tae see ye again. What's all this now, pointin' a gun at a mayoral candidate?"

"I'm pointing it at you, you blasted leprechaun!" Ron shouted.

A flash of light appeared over Ron's hand, and the gun vanished from his grasp. The weapon promptly materialized in Flaherty's hand. "As I said, ye were threatening a candidate." Lowering the gun, the leprechaun handed it to Silcox, along with his sheet of paper. "Michael James Flaherty, delivering me nomination."

The last statement caused a stir with the crowd, as different factions took in the news. Everyone was surprised, to say the least.

"You can't run for mayor," someone shouted.

"And just why not?" Flaherty asked as Silcox examined the paper.

"You're a no good Irishman," the protestor replied.

"Irishman perhaps, but I got me citizenship in sixty-three. I was a founding member of this here settlement, and I be reclaimin' me residency at thirty-four Berkshire Street. That makes me eligible."

"Ain't nobody gonna vote for no Irishman," someone else said.

"Let alone one behind bars," Ron said, storming the stage. When he reached the top of the stairs, he was enveloped in light, and promptly found himself back beside Fiora amidst the crowd.

"What's with all the hostility? You're not still harboring a grudge over our little trip in June."

"You bet I am. You kidnapped me and the sheriff!" Ron challenged. "I ought to arrest you!"

"I don't believe you want to be going that route," Flaherty said, eyeing Silcox. "It might bring about a whole host of unpleasantness."

Silcox caught the leprechaun staring at him and gave the

look right back. "Whatever you've done, I think you'd best pay for it."

Flaherty grabbed his chest in an outlandish show of betrayal. "You wound me, old friend, and after all we've been through."

"You know this miscreant?" Ron asked, walking over to the stairs again. This time, he managed to get to the stage without a spell sending him away.

"Michael here is an old acquaintance of mine, and of Marshal Rodgers," Silcox explained.

"I see," Ron said, stepping in front of Flaherty so he could look him in the eye. "Then I suppose you were working for Rodgers when you waylaid me and Doliber."

The leprechaun narrowed his gaze and lowered his voice. "If ye take me to court, perhaps ye'll find out the hard way."

Ron whispered back, "What's that supposed to mean?"

Flaherty raised his voice and answered loudly, "It means I'm running for mayor! Let's get on with the debate!"

Ron felt like dragging him off the stage in handcuffs, but a voice echoed in the back of his mind. *"You should wait."* It took him a minute to realize it was Sheriff Doliber sending him a telepathic message.

"Damn it, Doliber, you know how I hate your prying mind," Ron replied with an angry thought.

"Occupational necessity," Doliber's disembodied voice said. *"I don't want to confront Flaherty. Not yet. We need to see what he's up to, and the best way to accomplish that is to let him run wild a bit."*

"Give him enough rope to hang himself, and his accomplices?" Ron asked.

"Precisely," Doliber replied. *"Now, stand down and watch the show. I'll be over when I can."*

Ron knew better than to protest, and did as he was asked, clomping off the stage without acting too upset. He went back to his seat and stared at the candidates as they each got up to make their initial presentations. Their words didn't really interest him at the moment, as his thoughts continued to churn through what facts he had. Flaherty was certainly up to something, and he was determined to figure it out.

All the while, Fiora Silcox sat beside him, cheering the speeches and prompting Ron to do the same. She helped him keep pace with the happy crowd as his mind wandered.

He was going to see that dirty leprechaun in jail, if it was the last thing he did.

* * *

As half the town was occupied at the political rally, Joella found herself on corpse watch. After careful consideration, Doliber had decided it was unwise to leave the body of Jesse James unattended. *Who knew what Solen might do to the man?* So, to make sure things weren't disturbed, he sent the first available deputy.

Joella didn't mind the job. In fact, she rather enjoyed the task, as it gave her the chance to razz Solen. The arrogant saloon owner had made his interest in her clear on occasion, though never in a sappy manner. He was more the playful sort, who made light of his potential conquest. Whether a defensive mechanism or his natural, carefree attitude, Joella took pleasure in shooting down his thinly-veiled advances whenever the chance presented itself.

The Lucca Saloon was practically empty at two in the afternoon, which was unusual. Even at mid-afternoon, there were usually a few gamblers playing cards or a drover taking an early dinner. The absolute absence of anyone besides a couple of whores made the place feel even more dead than the blood-stained body in front of the bar.

"Aren't you going to take him out of here?" Solen asked as Joella continued to stare at Jesse's lifeless form.

"He can do it himself... eventually," Joella answered, followed by a smile.

"Not before he scares off more customers," Solen said, slapping a damp rag down on the counter.

"What customers? Everyone's at the rally."

"Yes, speaking of which," he said as a thought crossed his mind. He turned to the three girls who were playing with their makeup. "Why don't you ladies get down there and rustle up some clients."

"We don't work outside the house, Solen," the dark-haired one replied snottily.

"Lose the attitude, Sally. One of these days you'll get me in the wrong mood, and I swear you'll be looking for fresh accommodations."

"Right, Solen. Only, then who would you vent to?" Sally asked. Deciding against an escalation of hostilities, she grabbed her makeup kit and trotted upstairs.

Solen shook his head and turned back to Joella. "Get that body out of here, before I get a shovel."

"You'd actually attempt manual labor?" Joella asked, feigning surprise.

"Fritz, get out here," Solen shouted to the teenage waiter hiding in the kitchen. "Deputy Talus has a hole for you to dig."

Joella folded her arms and looked disappointed. "That's one of the things I really dislike about you, Solen," she said. "You've always got somebody else to do your dirty work for you."

"I'm sure you know how that is, being a Talus of Clan Talus," Solen replied, setting his cleaning rag aside. "No doubt, you had plenty of pampering growing up, which is why you're so tough and capable now. You think you've got something to prove."

"I don't have to prove anything," Joella said. "I just know the value of independence and hard work."

"You know, we could do some *hard work* together," Solen suggested with a jerk of his eyebrows.

"Perhaps," Joella replied, looking down at Jesse's stirring body, "but after I stabbed you, I doubt you'd rise from the dead."

The slight twitch turned into a full spasm, as Jesse returned to life. The stab wound in his shoulder was completely healed, and his eyes flickered, as consciousness returned. With a stiff roll, he managed to get into a sitting position and breathe deeply.

"Feeling better?" Joella asked as he took note of his surroundings.

Looking down at his blood-stained shirt, he replied, "It seems I need another set of clothes."

Joella reached down and gave him a hand up. "Maybe if you weren't intent on getting yourself killed, you'd get more mileage out of them."

"Dying is never my intention," Jesse replied. "That Yankee coward made some disparaging remarks, so I made my own in return."

"What did he say?" Joella asked.

Jesse paused and thought about it, looking oddly amused. "I don't seem to recall."

"Then it probably wasn't worth getting stabbed over," Joella said. "Come on, let's go get you cleaned up."

Jesse rubbed the kinks out of his shoulder as he followed Joella out of the saloon. His body was always stiff after a revival, though no more than he'd get from a bad night's sleep. It would prove to be a deterrent if it were much worse, but he wasn't one to shirk from pain.

They didn't say much as they made their way down the street, and they got a number of shocked expressions from the people they passed. Jesse always got stares when he had blood on his shirt, and word was getting around about his unnatural nature. Nobody had yet complained about a "shadowganger" being on the sheriff's staff, though it was only a matter of time—especially considering that that shadow was also a wanted outlaw.

"I assume the man who stabbed me is locked up," Jesse said as they neared the Sheriff's Office.

"He'll get his day in court," Joella confirmed, waving at a passing pair of parasol-twirling ladies who turned up their noses at the uncouth law officers.

"Doliber should've let me shoot him and be done with it."

"And how would that fit in with your path to redemption?" Joella asked, walking up the steps to the office.

"I've been doing good for a while now," Jesse said, opening the door for Joella. "Feel I can afford a detour now and then."

They came in to find Doliber sitting behind his desk, eyes closed and seemingly asleep. Keeping quiet as she approached the desk, Joella waited until she was right beside him to stomp her foot and call for his attention. He didn't budge to her noise, even after she shouted his name twice.

"Is he all right?" Jesse asked, sliding the black jacket off his shoulders. He started examining it, and saw there wasn't much blood on it—seems he'd lucked out there, and would only need to replace his shirt. Jackets could get expensive.

"He's in a trance of some sort," Joella replied. "I think."

"I'm busy," Doliber answered, remaining still except for the movement of his lips.

The words startled Joella, and she felt silly for being tricked so easily. "You could have said something. What are you doing?"

"Watching the mayoral debate. Now shush."

Seeing Doliber had things well in hand, the two deputies turned to leave. Jesse headed upstairs to find a clean shirt, and Joella felt it wouldn't be a bad idea to head down to the rally and see the proceedings firsthand. Though, as she made for the front door, the sheriff's voice caught her attention.

"You have a telegram, Joella," Doliber said.

"Oh?" Joella asked, moving back toward the desk and looking for a sheet of paper. "When did it come in?"

"About twenty seconds ago," Doliber said.

"How do you know?" Joella asked. She felt she knew the answer, but wanted to hear confirmation.

"Call orb," Doliber replied. "The telegrapher on duty just activated it."

"So, what does the telegram say?" Joella asked.

"I didn't read more than the address," Doliber said.

"Thank you," Joella said, feeling less than eager to receive the message. There weren't many people she could think of who would spend the time or money to send her a telegram, and none of them would be sending a kind word. Whether it was Mactus Sellius—her deceased husband's cousin and her would-be husband—or her parents condemning her for rejecting him, this was not going to be pleasant.

Joella walked over to the telegraph office, her head hung low as she remembered the hard choices she'd had to make, and the consequences she knew were coming. Elvish Clan Law mandated that she marry her dead husband's first cousin, though she'd done everything possible to avoid it, and finally refused. Though legally the clan could not force her to do anything, her actions would see her shunned by any who followed the old ways, including her family.

Joella's relationship with her parents had been strained for years, as she hadn't settled into the lifestyle of a good elvish housewife. Of course, they'd raised her on the frontier, and taught her all the independence necessary to survive in the wild. As soon as civilization took hold, however, they'd forgotten all of that, and expected her to conform to polite society. Yet, she had already been conditioned for the rugged life, and fate had delivered her away from the comforts of a submissive existence.

That, and the fact that her late husband had been a half-breed outlaw, made the prospects of her becoming a homemaker rather unlikely.

There was nothing in Clan Law that mandated the way a wife had to live, and while married to her often absent spouse—the scandalous half-elf bandit Vincent Lafayette—she'd been free to run her own affairs. That meant riding the range and playing cowgirl on the family spread much of the time.

While Law didn't dictate the behavior of a wife, it left that right to the husband, and Mactus wasn't the sort to tolerate unladylike behavior from any wife. He had three already who served in the traditional ways, and Joella would have simply been number four in his polygamous harem if she'd obeyed the ancient ways of her people. It was something she could never accept, and now she would have to live with the consequences of her rejection.

Stepping up to the telegraph window, Joella caught the attention of the junior operator, who promptly handed her the telegram. She stepped out from under the small awning so she could read the message in full sunlight.

The message wasn't from Mactus or her parents, but from her cousin, Doreen. Before she'd become the third wife of Mactus Sellius, Doreen had grown up with Joella, and they'd remained good friends into adulthood. It was understandable that she would be willing to defy her husband's wishes and bend Clan

Law by contacting her shunned relation, especially considering the circumstances.

Reading the telegram, Joella felt her heart sink. It was short and to the point. Mactus had arranged a betrothal to Joella's younger sister, Sara.

"The son of a bitch actually did it," Joella whispered to herself, sickened by the move. He'd threatened to do it, but she'd always figured it was just a negotiating tactic, to force her into marrying him. She never thought he'd really go so far.

When it came to Joella, Mactus had never wanted the love and commitment of a real marriage. He already had three wives for that. With her, it had always been a matter of standing. Joella was the eldest heir to the Chieftain, and her heirs would someday rule the clan—or they would have, had she not refused Mactus and gotten herself excommunicated. When she did that, the bloodline shifted to the next in succession, namely her sole sibling.

Mactus was ambitious, and would stop at nothing to assure that his children would lead Clan Talus in the next century.

Marrying Sara was a new low, Joella thought. Mactus was a man pushing forty, and Sara was barely sixteen. How could such an arranged marriage be permitted in this day and age?

Joella couldn't believe it. How could her parents be so heartless and complacent? Signing their youngest daughter over to Mactus like that; how could they? Yes, her folks had been close with Mactus' parents, but that didn't mean they had to trade offspring like chattel.

There had to be a way to stop it. Sara was still more than a year away from traditional marrying age, and nothing was set in stone. Her parents could revoke the betrothal at any time prior to the wedding day, and barring that the bride could always refuse. This wasn't the old country, it was America, and an elvish woman had the right to reject an arranged marriage, even if that meant turning her back on her people. It came with harsh consequences, but they were preferable to becoming a stepping stone to a man's ambition.

It wouldn't be easy, but Joella had to try. Somehow, she would save her sister from the dreaded fate that awaited her, and finally put an end to the ambition of Mactus Sellius.

Wasting no time, Joella hurried over to her room at the Bormans' Boarding House and packed her belongings, preparing for a long ride. It was pretty quiet around mid-afternoon, as most of the boarders were over at city hall hearing the stump speeches of the mayoral candidates. It was the perfect cover she needed to get away unnoticed.

Joella made her way down the stairs, ready to hit the trail with her rugged leather attire. She didn't want a big send-off, not when she wasn't sure if she'd be coming back. All she owned was in the pack on her back and the saddlebags on her horse. It wasn't much to show for the past four months of upholding the law, but she wasn't in it for the money. Nobody ever got rich fighting crime, and she'd known plenty of wealthy crooks. Fighting for what was right had to be a reason all in itself.

As much as she'd come to enjoy being a deputy, there was another wrong she had to challenge. Her sister needed her, so she was off to save the day.

Joella was on her horse and turning to head out of town when Sheriff Doliber appeared in front of her. The sudden arrival worried her, for she hadn't asked permission for this little excursion. She liked being a deputy, but when family business conflicted with her duties there was no choice in the matter. She couldn't risk him telling her no, so she hadn't given him the chance. Yet, now, here he was.

"Planning to say goodbye?" Doliber asked.

Joella felt guilty as sin, trying to sneak off without a word. Caught in the act, she realized what a mistake it would be to leave without clearing it with her employer. The stress of her sister's situation was making her reckless.

"You could have asked me," Doliber mentioned.

"My sister needs my help," Joella said. "I didn't think there was time to ask."

Recognizing the importance of family affairs, Doliber nodded and stepped out of the horse's path, saying, "If you need a hand, I'm there for you."

"Thank you, but this is something I need to handle on my own," Joella replied, wishing she could take him up on his offer, but knowing it would only make things worse. It was never wise to bring outsiders into personal matters.

"I understand," Doliber said, petting her horse's neck. "How long will you be away?"

"A few days. Maybe a week," Joella replied.

"I guess we'll manage without you," Doliber said. He kept his hand on the horse and gave Joella a thoughtful look. He always had so much on his mind, it was often difficult to gauge the meaning of his reactions, but there was something telling in the way he was behaving at the moment, something Joella had been searching for these past months; an affinity, a trace of love... or was she just imagining things?

"Well, I'd better let you go," Doliber said, stepping back. "Don't be gone too long."

"I won't," Joella said softly. "When I get back, we really should talk."

"Yes, I'm sure we'll both want to catch up and clear the air," Doliber said, quickly shielding himself. The longing in his eyes was gone, replaced with his usual, attentive glare. "Pleasant trip."

Joella gave a simple nod, and shook the reins. The horse started trotting forward as Doliber vanished in a flash of light, leaving her to ride away unobserved. The road west was dry and rocky, but she'd traveled it before. With any luck, she'd be able to cut the trip short with a quick teleport, though she hadn't tested her limited mystical ability since straining herself in a harrowing feat to save Doliber's life. That daring move had proven successful, but it could have killed her, and it left her with worries about tapping that ability now.

Doliber had been assuring her for weeks that nothing was wrong with her brain. It ought to be able to process magic energy just fine, though she had lingering doubts. She feared that something might be wrong the next time she tried to teleport, but she couldn't put it off any longer. The ride to Ravenna-West would take the better part of a week on horseback, while her teleporting skills could have her there within the hour.

Praying that she wasn't about to meet the reaper, she closed her eyes and prepared to take a leap of faith. Sensing where she wanted to go, a tingling sensation tickled the back of her eyes, as she activated the magic at her command. In a few moments, she'd find out if her skills truly were intact.

As the tingling stopped, Joella felt a gust of moist air on her cheek. Opening her eyes, she saw the arid desert was gone, replaced by the lush forests of eastern California. She knew this patch of woods well. She was barely five miles from home.

The first trial was over, and now she had to figure out her next move. What would it take to save her sister from the clutches of Mactus Sellius? She had five miles to figure it out.

* * *

After three long hours, the mayoral debate was nearing an end. The candidates had done their best to present their individual cases and highlight key issues to stimulate the voters. Many of the early attendees had since left, but new arrivals had kept the crowd substantial, even as things were winding down.

The leprechaun had just given his closing statements, swearing he had the connections necessary to guarantee construction of the Selwood rail spur, and Ron was feeling ready to sleep, even as the sun lingered in the western sky. He'd enjoyed hearing the arguments for a while, but he had his limits, and the candidates were all pretty much the same. They all had something different to offer Selwood, and each had a niche issue to tout, though none of it sounded very original. One man trumpeted his moral Methodism and the need for righteous leadership, while another decried the value of a working man's right to enjoy himself. Henry Currant played the fence and seemed uncomfortable on the stump, while Flaherty wasted time with his outlandish promises that nobody could take seriously. It grew tiring after a while, though most of the townspeople seemed to enjoy it.

With the final statements made, Silcox took the podium and concluded the candidate forum. Even as he shook the hands of the departing candidates, a new group of men stormed the stage, and the crowd remained to see what the new commotion was about.

A mustached man took Silcox aside and talked briefly, after which the cattle baron made a new announcement. "Ladies and gentleman, the debates are over, but you may all come back at dusk for a very special presentation by the Edison Electric Light Company."

The new announcement brought a lot of excitement to the group, even as they dispersed to attend their afternoon business. Many would return, and no doubt bring friends to this new event. Two major presentations in one day was more positive excitement than Selwood had seen in years.

Albert Silcox left the stage and made a direct line for his granddaughter and Ron. Fiora hopped up on the bench and gave him a quick hug when he arrived, seeming relieved that the debate was over.

"We aren't going to stay around for the Edison show, are we?" she asked.

"We've already stayed this late," Silcox replied. "I don't see we'll be riding back to the ranch today, at any rate. Might as well make a fresh run in the morning."

"That doesn't mean we have to sit around for another three hours," Fiora complained. She turned to Ron and asked, "Is it okay if Mr. Grimes shows me around some more instead?"

"If you wish, and he's amenable," Silcox said, sounding pleased.

"Hey, now, I don't mind spending time with you, but I'm pretty partial to seeing this Edison lightshow," Ron said. "I've read a lot about these bulb things over the last few years; feel I ought to see one for myself."

"So what?" Fiora said, sounding childish. "It's just another sort of magic. You want to see a ball glow, Grandfather can light one up any time. Isn't that right?" she added, looking lovingly at Albert.

The old man nodded and held her arm reassuringly. "Yes, it's true I can enchant an orb, but magic and technology are not really the same. From what I was told, Edison will be showing off more than just his electric lights this evening, things you might enjoy. There are wonders of modern science that even magic has not crafted over the centuries, and you'd be well advised to take notice. The world your children grow up in may be far removed from the life any of us have known."

Fiora looked up at her grandfather, then over to Ron and sighed. "All right, I guess I can sit around a while longer, but I'll want to stretch my legs first." She held her hand out to Ron and waited for him to take it. "Shall we?"

Ron took her hand and she hopped down off the bench. Before he could let go, she wove her fingers into his and dragged him along playfully, even as her grandfather looked on with a reassuring smile.

The picture was clear for Ron to see. The more he observed of Albert Silcox's mannerisms and attitudes, the more he understood what this whole thing was about; why the man had taken a shine to him in the first place. Silcox was trying to find a suitable suitor for his granddaughter. The concept left Ron feeling uncomfortable. As much as he'd considered the value of having a family in recent months, Fiora was not his type for various reasons—and he wasn't too partial to being set up by a would-be in-law, rich or otherwise.

Ron waited until they turned the corner onto Lexicon Street before asking, "Where are we going?"

Fiora stopped jogging and turned to face him, keeping her hand firmly within his. "I don't know. I just felt like moving after all that sitting. Where do you want to go?"

"I hadn't really thought about it," Ron said.

"I know," Fiora said excitedly. "Why don't you show me where you live? You must have a home or a room. Somewhere private?"

"How would your grandfather approve of that?" Ron asked with mixed emotions.

"He would trust me to maintain my Christian virtue, in any situation, and he wouldn't have left me in your capable hands if he didn't already trust you."

"I think part of that trust is trusting that I won't be taking you to my private room in the first place," Ron said, seeking to avoid a tricky situation.

"I don't know about that," Fiora said. "Besides, if anything were to happen, we wouldn't have to say anything, would we?"

Fiora moved in and planted a kiss on Ron's lips, forcing her way past the thick beard hiding his mouth. Before she could get more than a peck, Ron pulled her back.

"What are you doing?" Ron asked.

Fiora gave him a blank look and then started to blush. "I'm sorry. I thought that's what you wanted."

"You're pretty eager to give a man what you think he wants," Ron said, wary of her forwardness, even as he fought back primitive urges.

"I'm sorry," Fiora repeated. "I'm not usually like that, really."

"I find that hard to believe," Ron answered, considering the facts. She'd known him barely half a day and was already interested in having intimate relations? The only ladies Ron knew who would consider such action weren't the sort to act out of character, and were already in the habit.

"Oh," Fiora said, turning away. She took a few steps and stared down at her feet. "I ruined it. I knew I would."

Ron felt a twinge of guilt, but knew better than to fall into a potential trap. He'd known his share of women, and understood how manipulative the "fairer sex" could be. He wasn't going to play along. It was against his stubborn nature to give in to emotional blackmail.

"I think we should get you back to your grandpa now," Ron said, expecting it would put an end to this uncomfortable business.

"No, not yet," Fiora said. "Please, don't give up on me before we've even started."

Ron walked over and stepped in front of her, so he could see her eyes. They were red and damp, and it made him feel bad about his cold demeanor. "What do you expect to get out of this—out of me?"

"Nothing," Fiora said, wiping her tears, "and everything. Do you know I'm twenty-five years old, and no man has ever looked at me as more than a little girl? Twenty-five! I'm alone, Mr. Grimes, and I don't want to end up some old maid."

"That's nonsense," Ron said. "You're not even old yet,

and I can't believe you won't find someone who'll treat you right."

"You don't understand," Fiora replied, sounding ready to cry again. "You're normal, what you're supposed to be. You're a *real* dwarf. I'm just a shrunken human. Nobody wants me."

Ron understood completely, and the worst part was he agreed with her assessment of herself. She wasn't a real dwarf in his eyes, and his own genetic bias continued to color his feelings about her. He'd never once considered a romantic relationship with this girl, all because of his own racial pride. Despite their similar height, she wasn't *really* like him.

Seeing her sorrow made him feel sympathetic, but it would take more than a terse conversation to change his heart.

Putting a hand on her shoulder, Ron tried to ease her emotion. "Come on, why don't we get something to eat?"

"Oh, thank you, Mr. Grimes," Fiora said, starting to lighten up again. Her sadness was shifting to discomfiture, which left her acting stiff.

"Call me Ron," he said as they started walking again. He let her take his hand, and wondered how far he would be willing to go to appease her. However things turned out, he knew this was the beginning of an unusual relationship.

* * *

Dusk was a busy time in Selwood, even on an ordinary Saturday night. The streetlamps were being lit as citizens walked about their business. There was a local theatre troupe who often put on plays, though this night they took a bow from their regular routine, as a superior performance presented itself.

The outdoor stage was glowing, and not by magic or fire. The bright shine of glass bulbs strung along the stage and podium gave adequate illumination for all present to see the men standing near the podium, the central figure being Thomas Edison, himself. The power for the lights came from several small crank generators that whined in the background, and three men—Edison's employees—kept their arms rotating in rhythmic fashion.

"You see these lights?" Edison continued with his speech. "These are the product of science. Not of mental mysticism or primitive conjuring, but of true physical knowledge and innovation. It was a long trek of discovery to manufacture a functional light bulb, but now that the pattern has been uncovered it is simple and relatively cheap to reproduce it. In time, these electric lights of mine will be commonplace, superceding all their counterparts, and only rich men will waste money on candles or magic orbs."

Edison waved at the cranking men to stop, and the lights grew dark. There was silence again, as the spectators wondered what Edison was doing now, and they watched shadowed figures moving around on the stage. After a few minutes, two lights turned on again, powered by a large storage battery. It was enough light to show Edison standing there with another of his inventions. The long, cylindrical device with a crank and a horn sat flatly on top of the podium, and with a steady turn of the handle Edison made the device speak.

"Hello, I am a phonograph, a talking machine. I can be used to record sounds and replay them, like so. Mary had a little lamb..."

The voice was clearly that of Thomas Edison, though tinny and distorted by the playback. As the crank was turned, the light from the bulbs sparkled against the metallic cylinder as it turned about the core of the phonograph.

As the recording came to an end, Edison stretched his arm and one of his employees took the machine away.

"That is one of the original prototypes I made, almost five years ago," Edison explained. "Improved models are available for purchase, if any of you would like to be the first in your community to own one. Being ahead of the trends isn't a bad thing when it comes to technology. In a few short years, it won't be uncommon to see one of these devices in every household in America!"

"What's the point?" someone shouted from the crowd.

"Excuse me?" Edison asked.

"You heard me," the heckler persisted. "What's the point of these inventions of yours? We already got lights better than them bulb things. Half the homes in Selwood got magic orbs to see at night, and what good's a talking machine? Sounds like somebody's talking inside a tin barrel!"

The rest of the crowd remained eerily silent as Edison stared at them intently. It took him a minute to gather his thoughts and channel his anger before making a response.

"You want to know why I seek to advance the frontiers of science? To make inventions that improve the lives of people around the globe?"

"I asked *what's the point*," the heckler persisted. "Your lights ain't nothing new."

"Ah, you want to know why I seek to break our dependency on magic!" Edison said, looking pleased with the realization. "Isn't it obvious? Magic is an archaic form of energy, utilized by only a handful of people. It is limited in its functionality, and those who can use it extort large sums of money from all of us for their little trinkets. I seek to liberate us from that tyrannical system." He grabbed his lapels and stuck out his chest like a politician before continuing. "To cast magic, you have to be born special, and trained by other special men in order to adequately utilize your gifts. Yet, with true science, any man can learn to use its power. It doesn't take a Master of the Guild to make a light bulb. It only takes a man in a factory, copying a pattern, and the power that bulb needs is easily generated by scientific means, as well. As we speak, my work crews are setting up the first mass electrical distribution system, to supply power to customers in New York City. They aren't magic men using their minds to conjure that power. They are using science that anyone can utilize."

The heckler sought to continue. "Yeah, but..."

"You also asked about the phonograph, and there magic is sorely lacking. I have never encountered a magical device that can truly record sound and replay it. Yes, a skilled mentalist can speak into your mind or project a memory, but can any magician make a sound recording like the one I just played for you? No! Where magic has failed, science has succeeded!

"This is the purpose of my work; to advance the frontiers of knowledge, and invent devices that are built on sound principles that improve society. I seek to revolutionize the world with the truth of real science, not flighty mysticism."

The crowd came alive with applause, clearly impressed

with Edison's speech. The heckler had been thoroughly trounced in the war of words.

Edison stood there in front of the podium, looking smug and satisfied for a few moments before a sudden spasm struck him. His back arched, and he fell over onto his side, drawing the attention of his loyal employees. The cheers and clapping from the crowd ceased, as they saw the great inventor lying on the stage.

Ron Grimes made his way onto the stage and hurried over to the limp body. Checking him over along with the worried employees, he quickly discovered why the inventor had collapsed.

"Somebody, get a doctor," Ron shouted at the crowd. "Thomas Edison's just been shot!"

CHAPTER 3:
THE CHALLENGERS OF FATE

Edison's blood was soaking into the stage planks, as the crowd stood around waiting for help to arrive. It had all happened so fast, yet the short moments seemed to have lasted hours for Ron, as he knelt there beside the bleeding man, wishing he could do something, anything, to truly help. All he could do was wait, like everyone else. It was nerve-wracking.

Ron placed his hand in front of Edison's face, and came to a startling revelation. "He's stopped breathing!" the dwarf shouted, fearing the worst.

Time was approaching an end for Edison, as one of his men cried out to the crowd, "Please, is there anyone with the healing gifts? Anyone at all?"

The silence was deafening, as everyone waited for someone else to step forward. The power to heal was a rare gift indeed, so it was unlikely there would be a volunteer, but without a twist of magic it was clear that Thomas Edison would die here and now.

When all hope seemed lost, someone stepped from the crowd and climbed up onto the stage.

It was Clarence Davison.

"Let me see," Clarence said.

"You got the gift?" Ron asked.

"I've dabbled," the young man admitted. "Please, let me try."

Ron stood up and made room, allowing Clarence to kneel beside the dying man.

Looking over the limp body, Clarence took a deep breath, preparing to put his limited skills to the test. Placing his hands on the body, he closed his eyes and sent his senses wandering, probing the ethereal world through magic. His mind studied the bullet wound in Edison's body, and he soon understood what he had to do. Seizing hold of the power within himself, he commanded a spell to repair the wounded tissues and organs.

A dark green glow surrounded Edison's chest, and almost immediately the wounded man took in a deep breath, brought back from the brink of death. As the light intensified, a hissing noise sounded, and the tissue began to knit. A small spattering of blood began seeping from the healing wound, and after several seconds a lead slug emerged, pushed out ahead of the mending tissue. The bullet rolled off Edison's chest and rattled harmlessly against the boards of the stage. Ripping a handkerchief out of his pocket, Ron leaned over to retrieve the bullet, believing it may be of some later use.

The strain of such careful mystic manipulation left Clarence winded, and he knew his work hadn't been perfect. There was only so much magic his brain could process, but he'd been able to fix the major damage. Nature could take care of the rest.

Edison coughed and clutched his chest, and his struggle to stand brought a pair of his loyal employees to his aid. They got him on his feet, but had to support him to keep him that way. He'd lost a lot of blood, and there was still a little bit trickling out where the skin hadn't completely healed. The electric lights allowed everyone in the crowd to see the red stains running down his white shirt in grotesque fashion.

"You're going to be okay, Mr. Edison," one of the men holding him said.

"Thanks to a bit of magic," Ron said, amused that the man had been saved by a spell after his impassioned speech about scientific superiority.

"Magic has its place," Edison said, trying to get his legs to support him. "Now, if you'll excuse me, I'd better see a real doctor."

Edison's men stayed at his side, helping him along. As he passed Clarence, he thanked the young man and smiled at him in a peculiar way. The shock of the experience had made the grand inventor giddy, and their past encounter in the stagecoach added a note of irony to the miraculous save. Clarence hoped the man would be more open to the idea of God after he recovered, though he had his doubts.

As Edison departed and the crowd began to disperse, another man climbed the stage. Pastor Matt Jameson was well known to everyone in town, and he'd been sitting right beside Clarence the whole evening. The man's white hair looked extra pale as he entered the glow of the electric lights.

"Pastor Matt," Ron greeted him on approach, but the old preacher ignored him, heading instead for Clarence.

"Sir, I..." Clarence started.

The pastor cut him off. "Magic is the tool of the devil! How could you condemn yourself like this?"

"I just saved a man's life," Clarence defended. "I know, my ability must come as a shock, but please hear me out."

"I can't believe this," Jameson said, sticking a finger in Clarence's face. "To think after all I did for you, all the sermons we shared, how I practically raised you, that you could turn such a blind eye to everything I've taught you, and embrace the demonic arts. Sorcerer!"

"I am no sorcerer!" Clarence challenged. "How could you even think that of me?"

Jameson clenched a fist and shook his head. "I only know what I see, and what the Lord has taught me. Magic is not of God, and mortal man should not wield such dark power. You have been swayed by the lies of the misguided."

Clarence was at a loss for words, and simply stared at his old mentor with sorrowful eyes.

Jameson stormed off the stage, and a few members of the crowd followed him in the direction of his church across town.

Clarence knew this was bound to happen, but he still hoped his mentor would see reason.   Many Christian denominations were accepting of magic as one of God's gifts to man, while others felt it was evil trickery. Some, like his own Methodist faith, were divided on the issue, and in time the controversy might split the church in two.

How sad that a simple matter of interpretation could be so divisive.

* * *

There was a shooter on the loose, someone who didn't take kindly to Thomas Edison's anti-magic rant, presumably. It wasn't going to be an open and shut case, as nobody had spotted the culprit.   The bullet had come out of the dark, and during a time of such rancorous applause that nobody had even heard the shot fired. As it stood, the guilty party was liable to remain anonymous.

As the night grew long, Doliber met with Edison and his men at Doctor Redgrave's infirmary, which was little more than a living room with some beds in it. The young physician was relatively new to town, but he seemed pretty competent, even without magical healing gifts.

"I don't expect you'll be able to find the man who did this," Edison said from his sickbed.

"I wouldn't discount anything yet," Doliber said, pacing a little. "I have a mental record of the events, courtesy of you and several bystanders, and I have a metaphysical imprint from the bullet that hit you, which should help to positively identify the shooter when I find him. There are leads to be followed, and with a little luck this case may get cracked wide open."

"What leads do you think you have?" Edison asked, sounding less than optimistic.

"For one, there is that cynic in the crowd, the one who questioned the value of your work. He seemed pretty resistant to the idea of technological change."

One of Edison's men interrupted Doliber's explanation by clearing his throat. "Uh, that was me."

"It was?" Doliber asked, examining the young man. He didn't fit the description very well at first glance, but with a wig and change of clothes he just might.

"It's part of the presentation," Edison replied. "I need an antagonist to give my arguments the proper set-up. My men take turns wearing disguises and being the right kind of nuisance."

"That's a shame," Doliber said, feeling he'd really had something there. An angry traditionalist seemed like the most likely culprit, though there was no way to tell who that individual might be. There were any number of magic-trusting folks in the area, and plenty of backward-thinking souls who perceived Edison's innovations as a threat to their own way of life.

"Don't feel bad, Sheriff," Edison said. "I'm alive, and intend to stay that way. That'll be punishment enough for the underhanded scoundrel."

"Not by my reckoning," Doliber replied, heading for the door. He'd learned all he could from these men, and it was sorely lacking.

Stepping out into the night air, Doliber walked down the street toward his office. The street lights were getting dim, as the fuel turned to coals, and the lamp attendants were retired for the evening. Nobody else was out at this hour, most of them having to get up early for church. The excitement of the shooting had sent them all to their beds.

Turning a corner, Doliber felt his face smack against a wall. Stepping back, he looked ahead and saw no obstruction. Light sparkled out of several windows up ahead, as well as the smoldering streetlights, so he knew the way was clear. Yet, setting his hand forward, he felt the hard, smooth barrier; a magic force field!

"Good evening, Sheriff," a voice greeted him from the dark. It was clear, but accented with the mark of a Southern gentleman. "I do believe we should have a word, you and I."

"Who are you?" Doliber asked, casting a spell to enhance his vision. The faint light around him was amplified several times, giving him all the sight of a clear summer's day. There, leaning against a lamp post, was a finely-clothed, middle-aged man lighting a cigarette with a glowing fingertip.

"You are after the man who shot Thomas Edison," the gentleman said, stepping forward. He limped with each step, but didn't appear feeble.

"What do you know of it?" Doliber asked.

"I am the man you seek," he said, stepping up to the invisible barrier. A puff of smoke from his cigarette bounced back from the force field, revealing its continued presence.

"That is a very bold admission," Doliber said, scanning his surroundings for anything and everything. With a telepathic jolt, he sensed the minds in his vicinity, seeking to see if this man had any accomplices. At the same time, he activated a "mystic eye," allowing him to perceive the presence of magic in all its forms. He found no sign that this man had any colleagues nearby, though the vibrant glow of the man's body proved he was a powerful spellcaster.

After a moment of silence, the gentleman continued. "I am not afraid of you, Sheriff. While your magic tricks might be impressive to the common folk, they are nothing compared to the true power at my command."

"I've heard that before," Doliber said, ready to test the man's mettle.

A shimmering jolt of white light streaked out of Doliber's hand, and shattered the invisible force field separating him from his opponent. A second streak of red force came from his other hand, and wrapped itself around the gentleman's neck, seeking to find purchase in his flesh. The beam had the power to restrain and strangle, but as much as Doliber fought, he couldn't make his magical rope tighten. It was being repelled by a stronger force surrounding his opponent's body.

The gentleman smiled, and fire flared from his eyes. "How quaint," he said with amusement.

In an instant, Doliber's magic rope leapt from his hand and wrapped itself around his neck, while the other end relocated into his opponent's grasp. The spell had been reversed, a daring and difficult maneuver for a skilled warlock.

As the magic force started to strangle him, Doliber realized this man had genuine training on his side.

Stepping up to Doliber, the gentleman smiled in his face. "I could crush the life from your body any time I desire. I think it better that you live, for now."

The pressure vanished from Doliber's throat, and he fell to his hands and knees, gasping.

"I need you to know something," the gentleman said, grabbing Doliber by the collar and lifting him up again. "Edison will be the harbinger of doom for those who've wronged me and mine."

"I don't understand," Doliber said, hoping to get an explanation.

"You will," the gentleman said, releasing the sheriff and letting him stand on his own. "In time, everything will be revealed, and you'll be helpless to stop it!"

A puff of purple smoke appeared, and the gentleman was gone.

The odd after-effect of the man's teleport gave Doliber another piece of vital information. That wasn't the sort of teleportation spell the Guild utilized. Their training perfected a spell that produced light as an energy exchange. The most skilled warlocks could teleport seamlessly, without any visual effects, but purple smoke was never part of it, even for the most amateur apprentice. Smoke seemed more in line with a few sideshow freelancers, though their power was generally limited, while this man had strength to rival a Guild Master.

The investigation to find Edison's shooter had taken an unexpected turn At least Doliber had a face to link to the crime. Now he could start looking for a name, and a motive.

* * *

There were four churches in Selwood, plus the Catholic mission two miles south of town. Each building had a few hundred loyal attendees, though the Methodist congregation was exceptionally large after the chaos of past events. The pews had been filled to overflowing these past few months, as suffering and hardship had befallen so many in town. Certainly, the death of the Mayor and several other prominent citizens had had a positive impact on church coffers.

Clarence felt very out of place, sitting in the very church he had helped to build. The homecoming was turning bitter, as the truth of his magical escapades were the talk of the town. His fellow believers, those who had called him brother the day before, now saw him as an abominable sinner.

Before the regular sermon, Pastor Jameson asked for a special prayer, to save the soul of his wayward protégé.

"The false doctrine of superstition and sorcery has led Clarence astray," Jameson proclaimed, "but there is still hope. Let us pray that he sees the error of his ways."

Clarence wanted to walk out, but he still cared for the old man. So much he'd learned from Pastor Matt Jameson over the years; without the man's tutelage he never would have pursued a path to the Lord. Though, recent years had shown him that the path held far more wonders than some would readily accept.

No matter how much he pondered it, Clarence couldn't reconcile the rift that was growing between himself and his mentor. How could magic not be of God? The scriptures were full of examples of God-fearing men utilizing the mystic arts to fulfill His will. Christ himself practiced healings, and bade that his followers do the same. Yet, somehow, many Christians felt that *all* magic had to be demonic trickery, and there was no convincing them otherwise.

Magic was such an art of the heart and soul, contrary to what some perceived as the "rational" mind of God. Those with the ability to affect reality with spells had to "feel" what they cast, and no one person had the exact same results. Every user had to learn their own unique methods, and understand their inner senses, in order to be effective. Most of all, it was a rare gift, and those who weren't born with the ability could never understand it.

The original Methodists hadn't been opposed to magic, yet in recent years different churches had turned their back on mysticism in favor of science. Many preachers highlighted technological innovation as the true purpose of man, as part of understanding the truth of God's creation. They viewed magic as the antithesis of that true order, and therefore it had to be of Satan.

Clarence had always been torn on the situation, having been born with the innate talent to master magic, yet mentored by a man who despised mystic trickery. It wasn't until he'd gone out into the world and met with other believers—those like Professor Bennett, who didn't hate magic—that he came to understand its true value and compatibility with a Christian life.

If Thomas Edison hadn't been shot, Clarence might have broken the news to his mentor more gently, when the time was right. Without adequate preparation, it was doubtful that Pastor Matt would ever accept a mystic preacher in any form.

Clarence could have kept his gifts to himself, and enjoyed his visit in comfortable anonymity if not for Edison's attempted assassination. It seemed God had other plans.

Most of the congregation had to agree with Pastor Matt, or they would have worshipped in another church. The alternatives were numerous in Selwood. The Episcopalians were known to favor mysticism, and there was a non-denominational fellowship that the sheriff liked to attend... and there were always the Mormons. Though, for those who objected to the ways of magic, Jameson was the man.

The moment of prayer came to an end, and everyone picked up their hymnals to begin the morning worship.

As the organ began to play, the door to the meeting hall opened, and one by one the members of the congregation locked eyes on the latest arrival. A few people up front started to sing, but soon fell silent as the organ stopped, and the intruder made his way up front.

Stepping up to the pulpit, Sheriff Doliber offered a hand to the pastor.

"Forgive the intrusion, Pastor Jameson, but I need a moment with your congregation."

"How can we help you today, Sheriff?" Jameson asked coldly, keeping his arms folded across his chest.

"I'm looking for a man," Doliber said, looking out at the frowning parishioners. As a certified warlock, he knew he was walking into the lion's den here, facing those who deemed him to be the worst sort of sinner.

"Can this not wait?" Jameson asked. "You are interrupting our service."

"I'm sorry for the inconvenience, but I've already visited the other churches this morning and still haven't found what I'm looking for. This will only take a few minutes, if you'll indulge me."

Jameson rolled his eyes and asked, "What would you like us to do?"

Doliber closed his eyes, and sent a telepathic burst to everyone in the church. The sudden image of Edison's proclaimed shooter and a request for identification flooded the minds of the Methodists, sending many of them to their knees. A lot of mumbling and a few cries of fright came out as the people realized what had happened.

"You dare come into this church and assault us with your sorcery?" Jameson shouted, incensed.

"I need to know who this man is, before he tries to kill again or does something worse," Doliber defended. "Now, does anyone recognize the face?"

Nobody answered, and Jameson pointed toward the door, ordering the sheriff to leave. Doliber did as he was asked, but took his time, and perused the thoughts on everyone's minds. He didn't dig deeply, not wishing to pry into their personal memories, though if any of them knew the face he'd shown them, it would be right on the surface. Unfortunately, he found nothing. The shooter's identity remained a mystery.

As Doliber reached the door, Jameson shouted to him. "It's never too late to seek absolution, sheriff. We shall pray for you!"

"Pray that I find Edison's shooter," Doliber replied before stepping outside.

As the door shut behind him, the congregation was still in a state of disorder. The people were angry and upset about having the sanctity of their minds violated by the mystic intrusion.

"I won't pray for that man!" someone snapped. "Not after what he just did."

"Damn the devils and their magic!" a bearded fellow shouted.

"Pray for our own souls, Pastor," an elderly lady cried.

Pastor Jameson called for order, and the people obeyed, though it was clear they'd rather vent their frustrations than surrender their feelings as the Bible dictated. The mood of the room was far too hostile for Christian comfort.

Clarence knew he was now an outsider, and feared he would become a pariah. These weren't his people anymore, and it was wrong to remain among them. Standing up from his front row seat, he made his way down the aisle, getting shifty stares from people as he passed.

"Clarence, where are you going?" Pastor Jameson asked.

He couldn't respond. Nothing he said could make any difference here and now, and there was a good chance his words would turn negative. That would not serve God in any way. The door shut behind him, and silence gave the only civil answer he could provide.

The sun was shining outside, and it was getting hot at midday. Clarence had no idea where he was going until, starting down the street, he turned to see the iron railing surrounding the church cemetery. Something told him to stop for a visit.

It wasn't the largest plot of land, though the church was fairly new to the area, so there weren't too many believers buried in the graveyard. A few dozen well-kept graves stood atop the grassy field, and one toward the rear called to Clarence like a beacon. He stepped over and looked down at the hunk of marble, reading the words he had chosen to place there. *"Thelma Rebecca Davison, beloved wife and mother. May she rest with God."*

It had been three years ago that a virulent flu had taken her, a week before Clarence had decided to leave for college. The remnants of his mother's estate had helped him to cover the first year's tuition, and church donations had made up the difference thereafter until he left school to follow his calling. Now, recalling the bitter stares of his former friends moments earlier, he wondered if he was truly up for it. It was easy to spread the gospel to the willing, but in the face of fierce opposition he wanted to run. The joy and confidence was fading, and he wondered if the Lord might have other plans for him.

"I'm not sure what to do, Ma," he mused to the stone.

As he stood at his mother's grave, a lady's voice echoed inside his head. "Don't fret, my sweet boy. The angels will smile upon you."

It wasn't his mother, of that he was certain, but the

mysterious communication lifted his spirits.

Turning to leave, Clarence felt something hard impact the side of his head. The blow sent a wave of pain through his skull, and the next thing he knew he was on the ground, bleeding. His eyes were blurry, and all he could see was the faint outline of the gravestones around him, as a second blow put out his lights.

CHAPTER 4:
TROUBLEMAKERS

There was blood on the gravestones. Ron Grimes didn't like the looks of things, and wondered how this could have happened. How was it a man could be bludgeoned to the brink of death on a Sunday morning, in a church cemetery no less? It was unheard of, downright uncivilized. Most men had the good sense to stay respectable and moral on Sunday, even if they were less than perfect come Monday morning.

"Deputy Grimes, this is simply intolerable," Pastor Jameson said, exasperated. "To think, my former ward would be attacked directly after leaving service!"

"Just calm down, Pastor Matt," Ron said. "Tell me what you know."

"You? Where's that conjuring sheriff of yours?" Jameson asked. "He should be the one conducting this investigation... no offense, Deputy."

"None taken," Ron lied, feeling a twinge of resentment. The grizzled, old pastor was not the sort of man to befriend, though word of his firebrand sermons were the talk of Sunday dinner. "Doliber's chasing down a lead on the Edison shooting, and left me in charge while he's gone. Now, explain the situation."

"Very well," Jameson said.   "Clarence left the church shortly before the day's sermon began.   That was nearly two hours ago."

"Nobody was with him when he left?" Ron asked.

"No, he left alone," Jameson said, lowering his gaze.   "I fear we may have driven him off."

"You don't say," Ron said, recalling the hostilities of the previous night.   Jameson hadn't been very accepting of Clarence's healing gifts, and it wasn't surprising the young man would have fled a church full of anti-magic zealots.

"Now see here, Deputy, I care for that boy like he was my own son, but the way he's changed—it caught me off guard.   I tried to reconcile things this morning, called for prayer to help him see the error of his ways, but then Doliber had to show up and ruin everything."

"What did he do?" Ron asked.

"He invaded our minds, every one of us," Jameson said. "He sent an image into our thoughts without warning, and you know what we think of such demonic conjuring.   It inflamed the congregation, and drove Clarence away."

"I see," Ron said, understanding their upset.   He didn't much care for it when Doliber invaded his mind, and he wasn't against magic in principle.   He could only imagine how passionately the church goers must have reacted.   "Did you see anyone else get up and leave after Clarence did?   Somebody who might've followed him here?"

"No, and I'll tell you right now it wasn't a member of our church who did this.   They would never stoop to violence!   It is not the Lord's way."

"Naw, of course it ain't," Ron said, turning away.   He wasn't going to accomplish anything standing around the graves—not that he expected to get far investigating the beating on other fronts.   Without an eye witness, there was no way to tell who'd done it, and Sunday morning left the chances of a random bystander pretty slim.   Until Clarence woke up, his assault was liable to remain a mystery.

It was getting close to lunchtime, so Ron headed down the street and wondered which establishment would satisfy him.

There wasn't a lot of variety in Selwood, though each eatery had its own little quirks. He hadn't decided about a place when a voice called his name. Turning around, he saw Fiora Silcox with her grandfather crossing the street.

"I thought you two were gonna head out this morning?" Ron mentioned, surprised they were still in town.

"We just heard about Clarence," Fiora said, hurrying over to give Ron a hug. "How barbaric."

"Is there any word on the culprit?" Albert Silcox asked, looking upset.

"No," Ron simply said.

"To think, after saving a life last night, somebody saw fit to beat that young man," Silcox said, clenching his fist.

"It's all that preacher's fault," Fiora said, sounding sure of herself. "You saw how he reacted last night, and everyone's talking about how his flock hates the magically adept. One of his must be responsible."

"Don't go jumping to any conclusions," Ron advised. "Pastor Matt swears his people had nothing to do with it."

"And you believe him?" Fiora asked.

"Until I can prove otherwise," Ron replied.

"Oh, you will," Silcox replied. "I'm sure of it."

Ron could understand Albert Silcox's disapproval of Pastor Jameson, though the bitterness was something new, and it seemed out of character. Mr. Silcox was a calm and collected individual, and wasn't the sort to be calling for a lynch mob. The chaotic events of the past day were clearly having a serious impact upon him.

"Say, you've got the healing gifts, too," Ron mentioned to Silcox, recalling how easily the old man had healed a pair of broken fingers not so long ago.

"I don't know how much help I would be," Silcox replied solemnly. "If it were a bone fracture or a simple bruise, my power would suffice. But a severe beating..."

Fiora gripped the old man's arm and said, "You should try, Grandfather."

Silcox nodded and patted her hand as a half-hearted smile returned to his face.

With the conversation at an end, Ron was ready to bid them farewell, but before he could take his leave a new question halted him.

"So, what are you up to?" Fiora asked, sounding like she had something planned.

"Figured I'd round up some lunch," Ron answered.

"What a wonderful idea. I believe I'll join you," Fiora said presumptively.

Ron didn't mind sharing another meal with her, so he didn't object.

"You two have a good time," Silcox said, straightening his collar. "I have some business to take care of before I check in on Clarence. I'll meet up with you later."

As Albert Silcox walked away, Ron had to question what business the old man had. His cattle dealings had been concluded the previous day, and their carriage had to be fixed by now. Most likely, he was hanging around so his granddaughter could spend more time with a certain dwarven deputy.

The fix was still in, and Ron wondered if he would want to escape his fate when the time came, or if he would fall into the trap willingly.

"So, where are you taking me?" Fiora asked after her grandfather was out of sight.

"Can't say I've decided," Ron said, still weighing his options.

"I know. How about Lucca's?" Fiora suggested.

"You mean the Lucca Saloon?" Ron asked. "You been there before?"

"No, but my dad used to say it had the best food in Selwood." Her expression changed back to a more solemn look. "That's been a few years, though."

Ron could only guess about her father, but suspected the worst. Death was a constant companion for a lot of people, and life expectancy wasn't what it could've been. Everybody had a sibling or two who didn't live long enough to tie their shoes, and a lot of folks didn't live to see their kids grow up. It was the way things had always been, but things were changing, bit by bit. With the technological advancements of people like Edison, and the magical freelancing of people like Clarence Davison, the old tradition of death was nearing an end, or so Ron liked to think.

It was a short walk to the Lucca Saloon, and when they got there they found the place was packed. Sunday afternoons were often a time for people to dine out, as church served as a good excuse to bring them out of their homes. Even an establishment renowned for its liquor and gambling got a boost in business on the Lord's Day.

There was one small table in the corner that was vacant, and Ron found it to his liking. The neighboring tables had single men dressed in their Sunday best, who paid them no mind as they ate.

It took a few minutes before anyone came to take their order, and when that someone finally arrived it turned out to be none other than Solen, himself.

"Figure you'd want to be tending bar with all these people around," Ron remarked as Solen arrived.

"Selwood's own shrunken deputy found himself a match. This I had to see for myself," Solen said with his usual, flippant demeanor. "Are you going to introduce me to your lovely lady?"

"I shouldn't," Ron said.

"Fiora May Silcox," she said, offering Solen her hand.

"Rick's daughter?" Solen replied, patting her hand lightly. "You're just as he said you were, only shorter."

"Oh," Fiora said solemnly.

"Of course, that was ten years ago," Solen said, "but he's one to remember. I never met a man who could drink like that and still walk a straight line for the ladies, if you know what I mean," He ended with a smirk.

"My father was a God-fearing man," Fiora snapped suddenly. "You will not besmirch his good name!"

"Miss Silcox, your father's reputation has nothing to fear from me. I hold nothing but respect for the man. How is he these days?"

Fiora looked disgusted.

"Do you want to take our order, or should we find someplace else to eat?" Ron grumbled.

"Very well, would you like to have the special?" Solen

asked.

"Please," Fiora said, wishing to get rid of the annoying elf as quickly as possible.

"What is it?" Ron asked, less willing to commit to an unknown meal.

"Steak and mashed potatoes. Butter or gravy for the mash, your choice."

"Both," Ron said, enjoying a blend of butter and gravy.

"Both will cost extra," Solen said.

"Extra?" Ron exclaimed.

"Now, wait a minute," Fiora interrupted. "Steak for lunch? Isn't that a bit heavy?"

"It's the special," Solen said. "Didn't you know?"

"No," Fiora replied, looking flustered. "But I guess it'll have to do. You may leave."

Solen smiled and turned to fulfill her request.

"Hey, now, what about the butter and gravy?" Ron asked.

"You can afford the extra nickel, I suppose," Solen mentioned as he walked away.

Ron grumbled under his breath and accepted the inevitable. The charge was outrageous, but that was the way Solen would have it.

"That is the most disagreeable elf I have ever met," Fiora mentioned. "How is it he stays in business?"

"He only messes with people he likes," Ron replied.

"Does he *like* you personally, or does he simply have a thing for dwarves?"

"A bit of both, I think," Ron answered, as a commotion started a few tables over. A chair toppled over with its occupant still seated, and a large man started shouting insults toward him. Other men stood up and took positions behind each of the men, picking sides in the dispute. More words were bandied about, and different people began shoving each other and looking ready for a brawl.

Ron got to his feet and rushed over to break up the fight. It was a tall order for someone his size, but he managed to force his way into the center of the crowd and got up on a table for additional height.

"Hey, now, what's all this?" he asked.

"Nothin' need concernin' the law," a gap-toothed fellow in his Sunday best mumbled.

"Deputy, them men attacked me!" a scrawny lad with a patchy stubble replied. He couldn't be much more than fifteen, but he had the stink of booze on his breath.

"You asked for it!" a burly man shouted back.

"Says you, sons uh witches!" the youth rebutted.

The burly man stepped forward, ignoring Ron's protest. "Stand aside, law-midge. This ain't nothing a good rope can't handle."

"Yeah, they be hanging you, boy!" the gap-toothed fellow added.

Several people got up in support of the young man, and tried to stop the burly man from reaching his target. It only gave him an excuse to throw the first punch, and his friends joined in. Before Ron could blink, the brawl was on, and he found himself pushed off the table by one of the angry men. A pair of bystanders broke his fall, and he rolled out from under the angry crowd before anyone mistook him for a target.

A few respectable people were heading out the door, though most of the patrons were picking sides and throwing punches in a mad frenzy. All sanity seemed to have left the room without warning.

Ron rushed back over to Fiora, who was on her way out of the saloon. "Get on down to the Sheriff's Office," he told her. "Tell Jesse we've got a situation here."

Fiora nodded and hurried outside. Seeing she was safely out of the way, Ron turned toward the taps, to figure out his next move. Reaching the bar, he hopped up on a stool as a glass came flying past his ear.

Solen peeked out from behind the counter and asked, "Aren't you going to break it up? You are the law in town, aren't you?"

"You still gonna charge me an extra five cents for butter and gravy?" Ron asked.

"If you break this up before they do any more damage, you'll eat for free tonight," Solen replied in an uncharacteristic show of generosity.

Ron looked at his worried face, and wondered if the elf's purse strings would tighten again once the trouble was over. "Got a shotgun handy?" he asked.

"No," Solen replied.

"You should," Ron said, as a chair came flying his way. The wooden back smacked him in the side, but it didn't cause him any harm. Looking over the mad crowd, he spotted several other chairs being tossed about, and several remained in the air, as they were used to beat men into submission.

The fighting continued for another minute before someone got bold and drew a knife. Things escalated from there, as multiple people brandished blades and began stabbing at random rioters. The true bloodshed had started, and it was only a matter of time before guns would come into play.

"Damn," Ron said as he saw a bloody knife swing in his vicinity. "Now we're gonna have to hang some of them."

As the stabbings continued, Jesse James walked in, carrying a pair of double-barreled shotguns under his arms. He made his way to the bar, avoiding a few random punches along the way, and set the shotguns on the counter.

"Took you long enough," Ron said, grabbing one of the shotguns and cracking it open to confirm that it was loaded.

"I didn't hesitate," Jesse replied, looking over at the sour-faced bartender. "Pour me a bourbon, would you?"

"Not until you stop them!" Solen answered.

"Oh, all right," Jesse said, grabbing the other shotgun. Aiming it toward the ceiling, he let off a charge of bird shot that splattered harmlessly into the thick boards overhead.

Most of the rioters froze, and the few who didn't were quickly restrained by others. There was nothing like a shotgun blast in close quarters to get people's attention.

"Now listen up!" Ron shouted, keeping a shotgun tucked under his arm. "You've all had enough fun for one afternoon. It's about time you called a truce and get your asses off to jail."

The statement brought a renewed sense of anger from the crowd, and several men took the threat of incarceration as reason enough to finally draw their sidearms.

The moment they pulled their guns, Ron dropped the shotgun and drew his Remington. With lighting speed, he had the pistol up, cocked, and he sent a lead ball into the face of the first man to aim at him. A second shot dropped another would-be shooter, and after that the rest of the crowd had enough sense to put up their arms.

"Any of you get stupid like that again and I'll have Jesse send a load of buckshot into the lot of you!" Ron threatened, holstering his revolver.

The crowd wised up, and accepted their fate. The surviving rioters formed two lines and walked out of the saloon with Jesse's shotgun aimed firmly at their backs. Ron picked up the other shotgun and followed along as well, hoping he didn't have to kill anyone else this day.

Moving down the street with the two dozen subdued men, Ron felt his stomach grumbling. Killing was a hungry business, and he hadn't had anything since breakfast. Once the criminals were secured behind bars, he'd have to take Solen up on that offer of a free meal before the elf changed his mind.

Thinking of the meal reminded Ron that someone was missing.

"Say, Jesse, where's Fiora?" Ron asked.

"I left her at the Sheriff's Office," Jesse replied, looking pleased with the shotgun in-hand.

It was the logical thing to do, leaving her in safety while the trouble was resolved, so Ron didn't think anything of it.

They made it around the block, and down the short stretch of Commerce Street to reach the Sheriff's Office. Marching the men inside, they made a direct line for the back, and they filled several of the cells. They made sure to pat each man down and confiscate any weapons before sending them into lock-up. It was a tough crowd to deal with, and there was no telling who was getting locked up with whom, so punches might start flying before long.

Ron knew he had to get to the bottom of this fight, figure out why it had started in the first place, but that could wait an hour. He had a steak waiting for him, and a date to finish.

Fiora was sitting in front of the desk, looking calm and

collected as Ron walked over to her. "I see you have matters well in hand," she mentioned.

"Pretty much," Ron replied. "Feel like picking up where we left off?"

Fiora smiled and hopped off the chair. "I would be delighted, Mr. Grimes."

Taking her arm, he said, "Remember, call me Ron."

* * *

It was sunny in San Francisco, a stark contrast to the last time Doliber had visited the city by the bay. It had been cold and raining on that dismal day in May, though it had seemed appropriate, considering his business at the time. He'd delivered renegade warlock Tobias Sylvestri back into the hands of the Guild for disciplinary action. It was an unpleasant business, as Tobias was both a murderer and the Guildmaster's son.

Today's visit was no less important, though far less depressing.

The stylish house on Fulton Street was a pretty sight in clear sunlight, and Doliber made his way to the front door to announce his presence. Three firm clacks with the brass knocker was all it took to get the attention of those inside, and the door swung open with a trick of magic.

Nobody was immediately visible as Doliber entered, though that was to be expected. Pausing a moment in the entryway to take off his boots, the sheriff looked down the short hall that led to the Guildmaster's study. As if reading his mind, a voice called out from that room, beckoning him to come forward.

Walking into the study, Doliber spotted the aging form of Guildmaster Franklin Sylvestri sitting in a cushioned chair in front of a small reading table. The chubby man with round head was stroking his neatly-trimmed white beard as he studied a thick tome, seeming less than interested in his guest. "What can I do for you, Journeyman Doliber?"

"I need your help to identify someone," Doliber said, taking a seat across from the Guildmaster.

"I'm not sure what help I will be," the Guildmaster said, setting his book down and finally locking eyes with Doliber. "Tell me, have you considered the offer I presented you when last we met?"

"I am still considering it," Doliber replied honestly.

"Do not wait too long," Guildmaster Sylvestri advised. "The Master's Examinations are not offered lightly, nor often. If you delay much longer, your admittance to the program might not happen for some time."

"I understand," Doliber said, conflicted on the matter. It was something he wanted to do—expand his knowledge and power, and become a true Master of the Guild—but he was still uncertain of the cost. To become a full-fledged Master, he would have to accept the limits that came with his new station. No longer would he be allowed to impact society as a county sheriff. Guild Masters were banned from interfering in the affairs of *ordinary* men, and could not interact with society in general. The power and knowledge he would gain could not be used to benefit anyone outside the Guild itself, and that troubled him greatly.

Still, the allure of being a master of magic could not be denied.

"This man you need to identify," the Guildmaster stated, "why do you believe that I might be able to help you?"

"He's a very powerful mystic," Doliber explained. "I haven't seen strength like his outside a true Master."

"So you suspect he is a member of the Guild?"

"No," Doliber replied. "In fact, I'm fairly sure he isn't one of us, which is another reason I've come to you. It's doubtful a freelancer this powerful would have escaped the Guild's attention, but if he has, then what I can share with you will be ever more important."

"I see," Guildmaster Sylvestri said, looking thoughtful. "Show me."

Doliber closed his eyes and sent a telepathic burst into the Guildmaster's mind. The memory of the past night, and the confrontation with Edison's mysterious shooter, were replayed for the Guildmaster to see, giving the elder gentleman a clear, firsthand account. In an instant, he knew the events so intimately it was as if he had been there, himself.

As the Guildmaster reflected on the images, Doliber asked, "Is the man familiar to you?"

Guildmaster Sylvestri's eyes grew wide, as he continued to process the new information. "The face, no, but the magic! That sort of teleportation is not something a Master easily forgets. You will recognize it if you ever take your exams."

"What do you know of it?"

"It is the mark of the devil," the Guildmaster said morosely. "That sort of after effect is clearly the sign of black magic; the summoning of dark forces. This fellow you're after is an out and out sorcerer!"

"Then we have to stop him together," Doliber suggested.

The Guildmaster shook his head. "You know better than that. A Master of the Guild shall not interfere in the affairs of common man. Only under the most dire of circumstances would I be able to sanction any sort of precipitous action against a non-member."

"But you said it yourself. This man is clearly a sorcerer. Doesn't that make this a *dire circumstance?*"

"Not quite," the Guildmaster replied. "While the Guild does allow us to take action against certain magicians and sorcerers, it is only when it can be proven that those individuals pose a significant threat to the well being of large sums of people. What you have shown me, while troubling, does not equate to a serious threat at this time. He's a meddler, possibly a murderer, but until he begins stacking up bodies or summoning demons I cannot act. You, of course, are free to take whatever action you deem appropriate, as you remain a simple Journeyman."

Doliber clenched his fists and wanted to shout. The obstinacy of the Guild never ceased to amaze him. They were so set in their ways, beholden to their archaic codes of conduct that the world was suffering under their inaction. It was high time the Guild moved their thinking into the nineteenth century—though it wasn't likely they'd ever change.

Standing up, Doliber turned for the door, deciding it was time to look elsewhere for assistance. Turning back to face the Guildmaster, he said, "I'll bring you proof that this fellow is an imminent threat, assuming I survive."

"I'm sure you will," Guildmaster Sylvestri said, picking up his book and looking disinterested.

Doliber grumbled in frustration and went back to the entryway to retrieve his boots. As he sat on the small bench to put on his footwear, he saw another door swing open halfway down the hall. The sheriff felt his hair stand up on edge as he locked eyes on a familiar foe.

The tall, dark-haired figure of Tobias Sylvestri came stumbling out into the hall, and as the door shut behind him the young warlock felt his way forward with an ornately-carved hardwood cane. The man was still totally blind!

"Forgive the intrusion, Sheriff, but I believe we should have a word," Tobias said, his walking stick clicking against the floor in front of him with each step.

"What could you possibly have to say to me?" Doliber asked, uninterested in hearing a speech of remorse. No doubt, Tobias wanted to beg forgiveness for the trouble he'd caused, and the lives he'd ended unjustly. The fact that he still lived was a sign that the Guildmaster wasn't a true stickler for the Guild's rules. If Tobias had been anyone else's son, he'd have paid for his crimes with his life.

"I couldn't help but overhear the conversation you had with my father," Tobias said. "You have a sorcerer on the loose."

"That's my problem," Doliber said, tying his boots. "Now, why don't you go walk into a wall?"

Tobias smiled faintly, but otherwise kept a pretty neutral expression. "I understand your bitterness toward me. I did try to kill you, once."

"That's only part of it. If you'll excuse me."

Doliber stood up and headed for the outer door. As he wrapped his hand around the knob, Tobias' voice froze him in place. "I can identify him for you."

The claim struck Doliber like a bucket of cold water. What was Tobias playing at this time?

"What do you know?" Doliber asked.

"The individual you encountered, he seems familiar."

Doliber released the door knob and turned around. "You did more than listen."

"I may have intercepted that telepathic message you sent to my father," Tobias admitted. "Never mind the dirty details. I want to help."

"How?"

"Let me take you to the right people; individuals who might know your man."

Doliber studied the man before him, and a trick of magic allowed him to peer beneath the surface, searching deeper into the man's mind and soul. With a magically-induced empathic scan, the sheriff could sense Tobias' eagerness, and the sincerity in his thoughts. The truth was undeniable; the Guildmaster's son was trying to help, but why?

"What's in it for you?" Doliber asked continuing his interrogation. "What possible reason could you have for helping me?"

Tobias paused for a minute, as his emotions spoke for him. Doliber came to understand the answer even before it was spoken.

"I need to do something," Tobias finally answered. "I need to get out of this house, do more than sit around."

"That's your problem," Doliber said, feeling irritated by the admission. As usual, Tobias had a self-serving agenda, with no care of right and wrong, or the well-being of others. He didn't care to catch a criminal; he just wanted something to distract him.

Feeling the price of a possible lead was too high, Doliber turned back to the door, and started to twist the knob.

"Do you have any idea how utterly boring life can be as a blind man?" Tobias asked.

Doliber opened the door and looked out at the sunny day, ignoring the plea. Tobias had brought it all upon himself, and he'd have to live with his penance.

"You can't leave me here!" Tobias shouted as Doliber walked down the front steps. "You owe me. I'm only blind because I helped you."

"Helped me to fix a problem that you created," Doliber answered.

"That's only a half-truth, and you know it," Tobias challenged. "Regardless of what I did, if you want a chance at identifying your sorcerer, you'll need my help."

There it was again—sincerity. Doliber could feel it like a

warm breeze in the back of his mind. Whatever motivation Tobias might have, he actually did know someone who could identify the sorcerer. At least, Tobias *thought* he did. There were no guarantees.

"You want to help me? Give me a name," Doliber ordered.

"Hiram Mayer," Tobias said.

The name sounded familiar, though Doliber wasn't sure from where.

Tobias continued. "Morgan Winthrop, Peter Greenlaw, Horace Quinn, Nicholas Brandt."

Then, it struck Doliber like a bolt of lightning. He realized where he'd heard the names before, and it all made perfect sense. "The Northeast Light and Magic Company," he said.

"Precisely," Tobias said. "All freelancers, all with perfect motive to shoot Thomas Edison, their chief rival in the war between technology and magic. One of them likely hired your sorcerer, or knows who did."

The probability was too obvious to ignore. Most murders involved either love or money. Edison was upturning a lot of apple carts with his grand inventions, and none were so threatened as the purveyors of magic. Those who extorted huge sums from the public for their mystic devices would be out of business if Edison had his way, and that was a prime motive for an assassination.

Though, who could say which group of freelancers had hired the assassin? There were dozens of magic-selling outfits, any one of which might have been responsible. "What makes you think the heads of Northeast Light and Magic are behind this?" Doliber asked

"I've met them," Tobias answered. "More importantly, I've met Mayer. He's an unabashed sorcerer, who tends to disappear in a cloud of smoke. No doubt, he taught the technique to your shooter."

Though possible, there was no way to tell. It was purely circumstantial evidence, and it would be difficult to investigate. Doliber would have to go back east to confront Mayer and his associates, but a transcontinental teleport would take days and significantly drain his mystical powers. It would be unwise to interrogate powerful freelancers without an untapped magic arsenal at his disposal. Still, it had to be done.

"Of course, if you want to go up against Northeast, you'll need help," Tobias mentioned, sounding pleased with himself.

"You want to accompany me to Boston," Doliber said, getting to the point.

"More than that," Tobias answered. "I'll take you there."

"Really?" Doliber asked.

"I may be blind, but I'm still more of a warlock than you."

Doliber knew it wasn't an insult, but another truth. Tobias had been taking his Master's exams before turning rogue, and there were tricks he had learned over the years that made him more formidable than most other spellcasters.

"How long would our trip take?" Doliber asked.

"I could have us there in an instant," Tobias boasted.

Doliber climbed the stairs to reach Tobias, who lingered in the doorway. "Then let's go," he said, feeling ready to take the leap.

Tobias took a step back. "Oh, yes, there is one problem to overcome first," he said. "You'll need to sign me out."

Doliber felt like such a fool. Of course, the Guild wouldn't allow a murderer like Tobias to roam free. While unwilling to execute the son of a Guildmaster, it made sense that they'd put him under house arrest.

"What will I have to do to get you out of here?" Doliber asked.

"It's quite simple," Tobias replied. "Sign a Writ of Responsibility, and we'll be off."

It was a tall order, and Doliber wasn't sure he wanted to go that far. There was no telling how Tobias would react when he was released from this prison, and his power was more than formidable. Doliber wondered if he could actually keep him in line.

Speaking to the uncertainty, Tobias said, "It's either that, or you can hop a train and go by yourself. The choice is yours."

"I'd rather not wait that long," Doliber replied, knowing

how crucial timing could be in cases like this. It was dangerous to leave Selwood unguarded for a prolonged period. With a magically-endowed shooter on the loose, there was no telling the number of lives that could be lost in the coming days.

"Talk to my father again, and sign the Writ. I know you don't trust me, but think about it. I am blind, and wanted for murder. What possible incentive could I have to run off on you?"

"I can think of a few," Doliber said. "And I'd pay for it if you did."

"If I do not stay with my escort, the Guild will execute me for certain, no matter who my father is. Staying in this house with nothing to do is pure torture, but death is a journey I am not prepared to embark upon just yet. Trust in that."

There seemed to be little alternative. Doliber needed to get to the bottom of things, and catch Edison's shooter as soon as possible. If that meant enlisting the help of Tobias Sylvestri, so be it. He'd worked with worse men in the past.

Perhaps it would take a devil to catch a devil, Doliber thought, as he walked down the hall to see the Guildmaster.

"You won't have to wait long," Tobias said as Doliber neared the door to the study. "My father should have the writ filled out by now."

Doliber shook his head as he opened the door to retrieve the document.

CHAPTER 5:
FOR THE FAMILY

The farmhouse sat atop a gentle slope, amidst a stand of pines. Cultivated fields of grain stretched out in all directions, and in a few weeks it would be time for the harvest. Wheat grew well in the rich soil surrounding Ravenna-West, as did just about anything. The elves had helped this land to truly blossom in recent decades, bringing order to the wilderness.

Joella knew this spread well. She'd grown up here, and seen her parents turn this land from forest to farm. It had taken a lot of hard labor, and a lot of spare hands, but the end result had been worth it. Two hundred acres of golden grain and pastureland belonged to Errol Talus, Chieftain of Clan Talus.

It could have been hers, Joella knew. It *would* have been hers, if not for a few unfortunate circumstances. The death of her first husband and the twisted rules of Clan Law had condemned her to forsake this inheritance, or deliver it into the hands of Mactus Sellius.

She could hear the dogs barking from a mile away, as she rode up the slight incline toward the front gate. The large, wooden portal was opened wide, inviting her inside, though nobody was there to man it. The front fence wasn't used anymore, and remained merely for show. Twenty years ago, it had been used to corral horses, but as the farm grew and changed, so had the animal pens and roadways.

Joella kept her horse trotting at an even pace as she neared the house, and the large, hairy dogs came charging toward her in greeting. The gray haired breed of elven hound was a common inhabitant of western homesteads, bred to be even tempered and alert. They barked in low yelps as she came to a stop in front of the house.

Hopping down off her horse, Joella felt the front paws of the lead dog on her shoulders, as the happy animal gave her a friendly greeting. Its tongue stroked her face, and the hard licks felt strong enough to strip paint. Good thing they were kind-hearted beasts, or they could be deadly. She picked the dog's paws off her body and gave it a mild scolding for being so sociable. The dog and its companion wagged in response and followed her as she walked to the front door.

It was good to be home, if only for that fleeting moment.

She didn't need to knock on the door. By the time she reached it, someone had opened it, and she stopped to look upon the familiar face. The woman's name was Sienna Talus-Paness, though to Joella she always held a less formal moniker.

"Mom," Joella said, feeling flushed all of a sudden.

Joella's mother wrapped her arms around her daughter and gave her a reassuring hug of welcome. It had been nearly a year since they'd last seen each other, and despite the strain of recent events they still had a familial bond that could not be denied.

Stepping back and holding her daughter out at arm's reach, Joella's mother said, "It's good to see you."

"You too, mom," Joella replied. "I'm sorry I haven't been around."

"You've had your own life to lead, Joella," her mother said. "Now come. We should talk."

The last statement came off a little cold, and Joella knew the warm welcome wouldn't last long.

Beyond the door was the central living room, a long, sprawling area with chairs and carpets. A large, stone fireplace sat in the center of the room, and a player piano was tucked into the corner. There was enough room to entertain several dozen people, and the Chieftain occasionally had that many guests. There were many prominent citizens of Ravenna-West who liked to pay a visit on occasion, and the dinner parties were the talk of the town. Errol had the spirit of an entertainer at heart, and so long as you were sober and upright he was glad to open his home to you.

Passing through the now vacant living room, Joella recalled the many fond memories she had, growing up in this house and listening in on the adult conversations. Depending on the guest, her father could talk about anything. Philosophy, theology, politics, modern art, classical music, even rudimentary science; he was a very scholarly man. It had been his devotion to knowledge that spurred him to teach Joella to think for herself and turn her into the independent woman she was today. How ironic that such a logically-thinking man would remain tethered to the antiquated traditions of Clan Law.

They kept walking across the room and went into the kitchen. The fair-sized room was largely filled by the large cook stove, copper sink, and various cutting boards. The setup was designed to allow a chef to prepare a meal for a multitude of people, which the Talus family often did. Whether it was feeding their hired hands or entertaining the guests, Sienna always had her hands full.

Sitting down in front of a table covered with rooted vegetables, Sienna picked up a knife and began working. "I assume you're here about your sister," she said, peeling a rutabaga.

"That is why I'm here," Joella admitted. Feeling in the mood to lend a hand, she picked up one of the round vegetables and began peeling it with the large bowie knife she always had tucked under her jacket.

"You probably shouldn't be," Sienna said, keeping her attention focused on the work. The peels dropped off into a large basket in front of her, which was already half full of other rubbish.

"I couldn't stay away," Joella said, dropping a peel into the basket.

"Well, I'm glad you're here," Sienna said, braving a hint

of emotion, "and I'm sure your father will be glad, too, even if he won't show it. But you've gone too far, Joella. You're not going to be able to come around like you should. Clan Law says we ought to disown you for the shame you've brought upon us."

"For what?" Joella said, slapping the half-peeled rutabaga down. "For refusing to prostitute myself to the cousin of my dead husband, a man who doesn't care a wit about me, but wants the property and prestige that comes with my bloodline?"

"It is not our place to question Law," Sienna said.

"Why not? It isn't set in stone, and this isn't the Middle Ages any more. We're no longer ruled by feudal monarchs or nobles. Law has been adapted to accept the liberties of America. Why can't it be changed further, to permit the liberty of marriage?"

"That's not our place to judge," Sienna said.

"It should be," Joella said.

"Well, technically, it can be," Sienna replied. "We are free to make our own decision when it comes to obeying Clan Law, but those who choose to reject it also choose to reject those who still follow it."

That was the harsh truth Joella would have to accept. The price of freedom in her case was a high one, and it would be high for her sister, as well. Yet, how far would her parents go, if both their daughters chose to reject the Law? Would they really choose to be without a family, to shun their only children?

There was more on the line here than simply her sister's future. It could very well mean Joella regaining the favor of her parents in the process, and that could change the rule of Law itself! It was a lofty goal, and perhaps an impossible dream, but it seemed appropriate to think big. Nothing was ever changed by playing it safe or aiming low. Things were changed by bold people challenging the status quo. Nobody had really shaken things up in elvish society for centuries, and it was about time for an upheaval.

As chieftain of Clan Talus, Errol held a great deal of influence, especially among the traditionally-minded elves. If forced to reject the dictates of Law to maintain a relationship with his shunned daughters, it would make the whole of society reconsider the validity of such a ruling. In time, things would change because of it.

But it would only happen if Joella's sister played her part.

"Where's Sara?" Joella asked, hoping to get on with her mission.

"With your father," Sienna said, resuming her work. She hacked up the rutabaga she'd just peeled and tossed the hunks into a large, enameled pot.

"And where is he?"

"In town," Sienna simply said. "They'll be back any time."

"Good," Joella said. "I want to speak to both of them, separately."

Sienna shook her head as she started peeling another rutabaga. "That isn't going to happen."

Joella knew it wouldn't be that easy. Even if her mother was willing to bend the rules and associate with her shunned daughter, she wasn't going to let Joella talk Sara out of marrying Mactus. Errol would be even less inclined to entertain the daughter who had betrayed the traditions he loved and obeyed.

"Then I'll talk to them together," Joella said.

"I'm not sure how long your father will tolerate the conversation, if you intend to say what you're thinking."

"I'll say what needs to be said," Joella replied.

"You'll say what you *think* needs to be said, to legitimize your own defiance of the Law," Sienna said. "I wish you wouldn't. It will only cause trouble, and you know that."

"I'll do what I think best," Joella said.

"As always," Sienna said, sounding disappointed. "Really, Joella, sometimes I think you should have been a son."

"I don't want to be a man," Joella defended. "I just want the right to choose my own husband."

"While wearing pants, and a gun," Sienna mentioned, eying the pistol poking out from under her daughter's jacket.

"There's nothing in Clan Law that says a woman has to wear a dress and keep house."

Sienna sighed noticeably, and set her knife down. "I'm sorry I couldn't give Errol the son he wanted. Then perhaps he wouldn't have given you such wild ideas. That first husband of yours didn't help, either."

"Gee, I wonder whose fault that was," Joella jabbed. Her marriage to the half-human outlaw Vincent Lafayette had been arranged according to the traditions of Clan Law. Her parents had set it all up before Joella had even been born, trading her hand in marriage to the son of a family friend.

The irony seemed to escape Sienna, who didn't show any sign of remorse or regret in the affair.

"Please, Mom, can't you see that these arranged marriages are wrong?" Joella pleaded.

Sienna blinked nervously and picked up her knife, preparing to get back to work. "It's out of my hands," she said.

"Of course, Sara's betrothal to Mactus is all Dad's idea, right? He still can't see that the son of his old friend is a deplorable excuse for an elf, unworthy of his daughter's hand— either of them!"

"Mactus will treat Sara well," Sienna rebutted.

"Treating someone well and treating someone right are two completely different things. He'll give her a roof, and make sure she's well fed, but in the end she'll be little more than a slave, kept for breeding purposes. He'll never show her love or respect. How can you force that kind of life on Sara?"

"It is the best life she can hope for," Sienna said, her voice growing stern. The tone was something Joella had rarely heard, and it said her mother had heard enough. Their discussion had gone as far as it could.

Joella decided to leave her mother alone, and went out into the living room to wait. Finding a high-backed cushion chair, she put her feet up on a small foot stool and rested, enjoying the midday sun streaming in through the large windows facing south.

As Joella got comfortable, a flash of light drew her attention. The sudden flare appeared in the entryway by the front door, and when she turned to look, there stood her father and sister. Teleportation was a talent of Errol Talus, one that his oldest daughter had inherited. He could make short trips without much trouble, though his magical gifts ended there. Magic was inherent in most elves, though the extent of their abilities were varied and often limited.

Joella stood up as her father crossed the living room, and the second he spotted her he froze. This was not something he'd been anticipating, and it took him a minute to react.

"You're early," Errol finally said, tapping his younger daughter on the back, motioning for her to head into the kitchen. Sara complied, giving her older sister a sympathetic look in passing.

"I came as soon as I heard," Joella said, remaining stern. "Giving Sara to Mactus? Really?"

"I did what I thought was best for all of us," Errol said. "Sit down."

Joella took her seat, as her father claimed his regular chair beside it. His tall, thin frame slid down into the short-legged chair, and he kept his back rigid as he talked.

"You have brought a great deal of shame to our family," Errol started. "Pretending to marry a dwarf, refusing Mactus, turning your back on your people—I raised you better than that."

"You raised me to think, Dad," Joella defended, standing up. She wasn't in the mood for another debate about her decisions. There were more important things to do, and it was time she got on with them.

"Joella, sit down, please," Errol said, remaining firm, but sounding reasonable.

Joella fought back the urge to walk out, wondering if there might be a chance for reason to prevail. Her father was a rational man when it came to many things. It was only his blind devotion to tradition that kept him in the dark.

"I understand why you are the way you are," Errol said with a frown. "I'm sorry I dragged you around, out into the woods and fields when you were growing up. I should have left you in the kitchen with your mother, but life was different back then."

"Don't apologize for who I am," Joella said.

"Yes, I suppose that'll just leave us at odds," Errol concluded. "What's done is done. Nothing anyone says will change you, and I... must accept that." He struggled with the last words, finding it hard to admit.

"So, where do we go from here?" Joella asked.

"We live with it," Errol replied, "and we do what we can to mitigate the fall-out of your heretical decisions." Sliding his hand under his tan suit jacket, he removed a folded piece of paper and gave it to his daughter.

"What's this?" Joella asked, unfolding it.

"The settlement I arranged," Errol said.

Joella glanced at the document, spotting the gold seal of High Minister Ebenezer Fallios at the bottom of the page, accompanied by both Errol's signature and that of Mactus Sellius. Reading the four paragraphs above the signatures, Joella's jaw started to drop. When she finished, she breathed deeply and tossed the paper back at her father.

"You traded Sara for me?" Joella exclaimed.

"I handled the mess you made," Errol said, refolding the paper and tucking it back into his inner pocket. "In exchange for Sara's hand in marriage, Mactus has agreed to officially relinquish his marital claim on you, with the stipulation that your offspring shall be dispossessed of any and all inherited titles."

"Meaning Mactus gets what he wants," Joella said. "One of Sara's children will become chieftain someday, and Mactus will be the father."

"You should be overjoyed," Errol snapped. "These minor concessions prevent you from being outcast from the clan! I saved you from that!"

"At what cost, Dad? Sara's future?"

"Sara isn't like you," Errol said dismissively. "She's willing to follow the Law, and do what's best for her family. I suggest you show a little gratitude for the extreme lengths I've had to go to, in order to secure both your futures."

Joella stood up and headed for the kitchen. "I'm sorry, Dad. I can't be a part of this."

"Where are you going?" Errol asked.

"To see my sister," she replied.

Before Joella could go into the kitchen, Sara came out and stood in her way. The face was so familiar, Joella could imagine she was looking in a mirror ten years ago. Same round forehead, same flowing blond hair, same pointed chins; it was impossible to deny their shared genetics.

"We need to talk," Joella said, grabbing Sara by the arm.

Before Sara could reply, Joella utilized her teleportation talents, taking them both away from the living room in a flash. The sudden jump delivered them into thick woods, many miles from the Talus farm. There, they could talk in private, without interruption or coercion—or so Joella hoped.

"What have you done?" Sara asked, pulling her arm free of her sister's grasp. She took a step back, and stared at Joella, her eyes wide with bewilderment and anger.

"Like I said, we need to talk," Joella said, feeling light headed. The teleport had been a bit much for her, as she'd already crossed quite a distance earlier in the day. The mental pathways inside her brain that processed magic energy could only take so much, and she'd already reached her limit. It would be a trick to return to the house by dinnertime, though she wasn't thinking about that. Her sister's future was at stake.

"Where are we?" Sara asked, flustered. A gust of air shook the branches overhead adding an eerie punctuation to her query.

"Not far," Joella said. Seeing her sister's growing anxiety, she was about to say something more, to ease her nerves, but she never got the chance.

"No, I will not calm down!" Sara said, as if Joella had made such a suggestion. "You shouldn't be doing this, grabbing me out of thin air. Why couldn't we have talked at home?"

Joella was about to explain, but her sister continued without her.

"Oh, I see. You think I wouldn't agree to your little plan if our parents were around to pressure me otherwise."

"What do you know of my plan?" Joella asked, wondering how proficient her sister's perceptions had grown.

"I know whatever's on your mind. Every thought, every feeling," Sara replied, brushing a hand over her forehead and up onto her hair. "You want me to reject Mactus, just like you did, and for what? To prove a point and slight the man?"

"No," Joella defended. "To spare you a lifetime of empty

servitude."

Sara lowered her head, trying to calm down. "Don't
pretend your intentions are noble. I can read your emotions as
well as your mind. Oh, you might pretend this is a grand gesture
to change Elvish Clan Law, and spare me from a horrible fate,
but in reality you're doing it to win against Mactus. You are still
playing games with him."

"That is only part of my motivation," Joella said.

"It's the part that counts," Sara replied, looking cool and
collected at last. "It's about your personal pride, and a hatred for
a man who wanted to pin you down."

Joella was impressed. Her little sister had come a long
way in the past year, developing mental powers that rivaled the
best psychics Clan Talus had to offer. Sara could gather thoughts
and emotions as if they were her own, and process them with
apparent objectivity. It was almost frightening how much she
could perceive of Joella's intentions.

Considering what Sara was saying, Joella realized she
was right. The catalyst for stopping this marriage came down to
a rivalry that had sprung up between herself and Mactus. After
what that man had said to her, and how he had been willing to
hurt her for his own ends, she was not about to let him marry her
sister!

Still, that didn't mean she wasn't interested in helping
Sara. It was simply a secondary motivator.

"Don't pretend you're doing me any favors," Sara said, her
anger rising again.

"Fine. I won't," Joella replied, knowing she'd need a fresh
tactic to win over her sister. "Tell me what you want."

"I want to go home and make my own choice in the
matter," Sara said sternly.

"But you aren't making your own choice, are you?" Joella
continued. "You're doing what Dad wants you to do. You're..."

"I know what I'm doing, and I know what you're going to
do," Sara interrupted. "If I don't agree to your plan, you're going
to cry yourself to sleep a few nights, blaming everyone but
yourself. But you shouldn't blame anyone. This isn't such a bad
thing. Marrying Mactus won't be any different than marrying the

blacksmith's son I was betrothed to for years. I'm prepared for it, and accept it."

"How could you be so shallow?" Joella asked, feeling her eyes water. Nothing was going as planned, and it was eating her up inside.

"I'm not like you," Sara said. "I'm not out to pick a fight. I just want to get married and have kids, raise them in a traditional household like everyone else we know. Why do you oppose my right to choose that path?"

"I don't," Joella defended, wiping away tears. "But what choice do you really have?"

"The same choice we all have. Obey the Law and honor our traditions, or run away."

"That isn't much of a choice," Joella rebutted. "Why shouldn't we be able to decide matters of marriage for ourselves without losing everything else that's right and good about our people?"

"Because then we would lose everything else," Sara replied. "You fail to realize that all we have, the strength of family and tradition, all stems from the strict order given to us by Clan Law, including arranged marriages. Without that, we'd fall apart."

Joella wasn't ready to accept it, but there was a glimmer of truth behind Sara's words. She couldn't deny the wisdom her little sister held, though it seemed so odd and alien to hear the words coming from someone so young.

"How did you get so old, so fast?" Joella asked.

"Telepathy," Sara replied, tapping the side of her head. "I have so many years of other people's memories, sometimes I swear I'm already an old maid."

Standing there among the tall trees, Joella realized her sister really was different. Not only that, she'd become a veritable stranger. Being out of the house for nearly ten years, Joella didn't really know Sara at all, and that was the flaw in her grand plan. As much as she hated Mactus and arranged marriages, she couldn't make her sister feel the same way in short order. That was something Sara would have to learn on her own, if at all.

The whole thing still made Joella sick to her stomach, but there was nothing more she could do about it.

"Can we go home now?" Sara asked contentedly.

It was going to be a strain, but Joella felt confident she could summon the strength to make the teleport. It was only a few miles, after all... or so she thought until she mentally retraced her trail. It was then that she realized the distance. They weren't a few miles from home, they were a few hundred miles! How was it possible?

"Great job, Joella," Sara chided, continuing to read her sister's thoughts.

"I'm sorry. This has never happened before," Joella said, working it out. She hadn't done much teleporting over the last month, and getting to the Talus homestead had taxed her magic potential. Logically, she shouldn't have been able to teleport much more than a few miles after that, but somehow her calculations had been drastically off the mark. The lingering remnant of spellcasting ability had taken them so far, it didn't seem possible.

Then she considered the last time she'd strained herself, the teleport she'd made to save Doliber's life. With her magic processing ability all but exhausted, she'd dared to make the 'port over a hundred miles. The strain might have killed her, but she'd managed to escape with only minimal side effects, or so it had seemed at the time.

It was the only explanation that made sense. Straining herself that first time had somehow unleashed a previously unknown reserve of power. Yet, that reserve was now used up, and there was no way to know when it would be replenished.

"We're stuck here?" Sara asked, processing Joella's revelations.

"It's okay," Joella said, brushing it off with ease. Being stranded away from home seemed like the best possible outcome at the moment. It would give her time to convince her little sister to see things her way.

"That is a stupid way to look at this," Sara complained. "And it won't work."

"Stop that!" Joella snapped, finding her sister's constant

mind-reading annoying.

"I can't!" Sara shouted. "Don't you understand? I can't stop reading your mind!"

"Oh," Joella said, taken aback.

The situation was finally becoming clear. Her sister was suffering from Omnimentapathy. It was a rare condition known to affect the more powerful telepaths on occasion. Victims found themselves unable to shield their minds from those around them. Other people's thoughts became commonplace in their head, to the point where they couldn't block them out, any more than someone could stop from hearing a train whistle when they were standing right next to it.

Sara could not help but sense everything!

A crunching sounded in the nearby bushes, and the noise came on so suddenly Joella's heart jumped. She'd been so distracted with her sister that she hadn't noticed someone or something sneaking up on them. It was too late to run and hide, but her hand slid down to rest on the butt of her Smith & Wesson.

The source of the noise pushed through the underbrush, snorting and grunting all the while. The large beast with brown hair and claws was walking on all fours and jerking its head around nervously. At first, Joella thought it was a bear, but when the creature stood up on its hind legs, she clearly saw it was humanoid. The thing towered over seven feet tall and howled like a wolf at the elvish women.

Terrified by the beast, Sara turned and ran, distracting Joella for a split second. It was enough to give the creature an edge, and it swung a monstrous hand toward Joella, clubbing her on the side of the head. The impact sent a burst of throbbing pain into her skull and forced her to the ground.

Joella drew her revolver as blood began to pool in her mouth. She was seeing double, but the beast was so close she couldn't miss. It was moving in for a kill, she knew, and there was nothing else she could do but fire point blank. Three shots right to the chest brought another howl from the hairy beast, and enticed it to back off.

Forcing her eyes to focus, Joella stood up and aimed for the creature's left eye. Three more shots from her revolver did the trick, penetrating the beast's brain and stopping its rampage. With a soft whimper, the beast grew limp.

Once the immediate threat was over, Jella dropped to her knees and threw up. The spinning in her head had made her queasy, and that couldn't be a good sign. She'd once seen a man get kicked in the head by a horse, and he'd reacted much the way she was right now, only he'd been dead an hour later. What a miserable and meaningless way to die.

"Sara!" Joella called after spitting out the last of her vomit.

"I'm here," Sara replied.

Joella looked up and saw her sister standing right beside her. With all the pain and confusion coursing through her head, she hadn't noticed that she'd returned.

"I think I need help," Joella said, rolling onto her back. She was feeling tired, but knew she couldn't sleep. She feared it could be the last sleep she ever took.

Sara pulled a handkerchief out of a pocket in her blouse and started patting the side of her sister's head. She didn't say anything, but her pleasant expression told Joella it would be all right.

CHAPTER 6:
SAVING SARA

The crowd was gathered outside the Sheriff's Office when Ron and Fiora approached. Their lunch had been peaceful, eaten in the mostly vacant Lucca Saloon. It seemed most people weren't keen on eating with fresh blood stains on the floor and half the tables overturned. Ron didn't care, as other people's squeamishness had given him a more intimate venue for a date. He and Fiora had shared their meal while Solen and his employees cleaned up after the rioters. Other than a visit from the undertaker, nobody else stopped in.

Now Ron could see that a good many of the saloon's would-be patrons were, forming a mob. Though, as he neared the office, he saw it wasn't a single mob, but two distinct groups. Sympathizers of the rioters were gathering, split into dueling factions, and that could only spell trouble.

Walking up to the twin crowds that stood between him and the office, Ron demanded to know why they were there.

"Deputy Grimes, we been waiting for you," one of the men said, stepping forward from the left side crowd. The mustached youth was Billy Colfax, the son of a local carpenter. He seemed like an unlikely spokesman for a mob.

"Yeah? What for?" Ron asked.

"You got some men in there that don't belong behind bars," Billy said, and a few from his side of the crowd shouted similar affirmations.

"You got that right," someone from the other group shouted. "But they's ours, you mage killers!"

"Shaddup, you conjuring devils!" Billy shouted. "We oughta string you all up after what you did to Mister Edison!"

"And we oughta hang you for what you done to Clarence Davison!" someone in the other crowd snapped back.

The two groups started shouting at each other, and it seemed they were about to start a riot in the street.

Their motivation was clear, and Ron understood how the town could be split in light of recent events. However, the rage of the citizens seemed far greater than normal. There was something downright unnatural about it, as if someone or something was inflaming tensions, capitalizing on the tragedies.

"Fiora, you might want to go find your father," Ron suggested, wishing to keep her out of the trouble.

"No, not alone," Fiora said, sounding worried. "We should both go."

"I can't do that," Ron said, as the shouts of the angry mobs grew louder. "Somebody's got to break these people up before things get out of hand."

"How can you do that alone?" Fiora asked.

"I'm not alone," Ron said. "I've got Jesse James in the office, and there's a whole mess of respectable citizens who'll come out if we need them."

"I'd say you need them now," Fiora said as several men began throwing punches.

It was happening again, the same mad violence that had overtaken the Lucca Saloon a few hours earlier. Angry men were beating each other in a wild frenzy, and it wouldn't be long before knives and guns were drawn. The crowd outside was huge compared to the gathering at the saloon, meaning it would be hard to break up.

Stepping back from the violence, Ron turned Fiora's face toward Main Street. "Head over to the telegraph office. Tell the chief operator, Henry Currant, that I need him immediately for crowd control. Tell him to get anyone he can to help, as well."

"I'm afraid, Ron," Fiora said, seeing fists flying barely ten feet away.

"So am I," Ron replied, drawing his revolver.

Fiora started running down the street toward the telegraph office, as Ron wondered what to do next. There wasn't a whole lot he could do by himself, and firing into the crowd would only make things worse, and likely draw return fire from somebody. If he had a dozen armed men for backup, it might be possible to get things under control, but it was questionable if he had time to wait for help to arrive.

A dwarf alone wasn't much in the face of a bloodthirsty mob. A single warlock could make short work of them, but Sheriff Doliber was temporarily unavailable, tracking down the possible culprit behind these hostilities.

Worse still was the absence of his fellow deputy, Joella Talus. Her limited teleportation skills could really help in a pinch, sending a bunch of the troublemakers into lock-up in an instant. Her leave of absence couldn't have come at a worse time for the lawmen of Selwood.

"I sure hope it's worth it to you, Joella," Ron grumbled as he aimed his pistol at the crowd, waiting to take a shot.

* * *

The side of Joella's head still hurt, but her mind was clearing. The pain of the past hour was fading as the sun crept toward the western horizon. The trees blocked all sight of the sunset, but the sky was getting darker. Another hour and the stars would begin to peek out through the curtain of night.

Sara was busy preparing a fire, gathering pieces of dead wood from the surrounding forest. She had a decent pile already, enough to last them much of the evening, and work had begun on lighting the initial twigs. Setting a pair of sticks together, she sat motionless, breathing deeply to focus her limited mysticism and start the fire. After a minute, smoke began to pour out of the stick she was holding, and it wasn't long before the flames emerged. After that, it was simple enough to pile more twigs and larger sticks on top.

Joella watched with envious pride, amazed at how far her

little sister had come in the ways of magic. She'd inherited their ancestors' ancient proficiency in the mystic arts, and was well on her way to mastering many attributes of those archaic skills. Telepathy, pyrokinesis—what other talents would she reveal?

With the fire lit, Sara stepped back and admired her handiwork. After a moment of rest, she started on her next task. Taking Joella's knife, Sara hacked down several saplings. Removing a hunk of lace from her blouse, she tied the greenwood together into a brace for a makeshift spit. With the rack in place, she turned the knife on the hairy beast, carving off a leg and skinning it with the ease of a trained butcher. Stabbing the meat onto the stick, she placed it over the fire to cook.

"At least we won't starve," Sara mentioned, looking pleased with herself.

"You certainly know your way with a knife," Joella mentioned.

"Of course," Sara replied. "I am a Talus, after all. Maybe not as boyish as you, but carving game is a ladylike art, all part of keeping house. Same with lighting fires and tending wounds."

"That's not what I meant," Joella said, sensing a lingering resentment in her sister's voice.

"I know what you meant," Sara commented. "You think I'm pampered."

There was no sense denying it, Joella realized. Anything she thought or felt, her sister knew instantly. More than that, her sister understood their true meaning, the things Joella liked to pretend she didn't think or feel, the subconscious or biased opinions she wished to keep to herself, and some she didn't even realize. How annoying—and utterly unnerving—to be around someone who knew more about your innermost thoughts than even you.

"I'm sorry I haven't known you better," Joella said, feeling it was an honest enough expression.

"Well, I don't blame you," Sara replied. "Not really. You're twelve years older than me, so it's hard for us to relate to one another."

"I still should have been around more, but things are awkward. Mom and dad are so different these days. They aren't the same parents I had growing up."

"Yes, they are," Sara rebutted. "You're just too old to see it."

Joella didn't quite understand her meaning, but felt it was pointless trying to argue. Sara had the upper hand with her telepathy, and it made her conceited.

Sara sensed Joella's realization, and frowned in response.

The sisters sat in silence as the meat cooked over the fire. It wasn't cold outside in the least, so there was no need to get too close to the flames. It allowed Sara to keep her distance from her sister, which troubled Joella. She feared her own thoughts had alienated Sara, meaning her plan to win her over was at an end.

In her lone depression, Joella imagined the life Sara had to look forward to. A mundane existence, serving in the house of Mactus Sellius. There, she would take turns in the kitchen, or entertaining children, but that would be the happy side of the relationship. The grim truth of Mactus seeped into her imagination, the fat, arrogant man who considered his wives to be something less—servants to do his bidding, to stroke his ego, and satisfy his bodily desires. She could envision the nights Sara would sit alone, as Mactus took another of his wives to bed, or he stayed out drinking with business associates, more interested in whores than the women he already owned.

It was these ugly truths that had driven Joella to this course of action, to save her sister from a scandalous man.

Thinking about it made Joella depressed, but she wanted to be depressed at the moment. There was no sense hiding. Better to face it now, so she'd be accustomed to the situation when it actually came about.

"He can't be that bad," Sara said, breaking the silence.

"What?" Joella asked, stirring from her inner ruminations.

"Mactus can't be as dreadful as you imagine," Sara reiterated.

"Maybe not," Joella replied just to be kind. She knew the sort of man Mactus was. He was a Sellius, raised to be ambitious and ruthless, taught to disregard gentle emotions and considerations. Joella knew it all too well, for her late husband's mother had been a Sellius, the aunt of Mactus.

It wasn't hard for her to see the similarities in both men. The only difference between Mactus Sellius and Vincent Lafayette was that Mactus used his ruthlessness in a legal manner.

Sara took Joella's knife again and went over to the body of the beast. She continued the butchering, stabbing and hacking, working out a renewed frustration.

Joella saw she was finally getting through to her sister, but was careful not to feel too excited. It was time to stick with the depression and desperation, to keep the mental pressure coursing through the ether.

The silence stretched on as the sun set. And as the light faded Sara finished her butchering. The large beast was skinned and gutted, with several choice portions hacked off. The good meat was set upon the creature's skin, so the moss and dirt wouldn't soil it.

With darkness setting in, Sara checked the roasting leg, and sliced off a couple of slivers for testing. She bit one and handed the other to Joella, who bit down to find the meat stringy and gamey.

"This stuff's really good when it's marinated properly," Sara mentioned.

"I know," Joella said after swallowing. Chewing made her head hurt, as it flexed bruised muscles and sore gums. The blow hasn't broken anything, at least.

Things were finally calming down, as the sisters nibbled and prepared to settle in for the night, but as Sara removed the meat from the flames, a burst of light foretold renewed trouble.

As the light of the teleport faded, the fire's illumination revealed the new arrival, showing the stern face of Errol Talus. "There you are!" he snapped, thoroughly upset. "Joella, what were you thinking, making a blind teleport I couldn't trace?"

"Dad, calm down," Sara said, grabbing his arm. "Joella didn't mean to go so far. It was an accident."

Errol looked at his younger daughter's face, and breathed a calming sign. "Whatever the case may be, we'd best get you both home. You've caused quite a stir with this little stunt."

"What do you mean?" Joella asked, getting to her feet.

Standing made her head throb worse, but it didn't make her dizzy anymore.

"Half of Ravenna-West is looking for you two, since Sara sent a mental cry for help to every telepath in town."

"Sara?" Joella asked, stung by the apparent act of betrayal.

"I didn't mean to," Sara defended. "You grabbed me so suddenly... I was angry and worried. I didn't know what you had planned, so I sort of unconsciously sent a message. I told you I can't control my powers at the moment!"

"We can sort this all out later," Errol suggested, "but we'd better get both of you back to the farm now, before..."

A rustling in the bushes stopped Errol's speech, as a pair of elves came into the small clearing. The new arrivals were immediately recognized as High Minister Ebenezer Fallios and Mactus Sellius.

"Thank God!" Mactus proclaimed hurrying over to Sara. "You found my dear fiancée, and her kidnapper." He took Sara's hand and gave it a kiss.

"Hold on, Mactus," Errol said. "This has all been a misunderstanding."

"The only misunderstanding would be Joella's presumption that she could attempt to steal away my betrothed without consequence!" Mactus walked over and glared at Joella with a wicked smirk on his face. "I'll see you hang for this."

"No!" Sara shouted.

"Now, Mactus, kidnapping is hardly a hanging offence," Ebenezer said in his droning voice. He was always so austere, even in heated situations.

"Besides, Joella didn't kidnap me," Sara corrected.

"Then why are you here, two hundred miles from home?" Ebenezer asked. "And why did you call for help?"

"I just got spooked," Sara replied. "Joella wanted to talk in private, but didn't give me any warning."

"Yes, as I said, this is all a misunderstanding," Errol added.

"I think not," Mactus rebutted. "The evidence is clear. Joella abducted my fiancée, and I fear she will do it again unless we lock her up."

"I don't think I'd like that," Sara replied.

"Mactus is correct, and it is the law," Ebenezer interjected. "In a case such as this, the accused must be incarcerated pending an official hearing."

"But I'm telling you nothing has happened," Sara countered. "You can't arrest Joella if I confirm her innocence."

"I fear we must," Ebenezer said. "It is entirely possible that you are speaking under duress, or telepathic coercion. Or, seeing that the perpetrator in this instance is your blood relation, you may simply be biased, willing to accept abuse to protect her. Whatever the case may be, we must proceed with a proper legal investigation."

"That's ridiculous," Sara complained.

"It is the law," Ebenezer repeated.

"Then the law is wrong," Sara blurted out.

"Sara!" Errol exclaimed.

"It's the truth!" Sara persisted. "What kind of law presumes guilt, even after the alleged victim says nothing happened? What kind of law says you're not allowed to defend your own family? It's wrong!"

Seeing Sara protest against the inequities of Clan Law made Joella proud.

"Oh, shut up," Sara told her sister, hearing her thoughts loud and clear. She was further embarrassed to find herself conceding to all the points her sister had been arguing. Clan Law was flawed in many respects, and she couldn't deny it any longer—not when Joella's future was at stake.

"Like it or not, the law is the law," Ebenezer interjected. "We must all obey it, or suffer the consequences."

"Now, Eb, let's not be so hasty. There must be some middle ground here," Mactus said, suddenly sounding like the voice of reason.

"What would you suggest?" Ebenezer asked, playing along.

"Since the criminal act Joella committed was motivated by her desire to stop her sister from marrying me, I suggest we eliminate that motivation by holding the wedding immediately.

Once Sara and I are married, I'm sure Joella will see the light, and we can settle the ramifications of these rash actions without much fuss."

Joella wanted to punch Mactus, seeing him capitalize on the situation like the crafty snake that he was. However, her better judgment told her now wasn't the proper time. No sense feeding her foes more ammunition to use against her. Besides, with her head spinning, it was doubtful she could inflict much damage.

"How is that legal?" Errol asked. "Sara is not yet the proper age for marriage."

"Not exactly," Ebenezer rebutted, looking eager to support Mactus' position. "Though eighteen is the minimum age of majority for your average elf, the ancient statutes regarding noble heirs are still extant. According to Clan Law, the Chieftain's daughter may be considered a woman as early as she is able to conceive a child, with all the rights and privileges thereof."

"That's absurd," Joella protested, unable to contain herself.

"In such a case," Ebenezer continued, "the Chieftain will have full discretion to decide if his daughter should be wed."

"I'd say he's given it already," Mactus said. "He did sign the betrothal note today."

"I'm well aware, Mactus," Ebenezer replied. "I was there, after all."

"Now wait just a minute," Errol interrupted. "When I agreed to the betrothal, it was with the understanding that the wedding wouldn't be held until she was eighteen."

"The situation has changed," Mactus said. "I suggest you change your understanding with it—unless you want your precious Joella imprisoned."

"You bastard," Errol grumbled.

Mactus laughed at the insult.

"Enough has been said for now," Ebenezer said loudly to get everyone's attention. "I suggest we all retire for the evening, and continue these discussions in a more civilized environment tomorrow."

Everyone was quick to agree, though before they could depart for Ravenna-West, there was still a question concerning Joella' fate.

"We must incarcerate her, you understand," Ebenezer said. Seeing Errol's disapproving sneer, he quickly added, "Just for the night, until we can settle things in the morning."

"I'll not have my oldest daughter put in a cell with common criminals," Errol argued.

Mactus let out a disparaging sound and turned away from the chieftain. His reasonable persona was wearing thin.

"As a compromise, I will keep her at the temple," Ebenezer said. "That way, she will be under guard, but as my guest. Is that satisfactory?"

"I suppose," Errol conceded.

"Then we have an agreement," Ebenezer said with the faintest smirk on his lips. With the matter settled, the High Minister used his magic talents to teleport them away from the woods, to their respective dwellings, where they could each prepare for what the next day would bring.

* * *

Sara didn't sleep well. She had too much on her mind. The thoughts and worries of the future plagued her as never before, as her life threatened to be turned upside down. Marrying Mactus had seemed tolerable when it wasn't going to happen for two years, but being thrown to him now, when she was still getting used to the idea? It made her stomach turn.

The revelations Joella had shown her didn't make it any easier.

Marriage had always been beyond Sara's control. It was something elven parents decided for their children. As far as a prospective wife was concerned, it seemed as if one man was pretty much the same as another. You got married, took care of the house, raised the children, and grew old with grace. It was all any lady elf could want or expect. So what did it matter who the man was, so long as he treated you right?

Now Sara was starting to realize that being treated properly could mean different things. A man could provide all the riches of the world, but still not show his wife true affection.

It wasn't enough to be given a roof over your head and enough food to eat. There had to be more.

Mactus seemed kind enough on the surface, but what lay beneath was dark and ambiguous. His mind was one Sara couldn't read, and as she replayed the memories she'd received from her sister, it frustrated her greatly that she couldn't peer into the thoughts of her would-be husband. One of the few minds her Omnimentapathy didn't work with was someone she needed to read, for her own sake. Yet, fate wouldn't give her the slightest glimpse. What really was going on in his mind? Was it as Joella feared, or did he secretly have the capacity for love?

The answer would not be an easy one to uncover. In order to know beyond a shadow of a doubt, Sara would have to venture down a path from which there was no return. Elvish marriages were for life, with few exceptions. If she did indeed marry Mactus, a lack of emotional connection would never be grounds for a divorce.

Was it worth the risk?

As dawn came, she still didn't have an answer. Walking down the hall from her bedroom, her feet felt so heavy. It would be easier to stay in bed, but life couldn't be so easy. Yet again, the decision was not hers to make.

Light glowed out of the kitchen, as Sara made her way through the living room. The sun was cresting on the edge of the eastern woods, though not producing sufficient light for that amount of glow. The light she saw was the familiar illumination of a mystic orb, the small ball of glass that emitted magic rays as clear as day. Any who could afford the pricey objects had a few, though their charge wasn't infinite, so most people used them sparingly.

The Talus family had plenty of money, but only remained wealthy through financial frugality. It was uncommon for an orb to be glistening at this early hour—there were plenty of lanterns that cost less to burn. This was a most unusual morning.

Sara came into the kitchen and saw her mother sitting at a cutting board, chopping hunks of meat into cubes. The hairy beastman Joella had killed wouldn't go to waste. One large kettle full of water and glass jars was sitting atop the woodstove, while another sat at her feet to collect the cut meat. The food would be boiled, and then set in the sterilized jars for future consumption. Preserving food was a time-consuming process, something that kept many housewives busy for weeks on end during harvest season. Sara had learned to lend a hand since she was old enough to walk, and she expected to be doing it until she was in her deathbed. Such was life.

"Good morning, Sara," her mother greeted, pausing from her work.

Sara nodded and brought a chair over to the cutting table, to assist with the meat. Her help was expected, and she didn't have to be asked or ordered. "Where's dad?" she questioned, grabbing a hunk of the meat.

"Out with the men, tending the livestock," Sienna replied, resuming her cutting.

It was unusual for Errol Talus to be out in the morning these days. They had hired hands for that. It was clear he was troubled, as work was known to clear his mind. The thought of his sixteen year old daughter getting married couldn't sit well with him, any more than it could with Sienna.

"So, mom, what do you think about all this?" Sara asked, slicing the tough meat with a sharp knife.

"I think we'll be sick of stewed beastman before next winter's gone," Sienna replied.

"Not about that," Sara replied, feeling her mother was avoiding the obvious. "About my marriage."

"It was bound to happen sooner or later," Sienna said.

"Later being expected," Sara replied.

"We can't always choose," Sienna said, keeping a steady cutting pace. She was more interested in the work than discussing uncomfortable subjects.

"Do you want me to marry him? Now?" Sara persisted.

"We must do what we must do," Sienna simply said.

Sara slapped her knife down. "But this is wrong! I'm not ready to marry Mactus, and right now I don't know if I ever will be."

Sara's admission finally caused her mother to stop working. The middle-aged elvish matron gave her daughter a chilling stare.

"I'm sorry, but I just can't marry him," Sara said.

The intense stare continued with utter silence. Sienna's anger was so rare, and her powerful emotions were pumping through the air, stinging Sara's telepathic senses. It was overwhelming, and was bad enough to bring the girl to tears.

Seeing her daughter crying finally snapped Sienna out of her quiet frustration, and tugged at her gentler emotions. Getting up, she walked around the small cutting table and gave her daughter a reassuring hug.

"I'm sorry, dear. I forgot how sensitive you are at the moment," Sienna said.

Sara forced herself to stop crying, and reflected on the thoughts and feelings she'd received from her mother's mind. The anger and frustration was only part of the mix, the surface reaction. Underneath, there stirred the complex origins of those feelings, the memories that made her feel the way she did. Little bits and pieces of her past that helped Sara to understand.

It hadn't been easy for Sienna to marry Errol, but it had been arranged. At age eighteen, she married the rugged, young grandson of the clan's chieftain, knowing full well the trials she would endure. Uprooted from a comfortable life in Philadelphia, Sienna found herself being dragged across the country with a group of pioneering elves, eager to find a new homeland for their people.

Sienna had never wanted to be a pioneer, and would have been happy to stay in civilized settings, but Errol had been born to lead, and the council of Clan Talus had deemed it appropriate that he lead the first wave of elves to colonize the American west. So much pain and suffering had ensued during those first years, and so many colonists worked themselves to death to found this community of Ravenna-West.

Sara could see it all, as if she'd experienced it herself. All those years, committed to a man she barely liked in the name of honor and duty. In time, she had grown to love Errol, but not until their first child was born five years after the wedding. Joella's arrival had finally given Sienna a personal motivation to push forward in life, and brought her to love the man who worked so hard to win her affections. Yet, if she'd had it her way in the beginning, before growing to know her husband, Sienna would have never even considered marrying such a man. If left to her own devices, she would have stayed in the city and married some shallow aristocrat, never knowing the wholesome life she'd learned to appreciate.

Such was the origin of Sienna's personal beliefs, and her desire to see Sara follow the Law. It had worked for her, so why not for her daughter?

Yet, there was more to it than that, something that left a bitter resentment in Sara's heart. This marriage to Mactus was less about what was right for her, and more about what was good for Joella. Of course, she'd known all along that her betrothal was a bargaining chip to spare her sister from exile, though what she got from her mother's thoughts and feelings was even worse. It made her feel second best to be traded like property, and to know that her mother loved Joella a little more.

"I'm glad things worked out between you and dad," Sara said after her tears were dry, "but you can't expect them to work for Mactus and me."

"You must at least try," Sienna persisted.

"I can't and I won't," Sara said, growing firm in her resolve. "I'm sorry if you think it's childish or self centered, but I can't give myself to that man, not even to save Joella."

Sienna hugged Sara tighter and started to cry, herself. The hold lasted for a few lingering moments, after which she went back to her seat and started chopping meat in silence, her tears running down her cheeks as she continued with her work.

"We'll work this out," Sara assured her mother. "I'm sure Joella has a plan."

Sienna shook her head in disbelief, and almost laughed. She may not have thought much of the concept, but at least her tears were drying.

CHAPTER 7:
AFFAIRS OF HONOR

It was gloomy in the Temple's main meeting hall. The large, stone chamber was too big for the illumination of mystic orbs to sufficiently dispel the shadows. How fitting a place for an arranged wedding, Joella thought, as she stood at the speaking podium, staring out at the empty chamber. It was like the dismal castles back in the old country, the sort her people had left behind. How sad that Clan Talus still sought to cling to the ancient ways that man and elf had fought a revolution to overthrow barely a century ago.

"I trust you slept well," the High Minister said as he entered the chamber. He was dressed in his usual, drab robes that fit with the mosaic theme of the temple.

"As well as could be expected," Joella said, feeling her stomach grumble. Though a bed had been provided in the High Minister's private study, no breakfast had been served. It was either a very good or very bad sign. Either she wasn't being fed because her stay would be over shortly, or she was to be starved for strategic purposes. Joella wouldn't put it past Mactus and his allies to use such a scurrilous tactic to hurry the wedding along.

Joella didn't like being a pawn, and would have to rectify the problem. "When do I get out of here?" she asked, curious if the High Minister would divulge anything.

"Soon," was all he said, though his expression added meaning to the single word. There was something sinister up his sleeve, for certain.

Passing Joella, the High Minister took a seat at his desk, which sat in the center of a raised platform at the front of the large room. He began picking through sheaves of paper, going about his business as if nothing were out of the ordinary, paying no attention to his reluctant guest.

A beating sounded at the main doors, and the High Minister opened them remotely with a flick of his wrist. The magic at his command was often used for trivial actions like that, to prevent him from having to walk short distances.

As the doors opened, Mactus stepped inside, followed by his skinny stooge of a brother, Gregory. Both men walked with their head held high, seeming proud of themselves. They reeked of arrogant pretentiousness.

"Ah, Ebenezer, how are you this morning?" Mactus greeted the High Minister as he approached. Both men clasped hands in familiarity, after which they sat down on opposite sides of the desk.

As Mactus and the High Minister settled into their seats, Gregory walked over to Joella. "Lovely to see you again, Miss Talus," he said, sounding innocent enough.

"Under the circumstances, I can't say the same," Joella replied.

"Please, don't hold my brother against me," Gregory said, leaning against the front of the podium. His tall, slender frame was a stark contrast to the chubby form of his brother.

"Corruption of blood is forbidden under American law, so I'll judge you purely on your own actions," Joella said.

"Oh, how considerate and enlightened of you," Gregory replied. "So, are you planning to become a lawyer next?" he asked cynically.

Joella sneered at him and turned away, irritated by his obvious disdain for her behaviors. If he hadn't been a Sellius, she might have let it slide, as most people thought her odd to behave like a man. Upholding the law wasn't the job of a lady, or so she'd been told by just about everyone she'd ever met. She wasn't about to let it deter her from the independent life she was leading. Wherever it took her, she was going to see it through, and damn the naysayers.

Another pounding sounded at the door, and Errol entered with Sara. They were dressed in modest attire, nothing fancy or formal as one would expect for a wedding. It gave Joella reason to hope. Maybe things wouldn't go as expected, after all.

"Excellent, you're right on time," Mactus announced before the High Minister could speak. "Now we can get this marriage formalized."

"Do not act so bold, Mactus," Errol warned. "We haven't decided on anything yet."

"I don't see there's much to discuss," Mactus said, standing up to look Errol in the eye. "You agreed to the betrothal, and according to Clan Law the wedding may take place at any time. It is in everyone's best interest if we get it over with here and now." Leaning forward, he whispered in Errol's ear. "That is, if you want your other daughter to remain free."

Errol frowned but said nothing more, reluctantly subdued by the threat.

"May I speak?" Sara asked.

"You may," Ebenezer said graciously, "but choose your words carefully."

"I will," Sara assured him. Turning to Mactus, she asked, "Do you love me?"

Mactus smiled and took her hand. "You're cutting to the chase rather quickly," he said. "We must be married first."

Yanking her hand away, Sara stepped away from him. "I didn't ask if you wanted to make love, I asked if you loved me, emotionally."

"I will love you as I love my other wives—in time," Mactus replied. "Now, don't make a fuss over nothing."

"You expect me to marry you, and that we'll learn to love one another eventually?" Sara asked.

"That is our way," Mactus said.

"I'm sorry, but I want more," Sara said. "I will not marry you."

"What?" Mactus exclaimed, turning red.

"Sara, what are you doing?" Errol asked, looking worried. "You know your obligations."

"No, Dad, I can't. I just can't!"

Mactus stomped his foot and shouted, "You have no say in the matter. Your father and I have an agreement, and the law says you must marry me whether you like it or not!"

"In that case, I call for disassociation!" Sara challenged.

The statement brought silence to the room.

"You what?" Mactus finally said, as everyone continued to stare in wonder.

"I will not marry you, Mactus," Sara repeated. "If you insist, I'll disassociate myself from the clan. Is that what you want?"

"Sara, no!" Errol said.

"I must!" Sara persisted. "I won't marry a man I don't love, who only wants me as a trophy, or a tool to get back at my sister. If that means I have to leave the clan, so be it."

"You can't do that!" Mactus challenged. "You're not of age to declare disassociation."

"This is true," the High Minister confirmed, eager to back up his friend and regain control over the meeting.

"You say I am old enough to marry, but not old enough to disassociate myself?" Sara asked. "How can that be?"

"The statute that governs noble marriage predates willful disassociation. Therefore, a disparity of age exists. You may not choose to remove yourself from the clan before your eighteenth birthday."

Mactus grinned in triumph, as Sara broke down and cried.

Having held her tongue long enough, Joella asked, "Since when is there an age limit on disassociation? Since when does someone need to be an adult to be removed from the clan?"

The High Minister raised a finger as he answered. "Ah, it is only willful disassociation that is in question. A child is not deemed eligible to make such a crucial legal judgment, while the clan retains the right to disassociate those who wantonly refuse to abide by the law, regardless of age."

"How convenient for you," Joella said bitterly. "You can

make Sara get married, and assure she has no escape."

"Since when does an elf woman choose who she marries?" Gregory interjected.

"Enough," the High Minister said, bringing everyone to silence again. Looking at Mactus and Errol, he asked, "Now, how would you gentlemen like to proceed?"

"Clan Law is clear," Mactus said. "Errol has signed the betrothal, and Sara is of legal age to marry, so I propose we get on with it, immediately."

"I have already drawn up the papers," the High Minister said, grabbing the documents from his desk.

Sara covered her face as she continued to cry. Her fate was certain, unalterable.

"Wait," Errol said as the High Minister shuffled through the papers. "This is all happening too fast. Can't you see that my daughter is not ready for this?"

Mactus scoffed. "You should have thought of that before signing her away to me." His kind façade was gone, as it no longer served a purpose. His true, ruthless self was showing through for all to see.

"As the father, I have a right to rescind my approval, and stop your wedding," Errol stated firmly.

"Not on the wedding day," Mactus said.

"This is absurd!" Errol challenged. "No date has been set."

"It has now," the High Minister rebutted. "The marriage is scheduled for this time and place, according to my official records. You have no recourse but to agree."

"You dare treat me like this?" Errol said, incensed. "Me? The Clan Chieftain?"

"None are above the law, not even you," the High Minister stated.

"You abuse the law to suit your own ends," Errol snapped. "You are not fit for your office!"

"The Clan Council would disagree."

"Suck it up, Errol, you've lost," Mactus said, slapping him on the shoulder. "Now, accept me as your son-in-law while I'm still feeling charitable."

It seemed the game was over. Mactus had everything he needed, and there was nothing anyone could do to stop him.

Mactus grabbed the papers from the High Minister and looked them over with satisfaction, ignoring Sara's weeping and Errol's fuming.

Joella could barely contain herself. Everything she'd planned was for naught. Her sister had finally come around, but was now trapped. Everything would have worked out perfectly if not for crooked legal maneuvering.

She wasn't going to let them get away with it.

There was one last thing that Joella could do. It was unconventional and dangerous, but she felt confident she could pull it off. An official challenge in the name of honor!

Rushing over, Joella smacked the papers out of Mactus' hands. "You have dishonored my family enough. I'm calling you out!" Mactus had insulted and wronged her enough that she had reason to challenge him to a duel. Shooting him dead would put an end to his evil machinations, and assure that Sara remained free.

Mactus laughed in her face. "No woman has that right."

"But I do," Errol said.

The unexpected turn left Mactus speechless, as Errol nudged Joella aside and got in his face. "You've harassed my daughters enough. I've tried to be reasonable, tried to believe you were just a stickler for the old ways, but this goes beyond tradition and morality. You are a sick, twisted man, and I'll not have my heirs share your name."

"What are you doing, father?" Sara asked nervously.

"I'm doing what I should have done a long time ago," Errol said, poking Mactus in the chest. "*I'm* calling you out."

Mactus flinched, and stepped back away from Errol, unsteady in his movements. "Eb, do something," he asked, turning to the High Minister.

"He has just cause, I believe," the High Minister replied, "but first, the marriage."

"The duel first," Errol demanded, "or by God I'll put a bullet in you too, Ebenezer!"

The High Minister swallowed nervously and nodded his

head, finally purged of his austere arrogance.

Staring straight at Mactus, Errol asked, "How will you have it?"

Shaking off his fear, Mactus straightened up and replied, "Fine, I'll see you outside in five minutes!" Marching past the High Minister's desk, he disappeared through the doorway leading to the private study. Ebenezer and Gregory quickly followed him, and there was no telling what chicanery they were plotting. If any trick of magic was used to alter the results of the shootout, there would be hell to pay for the perpetrator, assuming they didn't cover their tracks too well.

As they waited, Errol's daughters each gave him a hug and words of encouragement.

Joella finally recognized the father who had raised her, the man who had never truly changed, but merely suppressed all the attributes that made him the man she admired. The political appeaser was gone. Now there was only the true elven man.

"Can you read their thoughts, Sara?" Errol asked, as Mactus and his cohorts remained in the back room.

"Mactus is blank to me," Sara replied. "I can only get faint bursts of feeling from the High Minister, but Gregory has some interesting ideas. He's feeling pretty confident, but there's nothing untoward going on. As far as he knows, this will be an honest duel."

"Good," Errol replied, drawing his revolver and checking the cylinder. "Then I'll be able to kill him fair and square."

"You talk a good fight," Mactus replied, emerging from the back door. "Let's go find out if you can back up those words."

The walk outside was tense and hasty, as everyone had their own reason to get on with it. The midmorning sun was warm and welcoming, and a lot of people were out in the street, going about their business. Ravenna-West was a growing trading center, not only for Clan Talus, but for several other elvish clans and even some human settlements. It was a shining jewel of civilization amidst the wilds of eastern California.

Joella felt sweat forming on her forehead, and it wasn't because of the heat. So much was pegged on this duel, she found herself feeling more scared and nervous than she'd been in ages. It wouldn't have been so bad if she'd been the one facing Mactus—she was confident in her abilities—but her father? He was a decent rifleman, but she had no idea of his skills with a six-gun.

The short street beside the temple was devoid of bystanders, so it seemed the appropriate place for the shootout. Even so, Gregory was sent out to make sure nobody was lurking in the path of errant gunfire, as the duelists took their positions.

Waiting for the word to turn, Errol looked over at his daughters and said, "Whatever happens, you take care of each other."

Joella nodded, but Sara stood frozen like a statue, unnerved by her own emotions and those she was receiving from others around her.

Gregory came back to the alley and gave the all-clear, after which the High Minister called for the men to turn and fire at will.

Errol spun around and drew his pistol, a dull, gray Vanguard .41 Special. Spotting his target and taking aim, he pulled the trigger as a burning sensation bored into his stomach. The pain made him cringe forward and drop his gun, even as he saw Mactus collapse twenty paces away.

As Gregory ran over to his fallen brother, Joella and Sara attended to their father. The blood was soaking through the shirt as they propped him up. Joella felt her father's back and noticed there was no exit wound, so the bullet was still in him.

"We have to get you to the hospital," Sara said urgently.

"Not until I know he's dead, and you're safe," Errol said, feeling throbbing pain with each word.

"Oh, no," Sara mumbled, as her face drooped with dread.

"What?" Joella asked.

"Gregory's happy," Sara replied. "It must mean Mactus is okay."

"Give me my gun," Errol said, fighting to get up. "I'll finish it."

There was no way Errol would be able to do it, so Joella decided it was her turn. Picking the gun up off the ground, she walked over to where Mactus lay, intending to put an end to him, legally or otherwise. She knew it would condemn her, make her a wanted murderer if she put a bullet between his eyes, but she didn't care. Sara would be safe if Mactus died, and the betrothal would be null and void.

Nearing the scene, Joella's concerns faded as she saw the puddle of blood forming around Mactus. He wasn't moving, and the bullet hole foretold his doom. It was straight through the heart and there was no recovering from that. Gregory was crouched there, making a convincing show of concern for his slain brother, though his eyes were clearly dry.

There was something quite satisfying at seeing Mactus dead, and Joella held no sorrow for the man's dependents. The wives would be taken care of by one man or another, and the children would have the chance to grow up to be something other than their pigheaded father. Truly, her heart felt like an alligator in springtime.

Returning to her father, Joella found him to be in great pain, but still living. The High Minister was standing over him now, checking his wounds.

"Is it done?" Errol struggled to ask.

"You did it, dad. Straight through the heart," Joella assured him. "Now, what about that doctor?"

"I have called for help," the High Minister replied, though Joella hadn't heard or seen him take any action to that effect. It took her a moment to recall that it was obviously a telepathic call he had sent, something she had grown unaccustomed to after years of living outside the elvish communities. Her late husband's properties and interests had sat further to the southeast, in the dry lands of Nevada and Utah. Wherever there was gold or silver to steal, Vincent Lafayette had been on the trail—until he'd met his doom at the hands of a vengeful dwarf.

The medics arrived moments later, a pair of young women in tight-fitting white suits. Their uniforms were designed to prevent the clothing from getting in the way during delicate surgeries and to prevent the spread of infections, though they had the side effect of looking a tad tawdry.

"The chieftain has been shot," the High Minister

announced.

"We know," one of the dark-haired ladies replied, kneeling down to examine the wound. "You know protocol; we must assess the situation on site before transferring any patient to hospital facilities."

"Have you assessed it yet?" Joella asked, irritated with the situation, "or should we wait for my father to die first?"

"Oh, hi there, Jo," the other orderly said pleasantly, flicking the back of her own ear. "Didn't expect to see you around again so soon."

"Mandi," Joella acknowledged, uninterested in talk. Her father's life was on the line, and childhood acquaintances could wait.

"How's that friend of yours, the sheriff you brought in a while back?"

"He's fine, I suppose," Joella replied. "Can you get my father to the hospital, please?"

"We're already there," Mandi said.

In the blink of an eye, Joella's surroundings changed. One second, she was standing in the alley, and the next she was in a bright, white room that stank of disinfectants. The teleport had been quick and painless, performed by a very skilled spellcaster.

Mandi and the other orderly helped Errol onto a surgical bed, and a haggard-faced doctor walked over to examine the wound. After using a simple spell to put the patient to sleep, the doctor helped the orderlies as they removed the bloody jacket and shirt to get at the bullet hole, and then the medical man performed his magic. Holding his hand over the wound, he extracted the bullet, levitating it into his waiting palm. Once the object was removed, he closed his eyes and examined the damaged tissue in his mind, then went to work to repair it.

"Perhaps you should wait outside," the standoffish orderly asked, directing the two sisters toward the lone door behind them.

"I'm not leaving my father," Sara said.

"Come on, Sara," Joella said, urging her to listen. "The doctor needs privacy to concentrate."

"No, he doesn't," Sara rebutted. "He's done already. He just wants us to wait a few hours so he can make it look more harrowing and pad the bill."

"What? That's absurd," the orderly shrieked.

"Then you are absurd," Sara said with a smile. "They're your thoughts."

"Nonsense. I'm a level five telepath. My mind is closed."

"Not to me," Sara argued. "Don't worry, your profiteering secrets are safe with me, but I'm not leaving my father's bedside.

"It is all right, Gladys," the doctor said in a droning voice. "I am done here."

Sara and Joella returned to their father's bedside, and saw him sleeping peacefully.

"He will be unconscious for a few hours," the doctor mentioned, staggering over to a nearby chair. He sat down and breathed deeply, looking exhausted, which was understandable. The effort needed to heal was taxing on the mind and body.

The sisters waited, having nothing else on their minds than seeing their father wake up and bask in his victory. Three hours passed, and as their inner clocks told them it was nearing lunchtime Errol stirred from his magically-induced slumber. "My chest is awfully cold," were his first words, as his eyes blinked at the brightness of the room.

"The doctor had to cut your shirt off," Sara said, grabbing his leather jacket from its resting place beside a garbage can. The blood on it had dried, and wasn't very noticeable on the weathered material. She draped it over her father, and he smiled, amused by her attention.

"That was the worst pain I've ever felt," Errol said, "but it was worth it."

"Thanks, Dad," Sara said, leaning over and hugging him.

As his younger daughter pulled away, Errol placed a hand on her arm. "I'm sorry I had to put you through this—either of you."

"You were just trying to do what you thought was right," Sara said.

"Not always," Errol admitted with downcast eyes.

"I know," Sara said, looking over at her sister, who stood on the other side of the bed. "You did what you had to do... for your family."

"We all did," Joella added, pulling Errol's gun out of her belt. She set the cold hunk of metal by his hand, but he shook his head.

"You hang onto that," he said. "I've got others, and I expect you could use it more than me, seeing that you're a sheriff's deputy, and all." He started to laugh, still amused by the concept of his daughter being a law officer.

"I don't know, Dad," Joella said, picking up the pistol again. "This is an ugly piece."

"Hey, that's genuine elven craftsmanship there," Errol said, scooting up in bed a little. "That was given to me last year by the chieftain of Clan Allyn, himself."

"Really? I didn't realize," Joella said. Staring at the pistol's six-inch barrel, she read the inscription: "Vanguard .41 Spl, Manufactured by the Allyn Arms Co., Mono Lake, CA. U.S. Patent Pending." Looking over the mechanism, she realized it wasn't much different from a Colt single action, only the frame was slimmer.

"It's made with a new nickel-steel alloy, making it stronger and rustproof, or so Felix told me."

"Felix?"

"Chieftain Felix Allyn," Errol said. "You really have been away too long. The eldest heir of Clan Talus should know such things."

"Well, maybe I'll come visit more often now that I'm free of that bandit you married me off to, and his wretched family."

"Yes," Errol said, clearly uncomfortable with the reminder. "Let us speak no more of arranged marriages, for either of you."

"Music to my ears," Joella said, to which Sara smiled appreciatively.

* * *

It was a peaceful evening at the Talus farm. For the first time in years, Joella sat at the dinner table, feeling comfortably at home. Her mother and little sister were bringing out the dishes, and the thought of fresh beastman stew was tantalizing.

The afternoon had been one long explanation for mother. Coming back after the great ordeal, Errol and his daughters had spent hours explaining the circumstances to Sienna. "Why did you have to shoot him?" she kept asking, unable to accept it. She'd always liked Mactus, and couldn't understand how her husband could kill him. Eventually, the message finally got through to her, and she had to accept that the duel had been for the best.

Errol and Sienna had their family back, and that's all that mattered.

As the table was set and they bowed their heads to bless the meal, a thumping sounded at the door. The hounds started howling at the prospects of an intruder, but the things would never bite anyone. Like many friendly breeds, elven hounds had a tendency to bark up a storm, but were otherwise harmless.

Errol said the brief prayer of blessing before getting up to answer the summons, and Joella followed him out of curiosity. Opening the door, they were greeted by a familiar yet unexpected face.

"Cousin Doreen," Errol greeted the lady in plaid dress. "What brings you out all this way?"

Stepping inside, Doreen answered, "What do you think? You shot my husband this morning." Slapping a piece of paper into Errol's hands, she said, "I'm here for my Widow's Rights."

Errol swallowed nervously and looked over the paper as Doreen walked into the living room. Joella chased after her, understanding her father's discomfiture.

"Doreen, you can't be serious," Joella said.

"I'm entirely serious," Doreen confirmed, looking around.

"But we're cousins," Joella said.

"It's either this, or I'll be forced to marry that creepy brother-in-law of mine. Personally, I'd rather marry your father." Staring at the wall of windows, she remarked, "I always loved this living room. Now it'll be mine."

"This is just wrong," Joella said, shivering in revulsion.

"Don't worry, you'll always be Cousin Jo to me," Doreen said. "I won't make you call me Auntie or anything."

"Yeah, thanks," Joella said, "you're all heart."

"Hey, I'm the victim here," Doreen whispered harshly. "I have four kids, and my husband is dead. What other option do I have?"

"Other than creepy Gregory?" Joella mentioned, thinking about the alternative.

This situation wasn't all that different from the one Joella, herself, had been in not so long ago. Faced with the choice of marrying Mactus or the dwarf who'd shot her husband, she'd opted for the dwarf, though she hadn't been willing to follow through. The sham marriage had never been consummated, and was presently null and void.

However, Doreen wasn't the sort to take half-measures. If she married Errol, it would be for real, with all the legal and physical requirements fulfilled.

Joella couldn't imagine her father having another wife, and the thought of him being with a woman other than Sienna made her sick to her stomach. God only knew what her mother would think of it.

As Joella tried to come to terms with the inevitable, her father stomped over, having worked up the courage to face Doreen. "Young lady, you must reconsider this," he ordered.

"There is nothing to consider," Doreen rebutted. "You shot my husband, therefore I have the right to claim you as his replacement."

"But I'm nearly twice your age, and your own blood!"

"First cousin, once removed. It's legal... in most States."

"Oh, what have I done?" Errol asked, slapping a hand over his forehead.

"Dad, I'm so sorry," Joella said.

"It's not your fault," Errol said.

"I'm sure it is," Doreen said, looking mildly amused, "but it won't be so bad. The kids and I will more than pull our own weight around here. Oh, and I expect Hittie will come around, too, just as soon as she stops mourning. She was the only one who really loved Mactus. The rest of us were just stuck with him."

"What about Yuba?" Joella asked.

"She's already fawning over Gregory. The trollop," Doreen replied. She had such a low regard for her brother-in-law that her ill feelings oozed onto her former marriage-sister for even liking him.

"What am I going to do?" Errol asked, looking at his daughter.

"It's the law, dad," Joella said, finding the words strange coming out of her mouth. "You don't have much choice, do you?"

"That's right," Doreen said with a satisfied smile. "Now, let's go see the rest of the family, and share the good news."

Joella rolled her eyes and followed them into the dining room. Home would never be the same again.

CHAPTER 8:
THE PURVEYORS OF MAGIC

It stank down on the Boston docks, the scent of old fishnets rotting in the sun. It had smelled like this for centuries, ever since the first European settlers had built the first wharf. Life by the ocean had its downsides, but it was a living for a lot of men.

Doliber had never appreciated salt water. The sea was so alien to him, a vast expanse that he left for other men to cross. The wind and the sail remained as mysterious to him as magic was to most others, and he decided to keep it that way. You wouldn't catch him boarding a schooner at any time.

It wasn't the tall ships that brought him to the docks this sunny August afternoon—it had been a blind man with grandiose claims and the desire to escape captivity. Renegade warlock Tobias Sylvestri had brought Doliber straight across the continent in an instant, promising him answers and clues. The men responsible for plotting the assassination of Thomas Edison lurked in this east coast city, or so Tobias thought.

"Look at this," Tobias said, turning around. "I've always loved the sea. You know, when I was a child, I'd go down and watch the ships sail into San Francisco Bay. I can't tell you how many times my father scolded me for wasting hours daydreaming, when I ought to be studying my magic books."

Doliber locked his eyes on Tobias, breaking the blind man's perusal of the harbor. "You can see."

"Of course not," Tobias said, "but you can."

Doliber flinched as he realized the implication. "You're tapping into my thoughts."

"How else am I supposed to find my way around? Now, would it kill you to look at the ships a bit more? I thought I spotted an old Brigantine up ahead that piqued my curiosity."

"Does it have anything to do with the men we're looking for?"

"No, but..."

"Then it can wait," Doliber replied.

Tobias grumbled but accepted his fate. "All right, we'll get on with it, but I expect a chance to see the ships again before we leave."

"If there's time," Doliber answered. "Did we come to the docks as part of our mission, or were you just here to sight-see?"

"Oh, no, Northeast Light and Magic has a warehouse around here... just over there, I believe." He pointed inland, toward a block of square buildings. "Take that alley there, and we should be right on their doorstep."

Turning down the cluttered alley between dockside warehouses, the two men bumped into a burly fellow who stank of liquor and urine. The guy hadn't shaved in a week, and his clothes were tattered, making him out to be a vagrant. Doliber and Tobias tried to get past him, but he was smack dab between two large stacks of crates, so the only way was through him.

"Beautiful day, gents," he said, sounding cogent enough.

"Indeed," Doliber replied.

"You fellas look like you know how to have a good time," the man mentioned happily.

"I suppose," Doliber answered.

"Then you'll have money for it." The smile vanished from the grungy man's face, and he drew a knife from under his tattered jacket. "Give it to me!"

Before Doliber could respond, a startled look flashed over the grungy man's face, and a moment later he stabbed himself in the eye. The man collapsed to the ground and began twitching in the throws of death.

"Oh, how sad. He killed himself," Tobias said, sounding amused.

"You did that!" Doliber accused, shoving Tobias against a stack of crates.

"Of course I did," Tobias admitted. "He was threatening us."

"You didn't have to kill him," Doliber argued. "His knife was no threat to us, and you know it."

"Don't act so offended," Tobias replied. "This piece of trash has no doubt been preying upon innocent people for some time. Who knows how many lives he would have taken if we'd left him alive. I've done society a favor."

"It's not for you to decide," Doliber rebutted, moving on. The alley widened out past the body, and the risk of being accosted again seemed minimal in broad daylight.

At the end of the alley was a narrow, cobblestone street with wagons blocking the way in all directions. There was one large, three-story warehouse that appeared to be the only structure that might use this particular avenue, and it was the building that Tobias had led them to.

"This is it?" Doliber asked.

"Northeast Light and Magic Company's main headquarters, manufacturing plant, and distribution center, all rolled into one," Tobias confirmed.

"They think it's wise to keep all their eggs in one basket?"

"I suppose that helps them keep a handle on things," Tobias replied.

They weaved their way through the maze of carts until they reached the side of the building. There were two large doors for cart access, but they were locked tight at the moment, so they had to look for another way in. Walking all the way down to the far corner brought them back in sight of water, and to a regular door with a uniformed employee standing guard.

Moving to enter, Doliber found his way blocked by a forcefield.

"Employees only," the guard said with arms folded across

his chest.

"Oh, excuse me, but we're here to see your boss, or possibly his boss," Doliber replied.

"Employees only," the guard repeated, sliding in between the doorway and Doliber, further blocking the way. The man's position placed him within the field's range, so he obviously had an immunity to the magic at work.

"Clever," Tobias mentioned, examining the scene through Doliber's eyes. "You're no magician or warlock, but your bioelectric field has been uniquely adapted to resonate at the precise frequency of the factory's protective field. Isn't that impressive, Jimmy?"

Doliber turned and saw the smirk on Tobias' face. "If you must use my given name, it's James," he said. "Remember, Toby?"

The amusement left Tobias' face and he returned to his neutral pose. "You're right, of course, *James*. Now, how do you propose we get around this field?"

Without answering, Doliber blinked his eyes and cast a spell, punching a tiny hole in the mystic barrier. The powerful jolt made a momentary humming sound, as the tangible field was breached. Further humming followed, along with a shimmering ripple that appeared where the forcefield was peeled back by the counterspell. When complete, Doliber had an arch-shaped opening formed, allowing them access to the door.

The guard's reaction was one of awe, and he stepped aside as the warlocks approached. "Really, you shouldn't go in there," he suggested shakily.

"We'll be all right," Doliber assured him. "Like I said, we've got business with the owners."

Entering the building, Doliber and Tobias found themselves in the loading bay, a large, open room with rows of tables covered with boxes and goods. This was where the finished products were shipped out to the various merchants, to be sold to the well-to-do. Magic trinkets were a booming business.

Dozens of packers were standing around the tables, putting various objects into the boxes. The workers gave no notice of the two strangers who walked amongst them. Obviously, they weren't paid to notice such things.

A bright flare almost blinded Doliber as he passed one particular table. A resolute curse resounded from a worker standing there.

"What's the matter, Seamus?" one of the workers asked.

The cursing man standing near Doliber replied with an Irish accent. "I set off one o' me orbs!"

"How'd you manage that?" another worker asked.

"I don't know," Seamus replied. "I was careful like they taught us, but me thumb slipped."

"You'd have to be strokin' her like she was yer groin, lad," someone remarked, bringing a stir of laughs from several workers.

The situation caught Doliber as peculiar. The orbs were designed to glow at an even light for several hundred hours. If used improperly, they could expel their magic charge all in one burst, but it was difficult to make it happen. A flare of the magnitude he'd witnessed wasn't liable to come from a mystic orb without extreme rubbing, unless something else was going on.

"Let me see," Doliber said, sliding up beside the frustrated worker.

"Who are you?" Seamus asked.

"Oh, just a visitor," Doliber said, taking the affected orb. Activating a mystic eye to perceive the otherwise invisible workings of magic energy around him, he found himself bathed in color. The air around him seemed saturated with leftover spells of different magnitudes that cast a thick haze of residue. The charged orbs piled on the tables around him glowed brightly, as if through a rainbow fog, while the one in his hand was dark and lifeless, completely spent.

"No wonder it went off," Tobias mentioned.

"What?" Seamus asked.

"The room is so saturated with magic residue, it likely reacted to the orb's charge," Doliber explained. "I'm surprised this doesn't happen more often. Your bosses really should dispel more often."

"Are ye some kind of inspector?" Seamus asked.

"You could say that," Doliber answered, setting the orb on the table. He flicked his fingers at the glass ball, sending a new charge of magic into it. "Carry on."

Seamus shook his head and set the orb into the waiting box. The small box then went into a larger crate that would hold fifty such containers. The crate was marked "Hundred Hour orbs," meaning the contents could fetch upwards of a thousand dollars in your average market.

"That was kind of you," Tobias mentioned.

"One of those orbs would cost that guy a week's pay, at least, and it wasn't his fault. This damn room is a powder keg waiting to explode."

Another orb flared as Doliber passed a new table, and the worker there shrieked in frustration. Amidst the laughs of the other packers, a loud shout carried through the air, and a tall man came over to investigate.

"What are you boys playing at today?" the lanky guy asked. "Two flares in as many minutes? That can't be coincidence. I should have you fired, O'Malley"

"It weren't me fault, MacTavish," O'Malley said. He was a short Irishman with curly red hair and a tiny nose.

"That's *Supervisor* MacTavish, and you'll not take that tone with me, Irish scum!" Catching sight of the two warlocks, he asked, "Who the hell are you, and how'd you get in here?"

"I'm James Doliber, Certified Warlock, Delta Grade, and I'm here to see the owners of this sweatshop."

"Bloody warlocks," MacTavish grumbled. "You haven't any active spells on you, per chance?"

"Why?" Doliber asked.

"Aw, damn!" MacTavish said, swiping a hand in front of Doliber's face. A moment later, the tall man collapsed.

The whole room grew quiet, as everyone pondered what had happened.

Tobias lurched forward and fell on Doliber's shoulder. "I can't see," he said repeatedly.

The meaning was obvious to Doliber. The magic spell Tobias had been using to see through Doliber's eyes had been dispelled, leaving him in the dark again. MacTavish must have cast a broad spectrum counterspell to remove it, and that also explained why he'd collapsed.

"The fool," Doliber mentioned. "He didn't think to ask what kind of active spells we had on us."

"What are you talking about?" O'Malley asked.

"Let's just say, your supervisor tried to counter a spell that was above his pay grade," Tobias said, recovering from the shock of being blind again.

Doliber started walking again, and Tobias did his best to keep pace with a hand on his escort's shoulder. It would be a while before he could reestablish a mental connection to peer through anyone else's eyes.

At the back of the loading bay there was a barred door with a magic ward placed on it, barring unauthorized access to the room beyond. Unlike a forcefield, a mystic ward had the potential to inflict pain, unconsciousness, or even death upon anyone who touched it. Based on the strength of the ward, Doliber discerned that it was a non-lethal spell, and one he could easily remove.

Opening the door and stepping through, Doliber stared at the manufacturing center of Northeast Light and Magic. The center of the factory was set up like a honeycomb in three levels, with ladders and stairs leading to different platforms and rooms. The end they were standing at was open all the way up to the roof, allowing the finished goods to be brought down from the upper levels via a complex pulley system, which deposited the items in this lower sorting area, where they'd be subsequently sent to the loading bays.

"Where now?" Tobias asked after a prolonged period of immobility.

The answer didn't come from Doliber, but an equally magical source. As Tobias tried to move, he realized why they weren't proceeding, as his legs failed to respond. Something was pinning them in place, just beyond the door's threshold.

"All right, you've made your point, whoever you are," Doliber said, scanning the mysticism that was restraining him. "Come out and let's talk."

A voice echoed inside Doliber's head. "Do not presume

to give me orders in my own factory, Warlock."

The field holding Doliber and Tobias in place began to contract, squeezing their muscles. The addition of pain gave Doliber the incentive he needed to find the right counteragent and promptly dispel the magic with a thought. He took three steps forward in triumph as Tobias collapsed to the ground, disoriented by the experience.

"Impressive," the telepathic voice said. "With tricks like that, I'm surprised they haven't made you a Master yet."

"They've tried," Doliber answered aloud. "So, are we going to stop playing games and get down to business?"

Stepping out from behind a flimsy partition on a second floor platform, an unassuming figure with small, round spectacles and thinning blond hair revealed himself. "I suppose it's either that, or you start tearing up the place. Really, you Guild members have no tact."

"I'm not here to cause trouble, but to prevent it," Doliber corrected.

"Oh, really?" the man said, climbing down a ladder to reach Doliber's level. "Then why didn't you just come into the shop?"

"What do you mean?" Doliber asked nebulously.

"The shop around front, that's where we deal with customers," the man said.

"I'm sorry, I didn't know," Doliber said.

"No, and I suppose the guard telling you to get lost wasn't a clear enough sign. As I said, the arrogance of the Guild is astounding."

"I don't believe we've been introduced," Doliber said.

"Horace Quinn, founding partner of Northeast Light and Magic. You may call me Mr. Quinn."

"I'll call you Hoar," Tobias interrupted.

"Of course you will, Toad Ass!" Quinn replied, sounding oddly amused.

Tobias stepped forward and Quinn latched onto his hand for a hearty shake.

"You two know each other?" Doliber asked.

"We were at the Academy together," Tobias confirmed.

"Apprenticed under the great Marcus Hilliard Wycliff our first year."

"Yes, but I was smart enough to drop out after that," Quinn added. "Toady here was too committed to following his daddy's footsteps to do the smart thing. Look where it's got you; blind and imprisoned. Well, let's see what we can do about that."

A burst of red light suddenly shot out of Tobias' eyes, and the renegade warlock fell to his knees in agony. He slapped both palms over his eyes, feeling the burn as a magic spell went to work on his corneas. The process lasted for only a few seconds, but it seemed like hours by the time it was finished. The end result, however, was well worth it.

Blinking furiously, Tobias saw with his own eyes. The blindness of the past months was totally reversed, something his father had said was impossible.

"How?" Tobias asked, looking up at his old friend.

"I didn't stop learning just because I left the Guild," Quinn said. "Those stuffed shirts think they have a monopoly on magic, but we freelancers could teach them a thing or two."

"You cured his sight?" Doliber said, disbelieving it.

"A complete restoration," Quinn said, and Tobias nodded confirmation.

"For how long?" Doliber asked.

"It's permanent."

"And just where did you learn such a powerful and complicated healing spell, Mr. Quinn?" Doliber asked.

"Hiram is a doctor," Quinn said, referring to one of his illustrious business partners. "His magical powers are actually limited, though he's figured out more about the human body and how it functions than one could learn from the best medical schools today. Amazing thing, microcellular introspection."

The term was fairly new, but the process was pretty old; the study of the microscopic world through mystical means. Many powerful Masters spent time examining the inner workings of the world, sensing reality on a different level entirely. It was a hard skill to perfect, and could drive an amateur mad, or so the Guild's masters had always warned. It was not to be attempted by anyone who had not completed their Master's exams, and learned the highest levels of magic. Yet, freelancers were under no such restriction.

"I can teach you one better, Hoar," Tobias said, sounding boastful. "Ever heard of subatomic omnispection?"

"Subatomic?" Quinn asked.

"The building blocks of existence, the elementary particles that make up the universe. I have seen them."

"If anyone else made such a claim, I wouldn't even consider it. Because it's from you... I still don't." Quinn smiled and looked dubious.

"You should," Tobias said, flinching suddenly. He got a discouraged look on his face.

"Are you all right?" Doliber asked.

"That damn MacTavish and his counterspell," Tobias said. "I won't have any telepathic abilities for a few hours."

"He did what he had to do," Quinn said. "You were running around in that room with active spells. They were interacting with the orbs, setting them off."

"That doesn't usually happen," Doliber mentioned.

"That's because you don't have a supercharged concentration of magic particles flowing though the air in most places. Your active spell was reacting to the residue, and making the orbs volatile."

"Ridiculous," Tobias said. "A telepathic link wouldn't react that way."

"But a high density mystic tether would," Quinn replied.

Tobias looked over at Doliber with an accusing eye. "We're tethered?"

"It was the only way your father would let me take you out," Doliber confirmed. "He cast the spell himself, just before we left."

"What's the range?"

"Fifty feet, roughly, and it's mono-directional, so only you will get paralyzed if you tread too far."

"How considerate of my father."

"You are a wanted murderer," Doliber reminded him. "You're lucky you're not swinging from a rope."

"Oh, yes, I heard about that," Quinn mentioned, looking

as pleased as ever. "Really, Tobias, I didn't know you had it in you."

"It's not something I'm proud of," Tobias said solemnly.

"Well, good," Quinn replied. "It would trouble me to think of you as a remorseless psychopath."

"The jury's still out on that one," Doliber rebutted. "So, tell me, Mr. Quinn, how much remorse do you feel about Thomas Edison?"

Quinn paused to consider his answer, giving Doliber reason to suspect his guilt.

"I read about that in the morning paper. Tragic, really."

"Tragic because he was shot, or because your assassin didn't succeed?"

"What? *My* assassin?" Quinn folded his arms over his chest and looked smug. "I swear, it's nothing to do with me or my associates. However, I might be able to point you in the direction of those who are responsible."

"How can you do that, if you're innocent?" Doliber asked.

"Having so many freelance mystics under my employ, you can understand I have connections," Quinn said. "I do business with just about everyone who's anyone in the magic fields, even the Guild at times."

"You say the Guild is responsible?" Doliber asked, having his own suspicions about his esteemed organization.

"No," Quinn said, shaking his head for dramatic effect. "It's far too underhanded and provocative for their tastes. You should know that. No, the real culprit is someone far more chaotic, and vengeful."

"All right, you've got my attention," Doliber said. "What do you know?"

"Not so fast," Quinn said. "First things first; namely, my price."

Doliber knew it could mean nothing but trouble when a man such as Horace Quinn talked about naming a price. Someone of his wealth and status wasn't liable to ask for cash, but something far more sinister. It was questionable whether Doliber would be able to bring himself to supply the payment desired.

"What do you want, Quinn?" Doliber asked.

"Tobias," Quinn replied simply. "I want you to leave him with me, and in return I'll tell you everything I know."

It seemed like a simple enough request, though it was anything but.

"Impossible," Doliber replied.

"It's my price. Take it or leave it," Quinn said resolutely.

"Why me?" Tobias interjected, looking more stunned than Doliber.

"Why you?" Quinn asked. "You have to ask?

"Yes," Tobias confirmed.

Quinn slapped him on the shoulder. "I'll not have a friend of mine locked up as his father's pet. No, you'll come work for me."

"And be *your* pet, eh, Hoar?" Tobias wondered.

"Don't be ridiculous," Quinn sneered. "You know me. Am I ever one to take advantage of people? Oh, sure, maybe a few wet Irishmen, but a friend? It wounds me that you could think so poorly of my character." He placed a hand over his heart in an exaggerated show of sadness.

Tobias lowered his eyes a moment, but quickly hid his regret.

"Now, what's the problem?" Quinn asked, turning back to Doliber. "Afraid the Guildmaster will torture you for losing track of his son, or do you want some coin on top of the information I'm offering?"

Doliber didn't like to be disrespected, or to have his honor questioned. He wanted to tell Quinn where to get off, and give him as much consideration as any other charlatan, but it wouldn't do. The only lead he had to discovering Edison's shooter was this annoying little man, so he had to remain civil.

"I don't want your money," Doliber replied. "And if you have any ideas about grabbing Tobias against my will, good luck breaking the tether."

"Oh, that was taken care of with the eyes, in anticipation of your approval."

Doliber took a quick mystic scan and determined that Quinn was telling the truth. The tether was gone—a tether cast by the Guildmaster, himself! The magnitude of the spell had been such that even Doliber wouldn't have been able to dispel it, yet this freelancer cancelled it with no trouble at all. The power Quinn held was truly remarkable, and dangerous—yet another reason to stay on his good side.

"So, name your price. What is Tobias' freedom worth to you?" Quinn asked.

"We're still bargaining?" Doliber asked. Considering Quinn's power, it seemed like a formality. He could take whatever he wanted, and who could stop him?

"Never say I'm an unreasonable or unjust fellow," Quinn replied. "My friend is worth a great deal to me, so I believe it's only fair that you receive adequate compensation." Reaching into his breast pocket, he removed a wallet and began sliding bills out for exhibition. "So, how much is his freedom worth to you?"

Thinking it over, and realizing the position he was in, Doliber looked over at Tobias, seeing the stoic look on his face, as if he were oblivious to the negotiations. The reason for coming here was painfully obvious.

"You two had this planned all along, didn't you?" Doliber accused.

"Nonsense," Tobias defended. "I haven't been allowed any visitors or correspondence since you delivered me to my father months ago, and don't you think my father would have caught me attempting any telepathic calls?"

"Maybe," Doliber said, feeling Tobias was protesting too much. "Then again, maybe not. You learned things from Mortimer Blythe that even the Guild doesn't know; you were just boasting as much. Don't treat me like a fool."

Looking a tad nervous, Tobias quickly continued. "Well, whatever you may think, I was sincere when I told you my belief, that Northeast Light and Magic were either behind the attempt on Edison's life or they would know who was. Being freed from captivity, that is a bonus."

"You're worth it," Quinn replied, splaying a fistful of dollars for Doliber's perusal. "Two hundred. How about it?"

Doliber replied with a chilling stare. Was his honor to be bought so cheaply?

"You still haven't told me why you're doing this," Tobias said. "There has to be a reason beyond helping an old friend."

"It's all about profitability, my friend," Quinn said, placing an arm around Tobias' shoulders in a confiding hold as the money lingered in his free hand. "We need men like you; trained warlocks with the skills and power to make and create new mystical innovations. If we intend to keep pace with Edison and the other technological inventors, we need to come up with magical alternatives. You're just the sort of man for the job."

"I see. You want to buy yourself an indentured servant," Doliber presumed.

"Never," Quinn snapped, shooting Doliber a vicious stare in his first true sign of hostility. Turning back to Tobias, he continued. "I'm offering you a paid position, heading your own research and development team. You will unlock new secrets in the magic trades that'll put these so-called techno-men to shame."

"I don't know where I'd start," Tobias admitted.

"Start by making a better talking machine, one that doesn't sound like a screechy tin can," Quinn suggested. "Feeling up to it?"

Tobias smiled, warming up to the prospects. "What's my salary?"

"Twenty dollars a week, with bonus pay for every worthwhile invention you devise. Of course, we'll have to dock some of your initial pay to recoup the cost of your release. Bribing the Guild to secure your pardon won't be cheap, and we still have to settle on a price with your current guardian, of course."

"I don't want your money," Doliber rebuked, "and what makes you think the Guild will stoop so low as to take money in exchange for a murderer's freedom?"

"You really need to stop idealizing your superiors," Quinn replied. "They're far more materialistic than they pretend to be."

There was no sense arguing with Horace Quinn, as he would do whatever he wanted. Doliber knew he'd been foolish to bring Tobias along, but he was going to make the most of his mistake. If there were any answers to be gotten, he would get them, and hopefully more.

"All right, Mr. Quinn, you want something from me, and I expect something from you. Let's get on with it."

"At last," Quinn said, stepping over to face Doliber. "Shall I tell you what I know, or will a telepathic download suffice?"

"Not so fast," Doliber said. "Information is one thing, but from my own experience I know how powerful Edison's shooter really is. His mystic skills are out of my league, but I'm betting you'd give him a run for his money. You want Tobias, you earn his release by helping me capture this magic assassin."

Quinn started laughing. "You expect me to drop everything—and put my life on the line—to fight Ezekiel Wiley?" He gripped his belly as he caught his breath.

The name didn't sound familiar, but it was good to have one to put with the face. "What else do you know about this Wiley character? How do you know he's the man I'm after?"

"Are you ready to accept my offer?" Quinn asked. "I'll grant full disclosure about Ezekiel Wiley in exchange for Tobias. That's the deal."

"Only if you tell me enough to defeat him," Doliber replied.

Quinn paused a moment, giving Doliber the answer he needed. Whatever information there was to be had, it wouldn't be enough.

"Oh, come on, Hoar, help us out here," Tobias interrupted. "We can't have a six-gun conjurer running wild and murdering people, can we?"

Both Doliber and Quinn turned and stared in shock. Coming from Tobias, it seemed a ludicrous statement, seeing that he had caused more than his fair share of death and destruction not so long ago. Now he was one to talk of law and order?

"It would be dangerous and stupid to put our necks on the line, Tobias," Quinn replied.

"True, but what alternative do we have?" Tobias asked. "If we don't stop this conjurer, who will?"

"I'm sure Doliber will find a way," Quinn replied. "Barring that, the Guild will get to it, eventually."

"That'll be little consolation for Wiley's next victim,"

Doliber mentioned.

"And what of *my* family?" Quinn asked sternly. "What will you tell them when I don't come home? You have no idea who you're dealing with."

"Then show me," Doliber demanded.

Quinn closed his eyes and a second later a burst of new information flooded into Doliber's mind. The telepathic download lasted barely a second, but hours of speech and visual experiences played on and on. The flash of memory was enough to stun most anyone, and Doliber had trouble staying on his feet. Tobias had to grab him by the shoulders to keep him standing.

As the shock wore off and Doliber's head processed the new memories, Quinn asked, "You now understand why I'm not eager to throw my life away?"

"I think so," Doliber replied. "You're right; I have to do this on my own."

Tobias shot his friend an angry stare. "What did you do?"

"I gave him the data he requested. Nothing more, nothing less."

"And why didn't you show me?" Tobias asked.

"I will, once your brain is capable of receiving telepathic signals again. MacTavish, remember?"

"Far be it from you to interfere with his little tricks," Tobias chided.

"Oh, stop it," Quinn said. "Now, do you want the job or not?"

"Of course," Tobias replied. "Though I'd feel better if we did help Doliber first. I feel I owe him that much."

"No, you can't," Doliber said, shaking off a headache. "Neither of you can. You're too tainted."

"Tainted? But the only reason that would matter would be if..." Tobias froze as a realization came to him.

"That's right," Quinn said.

"Ezekiel Wiley is a bonafide sorcerer," Doliber explained. "Which means both of you would be susceptible to demonic manipulation."

"Correct," Quinn said. "While I'm sure Tobias and I are strong enough to repel the attacks against our minds and bodies, that would draw all of our attention, leaving us fairly useless in a direct-on assault. I'm afraid we can't be of much assistance in that regard. You'll need friends with purer hearts."

Doliber nodded affirmation, and consigned himself to the fact.

"Now, if you'll excuse me, I'd like to get my new employee up to speed," Quinn said, turning toward one of the ladders. "That door over there should lead you to the shop. Wait for me there, and I'll be sure you get a proper send-off."

CHAPTER 9:
THE STREETS OF CHAOS

Violence was spreading all across Selwood at mid-afternoon, as the citizens went mad. The two factions were at each other's throats, and most everyone was siding with one side or the other. You were either magic or anti-magic, with little exception.

Deputy Ron Grimes could do little more than watch as the town tore itself apart. Mobs of angry drovers and shopkeepers brawled in the streets, while their wives cheered from the sidelines. Before long, the ladies started catfights on the porches, all in a frenzy over nothing.

Two assaults were fueling the fights; the attempt on Thomas Edison's life and the beating of magic preacher Clarence Davison. Each group blamed the other for taking violent action against someone of their philosophical persuasion, and more and more people felt justified in knocking a few heads in retribution.

"What should we do?" Henry Currant asked Ron, as both men watched the chaos unfolding.

"Not much I can think of, short of shooting them all," Ron replied. There was little alternative, but he didn't want to start firing his gun. At present, the rioters in the streets were sticking to their fists and a few blunt objects. Once bullets started flying, there would be a whole mess of dead men to bury, and the longer that could be avoided the better.

A flash of magic caught Ron's eye, and for a moment he hoped it was Sheriff Doliber, coming to the rescue in the nick of time. However, as the light vanished, and the teleportation was complete, he saw it was a much smaller individual.

"Do ye be needin' a spot of help, boys?" Flaherty asked, the leprechaun looking as spiffy as ever in his tweed suit.

"Not your kind of help," Ron grumbled, disinclined to trust the magic-using dwarf whose intentions were questionable at the best of times.

"Well, tough, you've got it," Flaherty argued. "I"ll not see me adopted home town wrecked like this. Who'll vote for me then?"

Ron wanted to laugh. The leprechaun who would be mayor was more interested in securing votes than actually helping anyone. His valiant effort to quell the disturbance was about personal gain. If it could win him the election to join the riots, he'd be leading them instead.

Still, understanding Flaherty's motivation, Ron felt he could be helpful.

"All right, leppercon. Think you've got the power to bust up this pack of brawlers in front of us?"

"Aye, but you maybe want to be standing by to arrest the ringleaders after the fact. They'll still be stirring for a fight, and they'll get it outside o' jail."

With a wave of his hands, the leprechaun did as he promised. A great wave of white energy rippled out from his body and cut across the rioting crowd on Main Street. As soon as the magic struck them, the people collapsed instantly, shocked unconscious.

It was a bold move, and instantly noticed by observers from all around. Some made their way over to find out what had happened, while others hung back, waiting to see if the bold investigators got struck down next. At any rate, it stopped much of the violence, as curiosity overpowered anger.

Ron and Henry began walking through the unconscious crowd, looking for anyone they recognized as a ringleader. A few faces came to mind, but there was no telling who was ultimately in charge of the violent factions, or who would take over next.

"Where's your man Jesse?" Henry asked as he started rolling people over to identify them. While he gladly served as emergency backup for the sheriff's department, he was eager to get back to the relative safety of the telegraph office.

"He's guarding the jail cells," Ron replied. "Remember, we've already got a couple dozen miscreants locked up. Damn place is almost full."

"It seems like the town has gone completely mad," Henry confirmed.

"Aye, and where would ye have us put all these troublemakers after we arrest them?" Flaherty asked.

"This just doesn't make sense," Ron mentioned, looking at the mass of unconscious bodies around him. So many faces, so many honest, working men, and even some women in the bunch. What could have happened to make them turn on each other with such malice? There was clearly more at work here than a simple philosophical dispute. Someone had to be manipulating things, but to what end?

There was Edison's mysterious shooter, the one who had threatened Doliber. He was a likely suspect, and his magic prowess had been enough for the sheriff to go running for help. Yet, there was another troublemaker, much closer and within striking distance, that Ron had to consider.

"Flaherty, tell me you've got no idea what's happening around here," Ron said, seeking to gauge his reaction.

"What are you implying, my boy? Ye think I'm stirring people up or something?"

"I wouldn't put it past you," Ron said flat out.

"You're mistaken," Flaherty answered. "I'd never do such a thing to me own town, let alone at a time like this."

The leprechaun seemed sincere, though Ron still held him in contempt.

A new crowd was forming around the field of unconscious rioters. The various men and women mumbled amongst themselves, and many stared at the law men who were standing amidst the bodies. One man dared to step forward and confront Ron, and that man was none other than Leroy Falk, candidate for mayor.

"Hey, you there. Dwarf," Falk said, stepping around the bodies to reach him. "What's going on here? What happened to these men?"

"They were aiming to kill one another, so I had them put to sleep," Ron replied, staring up at the tall man with a salt and pepper mustache.

"You and that no good magician sheriff," Falk grumbled. "You both ought to be driven out of town at gunpoint."

"What?" Ron exclaimed, stunned by the anti-magic rhetoric. Falk was running as the common-man candidate, proclaiming a man's right to as much pleasure as he could afford. He was a favorite of the hard drinking gamblers, and if women could vote he'd have had every prostitute on his side, as well. For him to speak out against magic was unbelievable.

"You heard me, runt!" Falk replied. "This town's had enough of you devil worshipping magicians playing tricks. You ought to get going while the getting's good!"

"You'd like that, wouldn't you?" another voice interjected. The familiar fellow stepped from the crowd to confront Falk, and was quickly identified as Chris Williams, Prohibition Party candidate for mayor. "Then you'd really be in charge, wouldn't you?"

"What's that?" Falk asked.

"I know your game, Falk. Get rid of the magic sorts, so your drunken thugs can run roughshod over the people, turn Selwood into your own little fiefdom. Maybe that sort of behavior would fly south of the Mason/Dixon, but not here!"

"You calling me a Reb, Williams?" Falk snapped back.

"If the slave collar fits," Williams added.

Falk took a swing at Williams, and put him right on his butt. "Teetotaler hypocrite! Think it's wrong for a man to have an honest drink, but you got no qualms about playing with the devil's toys!"

"Magic is of God," Williams grumbled, sitting on the ground and wiping blood from his lips.

"Horse crap!" Falk barked. "You and that Davison kid both deserve what's coming to you!" He pulled his foot back for a kick, but suddenly had his second leg kicked out from under him by an invisible force. He found himself planted face down in the dirt, spitting curses like a drunken bandit.

"That's enough, all of you!" an authoritative voice called out.

All eyes turned to the rough and upright Sheriff Doliber as he came up the street, his rawhide jacket flapping in the breeze.

"About time you showed up," Ron said, walking over to greet the sheriff.

"Stay right there, Grimes," Doliber said, shooting a penetrating stare at the dwarf. Both men held their positions for a lengthy moment, after which the sheriff said, "All right, you're clean."

"Clean?" Ron asked brushing his shirt sleeves. "Yeah, I guess so."

"That's not what I meant," Doliber said, looking around at the group of people staring at him. His face looked haggard and grim, as he canvassed the entire crowd, searching for something Ron could not perceive.

"What's going on?" Ron asked, stepping up beside him.

"A sorcerer named Ezekiel Wiley, that's what," Doliber replied, completing his observation. "I'd say about half the town is under his sinister influence."

"Damn," Ron cursed. "I figured something was up, seeing how everyone was out for each other's blood. You said sorcerer?"

"Yes, Wiley's in league with Lucifer, himself," Doliber answered.

The claim sent shivers down Ron's spine, as he considered the ramifications. Though he wasn't one to attend church on a regular basis, he still believed, and knew the true power of the dark one. He'd once run afoul of a demonic sorceress, and the encounter had cost him dearly.

Poor uncle Brizban.

Ron still felt sick to his stomach every time he thought

back to that fateful morning, when his band of Union scouts had run into the sorceress in a Georgia swamp. She'd crafted dark magic to steal the souls of the spiritually impure, those who were open to demonic machinations. Only a handful of dwarves had survived that initial assault of demon mites, and following that the sorceress had woven another, more insidious spell, rewriting the hearts and minds of those who remained, including Ron's uncle Brizban. In the blink of an eye, they were turned from loyal Union soldiers into willful Confederates who mirrored the sorceress' political views.

Only Ron had remained unchanged, and he'd walked away from that encounter uncertain of why he'd been spared. The remaining months of the war had brought him further hardship, but nothing to compare with that frightening experience.

Knowing how dreadfully powerful a sorceress could be, Ron wondered if even Doliber could stand up to such might.

"Can you fix it?" Ron asked. "Cure the people here, so they don't hate each other anymore?"

"Not alone," Doliber admitted. "The only way to end this is to find Wiley and stop him. To do that, I'll need help. Magic help."

"Did someone call me name?" Flaherty asked, standing behind the lawmen. It wasn't clear if he'd done a short-range teleport or if he'd simply sneaked over without them noticing, but either way he was there.

"What do you want, leprechaun?" Doliber asked, as wary of the little warlock as Ron was.

"I want to help," Flaherty said. "I see what's going on, and heard what you said. There be a sorcerer about, and we can't have that."

"You really think you can help?" Doliber asked, doing a quick scan of the leprechaun's mind, seeking the truth.

"I'm in tuh Guild, went to an Academy, same as you. Seeing that our superiors don't be taking a proactive role in these circumstances, I say it's our duty to put an end to this evil, here and now."

"Says a man who saw nothing evil about abducting me

not so long ago, and delivering me into the hands of shady characters with questionable motives," Doliber said.

"Aye, that was a paid job, and I only did it for an old friend. You understand how such things go."

"What *old friend*?" Doliber asked, having his suspicions.

"Best turn our heads to more prevailing matters, boyo," Flaherty said, avoiding the question. "There be a sorcerer to catch!"

"You're right," Doliber said, deciding the past could wait. "How's your telepathy?"

Flaherty lost his usual smugness as he replied, "Not so good. I'm more the sort to affect the body, rather than the mind. Physical mysticism is me specialty."

"You'll only need rudimentary empathy," Doliber replied. "That, coupled with a mystic eye, can show you who's under the sorcerer's spell and who's not. Find those affected and knock them out for their own protection.

"I believe I can handle that."

"And if you find anyone with mystic abilities who isn't affected, get them to help you," Doliber said, turning to walk away.

"And where will you be during all this?" Flaherty asked.

"Hunting the wily one."

* * *

Fiora Silcox sat in the telegraph office, more scared than she'd ever been before in her life. The town was tearing itself apart around her, as people fought over things she scarcely understood. The violence was so random and chaotic, there was no telling what might happen next, and she had no idea who was on her side.

She was no stranger to violence. As a child, she'd seen the harsh reality of the wild frontier. Her first sight of blood had been at age six, when a band of wild Indians had come to raid the ranch. It was during the Civil War, and a lot of able-bodied men, including her father and uncles, were away fighting on both sides of the conflict, leaving the Silcox spread undermanned. It may have seemed like easy pickings for a band of raiding Paiutes, but her grandfather Albert had shown them otherwise, using a combination of magic and machinery to deliver a deadly message.

Observing from a knot hole in a shutter, Fiora had watched her grandfather thwart the raid. Using his shiny new Henry rifle, he'd dispatched six riders with deadly accuracy, and a few paralytic spells dropped the others from their mounts. A handful of ranch hands rounded up the surviving Indians and tied them up in the barn, where she was given the chance to see them in their pacified state.

"Look at the savage, and remember what this land is like without us," her grandfather had said, pointing to a scarcely clothed brave with paint on his face and chest. They were frightening to look at, even when tied up and unconscious.

"Why did they come, grandpa?" she'd asked, eager to get back to the perceived safety of the ranch house.

"Most likely for sport, though partly as a matter of pride. This barren land was theirs to roam, long before we arrived, and many of them aren't satisfied to let their way of life end. These men may have come to kill us, thinking that will scare the white man from living here. Then again, they may have come to take what we have, just because they can. Theft and murder are not crimes to them. In fact, many tribes respect and honor the brave who can steal the most from outsiders."

"They don't sound very nice," Fiora replied.

"Nice has nothing to do with it," her grandfather answered. "The Red Man has a far different definition of right and wrong, and no understanding of God's laws. They worship animals and spirits, pagan things our ancestors abandoned to the truth ages ago. Perhaps they are as we were thousands of years before Christ, during the dark times."

The lesson was one that stuck with Fiora now, as she saw the savagery of so-called civilized men. Were they so different at heart, or did her people just know how to hide their barbaric tendencies with more cunning disguises?

A hard knock sounded at the door, and Fiora almost jumped out of her seat. The assistant telegrapher got up from his post at the wire and answered the summons, and Fiora's heart calmed as she saw the aged face of her grandfather. He looked a bit anxious, but none the worse for wear, clearly having avoided the brawling mobs.

"Thank heavens you're all right," Albert Silcox said, grabbing his granddaughter in a brief hug. "I feared the anti-magic lunatics might have gotten you."

"Deputy Grimes made sure I was well protected," Fiora answered.

"Where is Mr. Grimes?" Albert asked, glancing around the telegraph office as if the dwarven deputy might be hiding in a corner.

"He's out trying to get things under control," she said, feeling a new sense of worry for the law dwarf. "You didn't see him, did you?"

"No, but I met that older telegrapher, the one who's running for mayor. He told me you were here, waiting for me."

"That's very considerate of him," Fiora said. "I wish there was something we could do to help."

"I know it may seem cowardly, but I believe it would be better if we depart," Albert said. "Though I might be able to lend a hand, I can't leave you here. You're all the family I've got left, and I will not lose you, too."

"Very well, grandfather," Fiora said, smiling at his concern. She understood and shared his feelings, and wanted nothing more than to run to safety.

Stepping out of the telegraph office, Albert and Fiora glanced up and down the street, seeking a safe path of escape. The road to the livery stable looked clear enough, and if they ran into any hooligans Albert's magic skills would protect them.

Heading toward the stable, Albert mentioned, "I expect we can make Yucca Junction by nightfall. We'll stay there for the evening, then return to the ranch tomorrow."

"Of course," Fiora said, knowing how her grandfather disliked night rides. His magical powers could give them sight the whole way, but he was set in his ways, and preferred the light of the sun. "I do hope Ron is okay," she added, feeling her mind ease as they reached the stable.

"I take it you enjoyed your time with him," Albert said as he spotted their repaired buggy sitting in the back.

"He was a gentleman," Fiora replied.   "When this madness is ended, I hope to see him again."

"I'll make sure you do," Albert said.

Despite the chaos in the streets, a group of stable hands were still on the job, guarding the property. They helped the aging man and his dwarf daughter to rig the buggy, and once the horses were in place the Silcoxes were on their way. The road to Yucca Junction was just to the right of the stable, so there was no trouble getting out of town from there.

The afternoon sun beat down on the dusty road, and there wasn't another rider in sight as they ventured north. A few hours drive, and they'd be safe in another town where men weren't at each other's throats...

...or so they hoped.

* * *

Doliber walked down the streets of Selwood, wondering how the Guild could permit such a wanton abuse of power. They were the guardians of magic, purported to be the ultimate arbiters of the mystic arts. Their skills and knowledge were unparalleled, yet they turned a blind eye to a potent spellcaster in communion with the devil. For shame!

There were still a few stray fights here and there, but Flaherty was knocking them out. One by one, or in small groups, they all fell unconscious to the shocking waves of energy expelled by the leprechaun. A few of the magically-endowed fighters tried to resist, but they were no match for anyone with genuine Guild training.

To an onlooker, it might seem odd that the sheriff was roaming the streets, when he should be rounding up the troublemakers, though there was a purpose behind his wandering. As he moved through town, his mind was attuned to another layer of reality, an ethereal layer of existence only perceptible by certain mystics and proficient telepaths. Looking around at the people and places of Selwood, Doliber was studying the mystic meddling of Ezekiel Wiley, and searching for clues to his whereabouts. It was his intention to triangulate the sorcerer's position, and catch him by surprise.

It should have been a simple task, as the magic at work

was excessive. A spell inflicting such mass hysteria and fury upon hundreds of people all at once was impossible to cast without leaving a clear trail back to the source. While that was true, Doliber found his search ever more difficult, as the spells at work varied in intensity and frequency. It was not a single spell at work here, but several, and they were not all from the same individual.

Like any art or craft, magic spells held a unique appearance, based on who was casting them. Each spellcaster left their own unique signature or footprint when they wove their mysticism, and any warlock worth his grade could identify the different patterns. Studying the magic at work around him now, Doliber could not escape the conclusion that there was not a single sorcerer at work here, but two!

Ezekiel Wiley was not alone.

Tracing the two sources would be difficult, but not impossible. Though the divergent sources caused some interference, someone of Doliber's skill could separate the signals and lock onto each individual caster. Only, what would he do when he succeeded? Did he stand a chance against even one of these sorcerers, let alone both? His brief encounter with Wiley had shown him how powerful the man truly was. How deadly would the sorcerer be with backup?

Doliber's careful study was interrupted by a sudden flare of magic very close to him. The burst of energy appeared as a shimmering yellow glow to his mental perceptions, and it stunned his senses. It would be a minute before he would be able to resume his scanning, which was frustrating.

"Well, hello there," a lady's voice beckoned from directly behind Doliber.

Turning around abruptly, Doliber looked upon the source of the voice. What he saw was a middle-aged woman with raven hair and weathered skin, a few streaks of gray and a few wrinkles showing her years. She was smiling at him with shimmering teeth, like a cat eager to play with a mouse.

It wasn't hard for Doliber to discern that she'd been the source of the magic flare he'd witnessed. The spell had most likely been a teleport, which explained how this stranger had suddenly appeared only a few feet away from him.

"So, you are the infamous Sheriff James Doliber. Guild warlock, Delta Grade, correct?" she asked with a sweet southern accent.

"That's me," Doliber confirmed. "I don't believe we've been properly introduced, Miss..."

"Elena Pelletier, Mistress of the Southern Wind, at your service," she said, extending her hand as if for Doliber to kiss it.

"Why are you here, of all places?" Doliber asked, ignoring her waiting hand. "What are you doing to my people?"

"*Your* people?" Elena started laughing. "I'd never have believed it possible—a humble Guild warlock."

Suddenly, her laughter stopped, and with unearthly speed her hand was wrapped around Doliber's neck. She began to squeeze ever so slightly.

"These are not your people any more than they are mine. The creatures of this town are so beneath us; it is insulting to use such a comparison. They are the chaff, and we are the true harvest!"

Doliber tried to reply, but her grip was crushing his windpipe. His repulsion spell was having no effect on her deadly grip, and the hand kept squeezing tighter, threatening to cut off all blood flow to his brain. In seconds, his brain would become starved of blood and oxygen, forcing him into unconsciousness. Under the circumstances, it wasn't hard to believe these were his final moments.

A gun fired, and Elena's hand suddenly fell from Doliber's neck. Gasping for air, the warlock watched as the sorceress staggered to the ground, wounded by a magic bullet.

Standing in the shade of a porch awning was Ron Grimes, a nickel plated Smith & Wesson in his hand. The weapon was not the dwarf's regular armament, but it was one especially endowed by the sheriff to counteract magic. It was one of the few guns around capable of stopping a proficient mystic.

Elena struggled to get up, grabbing at her left butt cheek. "You pathetic cretin. You shot me in the ass?" she said to the shooter, bewildered by the successful attempt.

Ron walked over slowly, with the pistol aimed directly at

her all the while. "Remember me, witch?" he asked.

Elena stared at the approaching dwarf and started to smile again. "Corporal Grimes, how good to see you again."

It was Doliber's turn to be surprised. "You know this woman, Grimes?"

"We've met," Ron confirmed. "Back during the war, she worked for the Rebels, killed some friends of mine."

"How is your uncle Brizban?" Elena asked with an evil smile. "Still waving the Stars and Bars, I assume."

Ron stood in front of her and fired at her chest point-blank. "He's dead!"

Elena fell back on the ground and laughed as blood oozed out of her chest. As she continued to act ridiculous, her mind found the proper bit of sorcery to counteract the effect of the anti-magic bullets, and the holes in her chest and buttocks sealed themselves shut. In moments, she returned to a cold demeanor, leaping to her feet and sending a bolt of magic force against Ron. The dwarf flew back, as if hit in the stomach by a massive club.

"You really think any weapon of this world can stop me?" Elena asked angrily. "I have lived longer than any mortal man. Greater enemies sought my destruction before you were even born!"

The sorceress stomped over to the dwarf, and with a magic spell levitated him to face her. With Ron in her mystic grasp, she began inflicting pain, shooting jolts of energy through his body, all as she relished the experience. Then, suddenly, her joy ended, as Ron vanished in a shimmering glow.

"That was a mistake," Elena said, turning back to Doliber.

"You think I would let you kill my best deputy?" Doliber asked, fighting back the growing fear in his heart. He could have saved himself, cut and run while the witch dealt with Ron, but he could never be so shameless and dishonorable. If saving Ron meant sacrificing himself, so be it.

"I wasn't about to kill him," Elena replied, wrapping a magic strap around the warlock's throat and yanking him toward her. "Someone as noble as Boron Grimes must suffer first, beg for release, just as you will before I'm done!"

The magic strap burned against Doliber's skin, as he was

lifted into the air. Nothing he did seemed to have any affect on the sorceress' wicked spells, and he feared she was correct. Her power was so strong he could hardly believe it possible.

The fire coursed through Doliber's body, along with jolts of stabbing pain. The quick death of strangulation would have been preferable to some, but the warlock didn't care to die. A long, agonizing demise was preferable, as it gave him more time to seek an alternative. Dying instantly could ease the pain, but it was utterly final. Life always left room for hope, even in the midst of suffering.

As the pain grew overwhelming, the spells affecting Doliber ceased, and he felt himself falling. For those few seconds, a soothing wave of peace covered him, but it ended as he hit the ground and the force of the impact sent new pain into his legs and back. He sat on the ground, feeling the fading effects of magic and physical strain, staring at the stunned look on Elena's face.

"I say, Elena, that's far enough of that," a new voice said.

Hearing the similar inflection, Doliber quickly remembered where he'd heard it before, and he looked over his shoulder to see Ezekiel Wiley standing there, the Southern gentleman still sporting his polished, white suit and hat.

"It's never enough," Elena replied with furrowed brow.

"The sheriff is mine," Ezekiel said, stepping around Doliber to face the sorceress. "The *dwarf* is yours. That was our agreement."

"But he took Grimes from me," Elena complained. "That warranted a bit of torture, I think."

"You were attacking the sheriff beforehand," Ezekiel complained. "That isn't a fair part of the game."

Elena shook her head and stepped backwards. "You don't get to set unilateral rules," she said. "We're in this together, after all."

"Then act like it," Ezekiel complained. "Stop playing with the sheriff and go find the dwarf. Tracing a teleport shouldn't be hard to do."

"Do not give me orders," Elena grumbled. "I was *your* teacher, remember?"

"A long time ago," Ezekiel answered. "We've been equals for far too long to quibble over seniority. Now get going!"

Elena shook her head and wagged a finger at the man. "One of these days, Mr. Wiley." Before she could say more, she vanished in a puff of smoke.

With Elena gone, Ezekiel Wiley turned his attention to Doliber, who was getting to his feet. "Well, Sheriff, it looks like you found me. Congratulations."

Doliber felt a strange sensation flowing over his body, as a peculiar form of magic coated his body. His vision blurred, as a gray haze formed over the street and buildings around him. It took a moment for him to realize it was a dark magic teleportation field enveloping him. Indeed, he had found the sorcerer, and the sorcerer had found him!

Where the spell would take him, only the devil could know.

* * *

Yucca Junction was a burgeoning settlement, built beside the train station that served as a center of trade and commerce. Several rail spurs met here, allowing shipments of ore and cattle to pass through to markets both east and west. Virtually every household good needed by the populace in southern Nevada was shipped here, and anyone coming to Nye County had to stop here first, before venturing to their final destination. There was no doubt that Yucca Junction would continue to grow, overshadowing the neighboring towns.

As the late summer sun set over the western hills, the buggy carrying Albert and Fiora Silcox crossed the train tracks. The Silcox Company had a large stable and corral set up adjacent to the rail station, where they commonly imported and exported livestock, so it was the place Albert stopped to deposit his transport for the night.

As the buggy pulled into the stable, the manager took charge of the horses and gave Albert a quick account of recent business transactions. It was pretty unremarkable stuff that didn't take long to tell—there were always a few riders who boarded their horses with the Silcox Livery, which covered the cost of having a full time employee to run the place between cattle drives. Satisfied with the report, Albert took his granddaughter and headed into town.

Yucca Junction consisted of three main roads; *East Street*, *Center Street*, and *Third Avenue*, with two connecting roads, *Hayes* and *Garfield*, named for the respective presidents. The buildings were laid out in straight lines on either side of the broad roads, making it very functional and well planned. There were no tight corners or cramped loading bays, but plenty of room for wagons and riders to move about freely.

The town had about five hundred full-time residents, including shopkeepers, merchants, cattle drovers, and assorted service work employees. In addition, there were generally a thousand or more people visiting for business or pleasure, so there was no way to tell who you'd meet.

Albert and Fiora headed straight to the Nexus Hotel, a five story brick building only a hundred yards from the tracks. The structure stuck out like a diamond amongst hunks of coal, appearing very alien when compared to the wooden buildings on either side. Inside, you could expect the sort of fine service you'd receive in any five-star establishment in San Francisco or New York. In fact, you'd get the same exact service, for it was the same hotel in all three places; a trans-dimensional convergence point existing inside a pocket of folded space. It was a unique trick of magic, the only known structure of its sort in all the world, built and positioned by the enigmatic restaurateur, Philemon Hawk.

There were low rent rooms on the ground floor, but the quality of the accommodations increased exponentially by floor. The upper suites were even beyond Albert Silcox's price range, but the fourth floor was extravagant enough for an aging rancher.

Stepping into the lobby, Albert tipped his hat to a fat man in a business suit who was on his way out. Turning a moment to watch the man depart, Albert saw the blurry image of New York's Fifth Avenue as the fellow passed through the door. The nexus had an uncanny ability to deliver people back to their proper city when they departed, and as much as Albert knew of the wonders of magic, he could not begin to understand the complexities of this magic hotel. He knew it worked, and that's all that mattered.

Stepping up to the front desk, Albert hit the ringer as a red uniformed attendant appeared from a back room. The fellow had a smile that shined almost as brightly as his brass buttons, and he looked as clean and formal as any aristocrat. A stranger to America might think the man an officer in the local army from his formal attire and fastidious attention to duty.

"Ah, Mr. Silcox, wonderful to see you again," the attendant said, grabbing the register and setting it on the counter. "We have your regular room open, if you'd like."

"Oh, thank you, Finn. That will do nicely, but is it at all possible you have a second room available?"

Fiora grabbed his hand and looked up at him. "That's not necessary, Grandfather. I think we're perfectly capable of sharing a room."

"Nonsense," Albert said, patting her hand. "There's no need for you to put up with an old man for the night." Turning back to the attendant, he asked, "Is there another fourth floor room available?"

"Several, in fact," the attendant replied, handing over a pen.

Albert signed the book and then helped his granddaughter up onto the counter so she could put her name to it. Fiora scooted back to the floor as quickly as possible, slightly embarrassed by the move.

"So, what brings you and your granddaughter to us tonight?" the attendant asked as he put the book away and searched for the room keys. "You've never come with company before."

"Yes, about that," Albert said, his expression changing abruptly. "There's trouble in Selwood."

"Is there?" the attendant asked, bringing a pair of keys out from under the counter.

Albert grabbed the attendant's wrists and stared into his eyes. "The anti-magic zealots are on the warpath. We must be cautious, my friend."

The attendant looked startled for a moment, but after a sudden shiver he nodded his head in understanding.

Taking one key, Albert held it up and thanked the

attendant. "Remember to tell everyone who comes in. Liberty or death!"

"Indeed, sir," the attendant said, leaning over the counter to hand Fiora the key. She yanked it from his hand, annoyed by his action. She wasn't that short, and could have reached it if he'd simply held it out.

Fiora followed her grandfather toward the elevator, a mechanical marvel of the industrial age. Before boarding the compartment, she looked back at the attendant and saw the curious stare he returned. He was different all of a sudden—there was something creepy and unsettling that she couldn't quite put her finger on.

"Going up, sir?" the elevator operator asked as Albert and Fiora boarded.

"Fourth floor," Albert replied.

The operator flipped a lever, and the cage-like doors slid shut. Yanking another lever, the car started to move upwards. It took a full minute to reach the fourth floor, but it beat taking the stairs. As the doors opened, the operator held out his hand, and Albert gave him a quarter.

"Be careful, young man," Albert whispered as he handed over the tip. "There are anti-magic forces about."

"Understood," the operator said after a nervous twitch. He smiled at Fiora, and she couldn't wait to get away from him. It was that same creepy look the desk attendant had given her. What was it with this place?

On the end of each key was an intricately inscribed number, and matching them to the doors Albert and Fiora located their rooms, side by side.

Fiora put her key in the lock underneath the door knob, and giving it a quick turn she heard the mechanism click. Grabbing the knob and giving it a turn, she found the door wouldn't open, causing her to stare at the key, wondering what was wrong.

"You just locked it," Albert said, coming over after opening the door to his own room. "The unoccupied rooms are left open, so the staff can service them without keys. Turn the mechanism again, and you'll be fine."

Fiora felt foolish as she unlocked the door and opened it.

"I'll see you in the morning, I'm sure," Albert said, kneeling down to stare at her tired face. "We'll be back at the ranch by afternoon tomorrow, and won't have to worry about the anti-magic lunatics anymore." He leaned forward to give her a hug.

"Goodnight, Grandfather," Fiora said, slipping out of his arms and into her room. For the first time in her life, she didn't feel right in her grandfather's presence. There was something decidedly different about him ever since they left Selwood. Perhaps the mad events there had impacted him more than he realized. Warning strangers about anti-magic extremists wasn't something she would ordinarily expect from him.

The room was clean and brightly lit with magic orbs. There was enough space to live in, if one had the inclination to stay more than a night. There were lacey blue curtains hanging over several windows that showed a clear starlit night looking out over a grassy hillside that led down to sparkling waters. Was that San Francisco or New York, or somewhere else altogether? The trans-dimensional nature of the hotel was certainly unnerving, enough to make Fiora want to sleep and forget about it.

The mattress was soft and springy, the sort she had at home. Hitting the pillow, she felt the delicate composition of goose down underneath the cloth coverings.

Sliding her clothes off and slipping under the silk sheets, Fiora relaxed and let her mind fall into the peace of sleep.

CHAPTER 10:
BLOODY SELWOOD

Despite the efforts of local deputies, the madness in Selwood was getting worse. Whenever one group was put down, it seemed two more formed to take their place, and bloodshed had begun. Guns and knives were shining as the sun went down, and bodies began to fall with the night.

Jesse James sat at the sheriff's desk, guarding the full jail cells. The prisoners were pretty quiet now, though they'd given him enough of a headache throughout the afternoon. He'd been tempted to put a few of them down, but killing wasn't going to spare him the living hell that awaited him if he didn't mend his ways. Being a magically-resurrected outlaw had its advantages, but also its pitfalls.

Smashing glass shook Jesse out of a half-slumber, and he jumped to his feet as a whiskey bottle rolled across the floor toward him. A second object shattered another pane of the front window, and Jesse grabbed a shotgun from the rack behind the desk before clomping over to the front door to confront the vandals.

As the door swung open, Jesse looked out at an angry mob; two dozen men ranging from teenagers to feeble fossils, all armed and out for blood. Holding torches and rifles, the mob looked ready to lynch whoever stood in their way.

"All right, boys, you've had your fun. Time to move on," Jesse said, straining to remain civil, his finger twitching at the dual triggers of the double barrel.

"You got our friends in their, shadow man!" someone shouted. "Outta our way, and we'll be pushing off with 'em."

Jesse smiled, peculiarly amused by the belligerent crowd. "Not gonna happen."

"Look here, James, we don't got no grudge wit' you," an elderly gentleman from the crowd said, stepping forward, "none wit' the sheriff, neither. He done his job, but there's a war brewing now. Time we magic folks figgered out we gotta fight together."

"War? Against who?" Jesse asked.

"Against them anti-magic technoids," the elder ringleader said. "Seein' how's they want us dead fer using magic, seems only fair we meet 'em in kind."

Jesse shook his head. "That's not the way it is. You all are just overreacting."

A stone came flying in Jesse's direction, smacking into the side of the building a few inches from the outlaw's head. He tried to see the source of the attack, but the light was fading and the crowd was close together, making identification difficult.

"Look here, Deppity James, you either fer us or again' us!" someone shouted.

If he'd still been a flesh and blood mortal, Jesse might have feared the mob, but knowing the truth of his existence, death was no longer his concern. Fighting back a laugh, he leveled his shotgun at the front of the crowd and said, "I'm not against you all, but my gun will be if you don't get going, now!"

The crowd answered by pulling their pistols, and Jesse let his shotgun continue the conversation. Two blasts from the double barrel sent five men to the ground, after which Jesse drew his pistols, ready to take care of the rest. As the bullets flew, he found himself cheering, thrilled to be back in the thick of a fight. Then, suddenly, the thrill was gone, as a dozen slugs sank into his chest and face. The burning agony lasted a few seconds before the wounds put him to sleep. His eyes went blank before he hit the ground.

The curtain of death was no longer permanent for Jesse James, but it would leave him a lifeless corpse for a few hours, at least—long enough for the angry mob to do whatever they pleased.

* * *

As the violence persisted across town, a small band of vigilant citizens stood watch over Doctor Redgrave's residence. Armed men were necessary to protect the two important men who resided within. Thomas Edison and Clarence Davison were the unwitting catalysts of this madness, and it was logical to assume the mystically enchanted rioters would seek them out sooner or later. So, the deputized telegrapher Henry Currant had had the foresight to assign trusted men to guard detail.

Pete Buist felt like his knees were going to shake themselves apart as he stood in the front yard, watching small groups of men moving and fighting with each other. They'd duck in and out of sight, going down side streets and alleys, though their voices often carried, and gunshots echoed from all directions. This wasn't the sort of scene the young rancher was prepared to handle.

"Buck up, Pete," Orrin Oatley said, stepping over. "They ain't gonna git ya."

Pete looked at the middle-aged cowpuncher standing beside him. The dark skinned man with an ugly scar across his chin was a frightening sight, though his personality was anything but, and Pete had known him long enough to trust him implicitly. The rugged, old Indian fighter was a veritable jack of all trades, and in this situation there was nobody better to have on your side.

"If you say so, Orrin," Pete said, shivering.

Orrin pulled a pair of cigarettes out of his pocket and offered one to Pete. "Go on, this here'll steady your nerve."

Pete took the brown tube reluctantly as the older cowpuncher struck a match against his fingernail. He inhaled deeply as the fire sparked the tip, and a curious cloud of hot smoke entered his lungs. It didn't burn the way he'd expected, and he felt his fears suddenly fade. Pete may have been young, but he'd smoked his share of tobacco, and it didn't usually affect him so drastically.

"Is my own special blend," Orrin explained. "I mix me in some sprite leaf with the tobaccy. Give 'un a good pick up."

As Pete sucked down another lungful of the stimulating smoke, a low, guttural voice uttered, "You shouldn't lead the kid astray like that, Orrin."

Pete coughed and almost spit out the cigarette as he noticed the owner of the voice sauntering up behind him. The gray-haired man with leathery skin and a bushy mustache was the boss of them both, senior ranch manager for the Tinney spread just outside of town. Old Clive Savoy always had a chip on his shoulder, and a somber temperament to match. You didn't mess around on the job when he was within sight.

Clive stepped up to the smoking men and eyed them accusingly.

"Aw, come on, boss man, what's the matter?" Orrin asked.

"This crap is dangerous," Clive said, yanking the cigarette out of Pete's mouth.

"What, jus' a little pick up," Orrin mentioned nonchalantly. "Not all of us can be as tough as you by our lonesome."

"The kid needs to learn to get tough on his own," Clive chided. "Getting hooked on this crap you're puffing will just keep him weak."

Listening to the lecture, Pete couldn't disagree more. For the first time he could remember, he wasn't nervous or frightened in front of this domineering overseer. Ordinarily, he was quaking in his boots at the mere sight of Clive Savoy, but now he didn't have a care in the world. The sprite leaf had that sort of effect, sapping the worry and fear from the mind.

Orrin's cocky attitude began to fade as the conversation continued. "Look, boss, this ain't no ordinary circumstances. Don't imagine the boy could shoot straight on his own."

"That doesn't give you the right to mess him up," Clive persisted. Turning to leave, he added, "Don't let me see him smoking that filth again."

Stimulated by the sprite leaf, Pete dared to challenge his superior. "I can smoke whatever I want."

The statement froze Clive in his tracks, and the old ranch manager turned sideways to eye the rebellious youth. His cold stare spoke volumes, shouting disapproval.

"Kid's right, boss," Orrin added, looking cocky again. "Besides, ain't you got your own habits?"

Clive shook his head and started walking again. Before heading back into the doctor's house, he said, "I keep my addictions to myself. That way, nobody can blame me for their own problems."

After the old rancher vanished out of sight, Orrin replied, "Yeah, least most of us ain't got your problems."

"Why is he like that?" Pete asked, finally feeling brave enough to ask the question aloud.

"Who knows," Orrin answered. "Some folks just is."

Pete started to laugh a little at the subtle humor of the moment. Orrin joined in, and before they realized it the pair of them were making quite a scene. In their amusement, they didn't notice the group of men coming down the street, a surly band of unscrupulous rioters eager for a fresh target.

As Pete regained his senses, a harsh voice shouted, "Look alive, boys!"

Pete looked over his shoulder to the fat man with a goatee who was standing guard in front of the doorway. The fellow was pointing toward the approaching mob, even as he checked the cylinder of his revolver.

There were ten of them, dressed in common miner's clothing. The blue denim looked pretty new, so they were either successful in their trade or fresh to it. Either way, their present intentions had nothing to do with prospecting, though a little digging might be involved when all was said and done.

Feeling bold with the lingering effects of the sprite leaf in his chest, Pete stepped up to the edge of the lawn and faced the group. Wiping his nose and taking a deep breath, he asked, "What can we do for you fellahs?"

A small, unassuming man stood in front of the mob, and had a hand sitting on his six-shooter as he replied. "We've come for Clarence Davison."

"Is that so?" Pete asked, fighting back a smile. Everything was amusing at the moment; a combination of the drug and his own nerves. "What do you want him for?"

"Seems all the trouble in this town started about the time

he showed up. No good magic spinner needs to be put down while we still got something left! Now, you bring him on out here, and we'll be on our way."

Pete just stared, finding himself at a loss for words. As the mob began to grumble amongst themselves, Orrin took over the conversation.

"You can't be takin' a man out of his sickbed for uh execution."

"Like hell we can't," the ringleader rebutted. "We're going to do just that. We don't want any trouble, but if you stand in the way we'll shoot you dead."

"Is that a fact?" the burly man by the door asked loudly.

"Say, is that Archibald Keith I hear?" the small man asked.

"In the flesh, Dubell," Keith replied.

"Well, I'll be. What are you doing with these magic-loving cretins?"

"Trying to make sure nobody gets hurt," Keith replied, keeping the revolver lowered but in-hand.

"Well, then, you should tell these fellows to step aside and let us by. Seems only right that we avoid any unpleasantness."

"Come on down," Keith said with a wave of his hand.

Pete and Orrin stepped aside, albeit reluctantly, and the ten men of the mob started toward the front door. They were ten feet from the front step when Keith raised his revolver.

"That's far enough," Keith said, staring at the ringleader.

"Don't," Dubell warned, looking ready to draw.

"Drop your guns and go away," Keith said. "This is your last warning."

Glancing from side to side, Dubell mentioned, "Seems we have you outnumbered more than three to one. Seems I should be the one to lay down terms."

"Think again," Keith shouted.

Following the loud call, additional men appeared. Several came around the side of the building, while others peeked out of open windows from inside the house. Every man was armed and ready for action.

The show of force would cause most men to capitulate, though the mystically infected mob held no fear of death. As sane and rational as Dubell seemed, his fellows were driven to irrational action, drawing their guns at the sight of opposition. There was no reasoning with them.

Keith took the first shot, even as Dubell raised his pistol. The mob's leader cringed as the lead slug sank into his chest, and he fell forward in a crumpled heap. The rest shared his fate moments later, as they met a hailstorm of bullets. Pete and Orrin took credit for a couple of kills, though there had been so many shooters it was impossible to tell who killed whom.

"Is everyone okay?" Keith called after the last of the mob had fallen.

A quick roll call confirmed that everyone was safe and sound.

"What a rush!" Pete mentioned, shaking in exhilaration.

"Heads up!" Clive Savoy's grumbling voice snapped, as the old man stepped out of the house. He carried a beat up 1866 Winchester with him, and was busy shoving cartridges into the loading gate as he moved to the front of the yard. In the fading light, it was getting hard to see details, though the shiny brass of the receiver clearly identified the rifle's make and model.

Everyone was watching Clive, and as the old man shoved the last cartridge into the rifle's magazine he cycled the action and nudged his head, inviting the men to look across the street. There were men over there, almost concealed in the shadows but visible to the vigilant eye. It was another mob forming, and their proximity to the doctor's house was a clear indication of their purpose.

"Keith, I want you and Pete to get inside." Before Keith or Pete could object, Clive continued. "Go get Doc Redgrave and help him move the patients out of here, before we're overrun."

"Take 'em out?" Pete asked. "Take 'em where?"

"The Lucca Saloon," Clive replied. "The elves were setting up their own little Alamo there, last I heard. Figure if there's any place in town that's defendable, that would be it."

"Alamo," Keith mumbled as he headed into the house. "That's a real comforting thought."

Pete didn't argue further, realizing the logic behind the plan. Elves were known to wield their fair share of magic, so if anyone could repel angry mobs it would be them. Only, would the proprietor let humans in at a time like this? They'd have to find out the hard way.

Pete hurried into the house, running to catch up to Mr. Keith, who was already marching through the entryway. Without delay, they came into the doctor's living room that was currently serving as a makeshift medical ward. There were half a dozen patients there, including the still comatose Clarence Davison and shooting victim Thomas Edison.

Spotting the sudden intrusion of the new men, the attending nurse hurried over to see them.

"No time to talk," Keith said. "We've got to get these men out of here."

"Sir, I'm sure Doctor Redgrave has explained his position," the nurse replied. "Several of these men are not suited to travel, and the chaos outside..."

"Is about to come in here," Keith snapped. "Now, I don't care what the doctor wants. We've got to move, now!"

The shout drew Doctor Redgrave into the room, and Mr. Keith explained the situation quickly. His words, coupled with renewed gunfire outside, convinced the good doctor to agree.

"Most of these men will need help walking," Redgrave mentioned, as his nurse helped two men up out of bed.

"I won't need any help," Thomas Edison said, standing on his own. He flinched from the pain in his shoulder, but fought to conceal any infirmity. "Assist the others."

"Davison will need to be carried," Redgrave added.

A bullet ricocheted down the adjacent hallway, and the agonizing shouts of wounded men carried from outside.

"I've got him," Keith said, leaning over to grab Davison.

Assisting a feverish man to his feet, Redgrave said, "We'll head out the back. Follow Nurse Tilton. She knows the way."

Passing through the kitchen, the fleeing men followed Nurse Tilton to the back door, where they hesitated. Behind the doctor's house was a wide alley, where ambush could be waiting. It was necessary that someone scout it first, and Pete took the initiative. Jumping out into the dark, he looked around and found nobody lurking there. It was then that he realized how quiet it was. The gunfire had ceased.

Moving to the corner of the house, Pete looked toward the front yard, but was unable to see much in the gathering darkness. There were a few lumps on the ground that were probably bodies, though he didn't see anyone standing there. After a few seconds, the rest of the fleeing men came rushing out of the back doorway.

"Let's move," Keith whispered harshly.

As the group of injured men passed, Pete could hear stomping feet from inside the building. Someone was in the house, looking for them. If it had been any of the defenders, they would have announced themselves to allay any fears. Their silence spoke volumes.

It was a long walk to the saloon, and it was anyone's guess if they'd make it there alive.

* * *

The violence continued to escalate as the sky grew dark. Anyone with common sense stayed indoors, but a few concerned citizens still roamed around, seeking to restore order, though their numbers were shrinking fast. Nobody wanted to get beaten up by the angry mobs, and a good share of the violence was now being perpetrated by people who weren't directly under mystic influence. People continued to pair off into the two camps as a means of survival.

Yet, amidst the madness, two men stood their ground, daring to challenge both sides. The unlikely duo of Henry Currant and Michael James Flaherty walked through the north side of town, seeking to curb the chaos as best they could.

"There," Henry pointed to a clump of shaded figures. Gunshots sounded, and muzzle flashes appeared in front of the dark figures, as they fired at a vacant storefront.

With a wave of his hand, Flaherty sent out a burst of magic, and the dozen armed men fell in its wake. The guns slipped from their grips as they dropped, and the unconscious bodies fell atop each other, as they'd been standing close together.

Walking over to the subdued men, Flaherty mentioned, "Have you any idea why they'd be shootin' in that direction?"

Henry looked around to get his bearings. "That's Racine's shop. She's a seamstress, known for her 'magic needle' embroidery."

"Then these be another band o' magic haters," Flaherty said between breaths.

"There can't be too many troublemakers left," Henry responded, rolling a man over onto his back to get a look at the face. It was nobody he recognized, just another anonymous drover passing through town.

"As insidious as it is, the spell's not our only problem," Flaherty said as he spotted another pack of men throwing punches down a side street. "Those boys over there aren't even affected, and you see how eager they are to fight one another. At this rate, I can't say how many more we'll need to be whacking."

"Scurvy magic peddler!" someone shouted.

Flaherty turned around to see a band of hoodlums coming toward him. They were very young, barely old enough to grow hair on their chins, yet they were raring for a fight. Their sympathies were clear, so the leprechaun wasted no time sending them to sleep. The bolt of magic force cut them down like a scythe, but would leave no lasting injuries.

After casting his latest spell, Flaherty swayed and grabbed his head, looking ready to collapse. He'd been throwing powerful spells around for over an hour non-stop and was nearing his limit. "I'm running out o' strength," he said, shaking his wrist.

"This is pointless," Henry said, watching a pair of angry citizens smashing out a shop window. "We can't police these people alone. Where's Doliber, or Grimes for that matter?"

"Chasing down the sorcerer, no doubt," Flaherty said, grabbing Henry's side for support as a wave of dizziness shook him. "You're right, we're outmatched. Best find a place to hole up."

"The Sheriff's Office is just over there," Henry said, finding it hard to see the turn-off to Commerce Street in the darkness. Night was fully upon them now, making their task all but impossible. The shadows worked to hide the brawling men, and allowed others to lie in wait, to strike without warning. There was no way to reason with the people, and no way to scare them into submission. The magic at work made their hatred overwhelming, to the point where they would rather die than let their perceived opponents live.

Flaherty and Currant made their way down the street, keeping their eyes peeled for signs of attack. They'd done a fairly good job of thinning the herd in this section of town, and the few packs of brawlers were too busy beating each other to strike at the temporary lawmen. They were able to get near the Sheriff's Office without incident, but coming within sight of the building brought them no joy.

The building was on fire.

The two men ran as quickly as they could to the scene, hoping to do something—anything—to stop it. By the time they were close enough for a full inspection, they saw it was too late. The Sheriff's Office was fully engulfed in flames, and a few dozen spectators cheered its destruction.

"Can you snuff the fire?" Henry asked.

"Not now," Flaherty replied. "If I had a fresh reserve o' magic, perhaps."

"I wonder if Jesse got out all right," Henry mused, listening to the cheering crowd. There was no telling whose side they were on—magic or anti-magic—but whatever their cause they didn't seem to care about fighting at the moment. The fire was a good distraction.

"Where do we go from here?" Flaherty asked.

"Doctor Redgrave's," Henry replied. "We should make sure that Edison and Davison are still safe."

"We put a dozen men on the guard," Flaherty replied. "You think that two more bodies will make a difference?"

"You wanted someplace to hole up. It seems as good as any."

"Doesn't seem any place in town's liable to be good tonight," Flaherty mentioned, as the fire from the Sheriff's Office spread. The buildings on either side were catching, and it wouldn't be long before the whole street was up in flames.

The two men made their way across town to Doctor Redgrave's home practice, only to find dead bodies in the front yard. Many of the dead men were those that Henry had left to protect the building.

Walking through the building, they found no signs of life. Windows were smashed and tables overturned, proving that the place had been ransacked.

"Oh, God," Henry whispered, staring at the devastation, and fearing the worst.

"No sense hanging around here," Flaherty said. "Best find another hiding place."

"There's only one place I can think of that might be safe," Henry muttered, kicking a broken chair out of his way. "If we're lucky, they haven't hit the saloon yet."

Hope was becoming an endangered commodity, as the pair made their way through the back alley, hoping to avoid the brawling packs of men on the wider roads. Reaching Main Street, they spotted a group of men outside the Lucca Saloon, hurling bottles and exchanging gunfire. So much for having a peaceful moment to drink.

"Let's see what I've got left," Flaherty said, preparing to cast another jolt of magic force. "If I don't survive, make sure I'm buried with me hat," he added tapping the bowler ceremoniously.

After a deep breath, the leprechaun expelled another wave of white energy, knocking out a dozen angry citizens. Those attacking the Lucca Saloon fell in a heap, just as Flaherty himself hit the ground.

Henry bent down and checked the limp Irishman. He was still breathing, so that was a good sign. Tossing the little man over his shoulder, Henry carried him to the saloon, only to find himself staring up at the muzzle of a rifle.

"It's okay," a voice shouted from inside. "Let them enter."

The owner of the rifle was a tall, muscular elven man with dark hair, who lowered his gun but never cracked a smile as Henry passed.

Henry carried Flaherty up the steps and into the saloon, finding the nearest vacant seat to set him in. Leaving the unconscious leprechaun with a group of attentive citizens, the telegrapher breathed a momentary sigh of relief, and looked around at the packed barroom. There were at least a hundred people there, most of them women and children. The Lucca

Saloon had turned into a refugee camp for those unaffected by the evil magic and unable to defend themselves.

"I take it things aren't going well," the elf behind the bar mentioned.

"No, they aren't," Henry said, looking over at Solen, the ever prim and proper elvish barkeep. Even in the midst of chaos, he remained relatively unscathed.

"Have a drink," Solen offered. "It's half-price tonight."

Henry sat down on a vacant stool but declined the drink. He felt insulted that he hadn't been offered one for free, considering the danger he'd just faced. "How long do you figure we'll be able to hold out here?" he asked.

"As long as necessary," Solen answered, grabbing a glass to polish with his rag. "We should have enough magic muscle to repel all comers, assuming the prevailing spell doesn't start affecting elves. So far, we've been lucky, but there are only twenty of us."

"We should keep more of your lot around," Henry mentioned, looking over the crowd. "How many humans are here?"

"Counting the ones upstairs and in back, maybe two hundred," Solen said.

Henry grew quiet and studied the many faces around him, feeling empty inside. How many people of the town had not been lucky enough to make it here? How many hundreds were still out there, huddled in their homes or dead in the street? How many were being manipulated against their will to commit heinous crimes against their fellow man? How many?

This sort of thing wasn't supposed to happen. This was America, a land of peace and prosperity. Such wanton violence was something best left for the more savage lands and Godless heathens of the world, or so Henry had always believed. To think his own neighbors were capable of this!

Looking at the crowd, Henry spotted a familiar face coming toward him, pushing through the huddled masses. The young man had been one of the dozen who'd been left to guard Doctor Redgrave's home. It was a relief to see someone had survived.

"Peter Buist," Henry greeted him as he came over. "I thought you were dead."

"I might have been," Peter replied. "It wasn't good, I tell you."

"I saw what was left of the doctor's house. What happened?"

"A group of anti-magic supporters got it in their heads to finish the job on Davison. They started shooting, and we gave as good as we got, but there were twice as many of them in the second wave. Old Clive Savoy and the rest held them off long enough for me and Mr. Keith to get Doc Redgrave and the wounded out—just barely. We heard folks were gathering at the saloon here, so we came over."

"Did you save Thomas Edison?"

"Yes, and Mr. Davison," Peter confirmed. "They're both upstairs."

Henry felt great relief after hearing that both men had survived. There was still a glimmer of hope that he could cling to in this god-forsaken situation.

Knowing that his old friend was still alive, Henry wasted no time heading upstairs to find the room where Thomas Edison was resting. It was a bit of a climb, stumbling over people who were sitting on the stairs and standing against the walls, but there at the end of the hall Henry spotted a familiar face. It was one of Edison's employees, a tough-looking gentleman standing guard over the last door.

"Sorry, pal, no admittance," the guard said as Henry approached. "Mr. Edison does not wish to be disturbed."

"I expect he'll make an exception for me," Henry said.

"No, Mr. Currant, not even you," the guard confirmed.

"This is madness," Henry complained. "I want to see that my friend's all right. Step aside."

The guard put a hand on the butt of his pistol. "You're not going in there."

It struck Henry quite odd that the man would be resisting so fiercely. Perhaps he was simply being overly protective, or perhaps there was something sinister afoot. Either way, the telegrapher was determined to go by. After all he'd done, he felt he deserved that much.

Moving swiftly, Henry punched the guard in the throat, while slamming his right arm against the door, forcing the man to drop his gun. With the guard distracted and weakened by the blows, the telegrapher managed to push him aside and open the door, assuming that Edison would put an end to the hostilities after seeing it was him. Though, as Henry looked inside the cramped room, he soon realized that wouldn't be the case.

There were almost two dozen people in the cramped bedroom, but Thomas Edison was not among them.

A hard object slammed against the back of Henry's head, and he could ponder the situation no longer.

CHAPTER 11:
THE TENETS OF DOOMSDAY

There was no light whatsoever.

Trying the best he could, Doliber couldn't see anything, not the faintest gleaming of illumination, but that wasn't the strangest part of this place. Feeling around with his hands, he found nothing solid around him. No walls on either side, no ground or floor beneath. It was a creepy emptiness that left his mind searching for understanding. What sort of place was this?

"Hello?" he called, hoping someone would hear his voice. The word came out, but it didn't seem to resonate beyond his throat. This strange realm of emptiness continued to confound him.

What layer of purgatory had that sorcerer sent him to?

Where physical senses failed, Doliber hoped mysticism would prevail. With a mental command, his eyes flared blue, allowing him to perceive the existence of magic energy. In an instant, the world around him came alive, a bright swirling of colors all around, streaming in rivers and pools. So, there was something to this immaterial realm. It was pure magic!

"Making yourself at home?" a voice asked from out of the blinding glow.

Doliber searched for the source of the voice, but he

couldn't find any perceptible figure amongst the light. Try as he might, his perceptions were all a meaningless blur. Still, the tone and accent of the voice was a dead giveaway. In this place, at this time, it could be only one man, though doubt had to linger, as with mysticism anything could be faked.

Eventually, the owner of the voice made himself known, appearing in front of Doliber like a gray specter amidst the magic void. The sinister form of Ezekiel Wiley stood on what appeared to be solid footing, even though nothing but colored light existed beneath his feet. Clearly, the sorcerer had some mastery over this domain.

Doliber struggled to claim an equal footing, flailing around as his mind searched for a mystical answer. No matter the effort, he couldn't break free, so he remained floating there, trapped like a ghost.

"Don't try too hard," Wiley said, amused by the display of defiance. "Wouldn't want you to pull a muscle."

"What is this place?" Doliber asked. "Where have you brought me?"

Wiley smiled and answered, "You might call it a stepping stone between heaven and hell."

"I'm not sure I understand," Doliber said, hoping for a better explanation.

"Oh, I'm sure you don't," Wiley said. "You are, after all, a simple journeyman. The Warlock Guild does not teach its underlings about such realms. Only a Master might be able to conceive of the many layers of existence, and the true nature of mysticism!"

Doliber had to accept the answer as the best one he would get. Clearly, this magical realm was beyond his current education. The mystery ate at him, and left him feeling slighted, as a man denied an elementary truth.

"Why are you doing this?" Doliber asked.

Wiley observed Doliber's face in quiet contemplation, shifting between amusement and contempt. It was enough to disturb anyone, though Doliber kept a neutral expression throughout the uncomfortable examination.

"You amuse me," Wiley finally said.

"That's it?" Doliber said incredulously. "You expect me to believe that you're tearing Selwood apart, pitting neighbor against neighbor in a town I'm sworn to protect, merely to amuse yourself?"

"Don't pretend to be innocent in all of this," Wiley remarked, shaking an accusing finger at the warlock sheriff. "The sins of the father are an unsightly blemish upon the son."

"What does my father have to do with anything?" Doliber asked, genuinely curious.

"Your father was a Sergeant in the Union Army. He fought at Atlanta, and did kill many of my countrymen. Do you deny your heritage?"

"My father never talked about his service," Doliber replied.

"No doubt, he was ashamed of himself," Wiley snapped. "For all the death he caused, for the homes leveled by his artillery brigade... the widows he molested in victory."

Enraged by the slurs against his father, Doliber jerked his hand forward, attempting to cast a spell in the process. Under ordinary circumstances, the magic at his command would have sent a bolt of invisible force into Wiley's face, but in the ethereal realm all his effort was for naught. A thin streak of golden light flew out of his fingers, swirling harmlessly into the cloud of colors behind the sorcerer.

Wiley laughed obnoxiously.

"My father is a good and moral man!" Doliber shouted. "He fought for his country because it was the right thing to do, to preserve the Union."

"More to empower the carpetbaggers," Wiley rebutted. "You Yankee interlopers were not supposed to win the war, and you wouldn't have, if your Guild had stayed true to its word. Neutrality, they promised, but in the end they cheated."

"Only to stop the likes of you," Doliber answered defiantly.

"How true. Funny, how none of the Guild members felt enough sympathy for the Confederacy to take up arms on our side."

"Med-locks attended to your wounded, just as they did

ours," Doliber affirmed. "Other than that, the Guild remained neutral, except when it was necessary to level the playing field."

"It was not their field to level," Wiley replied, "but things will be different this time."

"This time?" Doliber asked, and then sudden realization washed over him like a foul breeze. "You're orchestrating a war. That's what the violence in Selwood is all about. You're hoping to pit the people against each other... for what? Revenge over losing the Civil War?"

"Hardly," Wiley said, looking pleased with himself again. "It is about dominance. The next war will not be a simple matter of nation versus nation, but a true conflict between the mystically endowed and the *lesser* beings. There will be no quarter given, no treaties to be signed. The sorcery I and Mistress Elena have woven will assure mutual destruction. Then, when both sides are crushed, we shall take charge, installing a new world order of peace and prosperity for the survivors."

Doliber could only imagine the sort of "order" a sorcerer would seek to impose. What little he knew of their ways was rumor and conjecture, but dominance in any form was deplorable to a free American. That a select few would seek to rule made the warlock's stomach turn, and his heart filled with righteous anger.

"You'll never succeed," Doliber challenged, even as he remained helpless.

"We shall see," Wiley said, turning his back on Doliber.

Waving his hand in an arch-like motion, Wiley formed an oval window amidst the light. The opening was dark, and it was difficult to see anything, but after a few moments the picture became clear. It was Selwood at night, an overhead view of Main Street, faintly lit by distant fires.

Wiley turned his hand, and the image through the window shifted, allowing for a wider angle up the street. As the display moved forward, the light of flaming buildings revealed the scene with greater luminosity.

"Watch Selwood burn!" Wiley boasted. "This is just the start. In a few weeks, the whole of the United States will be set ablaze—after that, the world! Tell me again that I won't succeed."

Doliber couldn't stand to watch, but he didn't dare turn away. The situation looked grim, but there was still a chance. Every spell had its counter, and someone, somewhere, would uncover the truth. Only would it be in time?

* * *

Ron materialized into darkness. It wasn't a starless night, but the total black of a stone cavern. There was a total absence of light, which left him unnerved. Where had he been taken, and by whom?

The agony was gone, at least. He was beyond the reach of that sorceress and her malicious spells, but whether this would be a long-term improvement, he had yet to discover. Being stuck underground didn't appeal to him, and it could result in a slow, painful death if he couldn't find a way out.

Moving around slowly with arms outstretched, Ron ran into a wall. The rough surface felt like the rock under his feet, but sliding his hand along it he bumped into something that felt more like wood. Working his way around the object, he discovered the square outline of a frame, perhaps a large picture or a mirror. This was no ordinary cavern, obviously. There were clear signs of life.

Ron continued along, following the wall, bumping into a few tables and chairs as he tried to get his bearings. At times like this, he wished for the barest inkling of mystic ability, so he could create even a spark of light. Of course, he could always buy a magic trinket to provide the light he desired, but those cost way too much for his liking. Maybe Edison would invent a portable light source of his own someday, something that an honest working dwarf could afford?

Stuck in the dark, Ron continued along the wall until he ran into a corner. Following the new direction, he soon found the outline of a door frame, but try as he might he couldn't find a knob.

A soft scuffing sound caught Ron's attention, telling him he was no longer alone. Someone or something was sneaking up behind him, and it was anyone's guess what they would want. It might help to know where this was that he'd been deposited, though he guessed he'd find out soon enough.

Turning around, Ron felt cold steel slide up beside his neck—the sharp, straight edge of a sword blade. He knew he'd recognized that scuffing sound; it was the noise of a sword being pulled from a leather-lined sheath, the sort preferred by true swordsmen who didn't like to announce their presence when drawing their weapon of choice.

"Hold, or taste my blade," a gruff voice said.

Ron immediately recognized the man's tone, and knew where he must be. "Myles Ferguson?"

"Aye," the man replied, keeping the sword to Ron's neck. "And who do you claim to be?"

"Boron Grimes. Don't you remember?"

"I remember fine," Myles answered. "Perhaps all too well. How did you get here?"

"I guess Sheriff Doliber dropped me off," Ron said.

"You guess?" Myles asked.

"Yeah, I was being tortured by a sorceress at the time. Doliber must have sneaked me out, but didn't have time to tell me."

After a few moments of silence, Myles asked gently, "What do you think?"

A lady's voice echoed a reply amidst the darkness. "I'm not reading any active mystical signals, and the psychegraph reads honesty. He is who he claims to be."

The sword was pulled away from Ron's neck, and the ceiling began to glow, producing a pale and steady light. With the lights on, Ron was able to see he was in a narrow sitting room with chairs and other furnishings prettying up the place. Half the walls were still rock, while varnished wood paneling covered the rest. Standing in front of him was the gray haired Scotsman, Myles Ferguson, sheathing his sword.

"Sorry about that," Myles said. "Had to be certain."

"Of course," Ron replied, finally sure of where he was.

"I assume this isn't a social call," Myles said, stepping over to the door. A metal sheet slid away from the frame, revealing a panel with numbers on it. He punched four of the numbered buttons and the metal door slid aside, revealing a spacious chamber beyond.

"Like I said, Doliber didn't have time to explain his intentions for sending me here, but I dare say we could use your help," Ron said as he stepped into the round room filled with glowing screens and colorful wires. The computerized world of the Fergusons was the most alien environment he had ever seen, far harder to believe than any of the wild mysticism he had encountered throughout his life. The industrialized world of modern man had yet to even glimpse the technological achievements that lay before him in this electrified room filled with wires and screens. It was all a frightening glimpse of another world.

Ron followed Myles across the hundred foot span that led to a large metallic pillar in the center of the room. There, sitting in a chair in front of several monitors was Nora Ferguson, a fair-haired lady with the looks of early middle age, though her true years were as mysterious as her other-worldly origins.

"Boron, it's good to see you again," Nora said, turning around in the swiveling chair. "How have you been?"

"Okay, until recently," Ron said, hopping up into a nearby seat. He glanced at the screen beside him, and became entranced by the flying stars. Nora's technology never ceased to astound him.

"What the matter?" Nora asked, breaking Ron away from the screen.

"Everything."

* * *

Ron spent the better part of an hour going over his recent experiences and the troubling events of the past few days. He went over the Edison shooting and Davison's beating, the mad riots in the streets, and the final confrontation with an evil sorceress he hadn't seen in eighteen years. Nora and Myles listened carefully to his retelling, shielding any emotional reaction until after he was done.

"So, the next thing I knew, I was out in that living room of yours," Ron concluded. "All together, I'm lucky to be alive."

"You've had your hands full, haven't you?" Myles remarked, standing up to stretch his legs. "Makes me feel glad we made the decision to step out when we did."

"We've been down here for the last two weeks, working on the quantum core," Nora added. "It's good to hear your news from the outside world. We haven't access to the latest papers, and your world's quite a few decades away from having cable news feeds."

Ignoring the otherworldly comment, Ron said, "Look, I know why Doliber sent me here. Figures he'd kill two birds with one stone. This place is shielded from most magic, right?"

"Correct," Nora said. "*Most* magic."

"So, he dropped me off in the one place he figured the sorceress couldn't find me, with the only people with the power to stop her."

There was a momentary pause, as Ron's hosts considered his final words.

"Well, dear, what do you think?" Nora asked, sending a sanguine look at her brooding husband.

"We don't have to help them, Nora. Not now," Myles told her.

"Myles, I think we do," Nora corrected, turning back to Ron. "We'll do whatever we can for you."

It was a great weight off Ron's shoulders to hear, knowing that if anyone could thwart a rampaging sorceress it was the Fergusons. Nora's other-Earthly origins gave her knowledge of technologies that innovators like Edison had yet to even imagine. While her husband, Myles, lacked an exotic background, he was a Knight of Wallace, with great strength of spirit and a fistful of magic up his sleeve. Together, they would pose quite a threat to any enemy.

"But we're so close, Nora! The affairs of this world should not be our concern anymore," Myles mentioned.

"Perhaps not to the world, but what of our friends in it?" Nora asked. "What sort of people would we be, if we abandoned them at a time like this?"

Myles groaned and shook his head. "We're never going to travel to other worlds, are we?"

"Of course we are," Nora assured him. "We haven't come this far, *twice*, to be stopped. Once we lend a hand to those in need, we'll be off."

"I thought you two were going to give up on world hopping," Ron interposed, remembering the last conversation he'd had with them.

"That feeling lasted for about a week," Nora said. "Once the trauma of our encounter with Mortimer Blythe faded, we realized how far we'd come, and knew we couldn't abandon our work. I promised my husband that we'd see the multiverse, and that's what we're going to do. However, we must see what we can do to save this world before we leave it."

It was the best news Ron could have asked for, and for the first time in days he felt reassured. All hope was not lost.

"It will take a few more weeks for the quantum core to initialize before we can make a successful crossing anyway, so in the meantime we'll do what we can for you, Ron."

"Thanks, it means a lot."

"Now, give me a few minutes," Nora said. "I'll need to launch a drone with a quantum spectrometer aboard to scan the area around Selwood and gauge the nature of the mystical incursion. It'll take me a few minutes to reinitialize my equipment, so be patient."

"Uh, okay," Ron replied.

Myles translated in a hurry. "She's going to send a flying machine to see what's going on in Selwood, and figure out how to dispel the sorcery involved."

Ron felt awkward whenever Nora started talking about her future science, so he left her and Myles to tinker, while he studied the rocky walls of the spacious chamber. What bothered him the most about her technology was it didn't mean anything to him. He knew it never would, and that realization humbled him. He was a practical dwarf who understood how the world was supposed to work, but what Nora Ferguson said often made him think that the world around him *didn't* work the way he thought it did. Her explanations of space and time forced him to consider that reality itself was an illusion, and that scared the pants off him.

Better to keep his distance, and leave the finer points of science to future generations.

After wandering around for the better part of an hour, Ron heard Nora's soothing voice call to him, saying her preparations were complete. Walking over to the center of the chamber with its lights and wires, the dwarf took a seat beside the otherworldly lady and watched as she tapped a few buttons, setting things into motion.

Suddenly, the screens around them came alive with imagery and colors. The "drone" as she called it was relaying data, visual and environmental. Several panels displayed real-time visual images from the low flying craft's perspective; one was dark and hard to see, as the sun had already set, but another screen compensated for the low light, revealing what the terrain would have been in broad daylight. The dry soil and scrub brush of southern Utah was rushing past, while several graphs revealed the invisible workings of magic in the vicinity. Spikes and bars on various panels were all gibberish to Ron, but Nora studied them carefully.

"It'll be about ten minutes before we're over Selwood, but I'm already getting some curious readings."

"Curious how?" Ron asked.

"It's faint at the moment, but the mystical disturbance is detectable even from a distance," Nora answered.

"Those readings aren't from Selwood," Myles mentioned, studying a screen that had colorful dots superimposed over the dimly-lit landscape.

"No, but these are," Nora replied, pointing to a screen displaying wave patterns. "The spectral readings are identical, which means this spell is spreading."

"Mystic plague," Myles uttered in disgust.

"Yes, and from what Ron has told us, one that attacks the mind," Nora added. "A magical plague designed to make people violent and irrational, but for what purpose?"

"The devil loves chaos," Ron said.

"Aye, and we all know where a sorceress gets her power," Myles affirmed.

"Perhaps," Nora said in contemplation, "though I'm not entirely sold on Satan's influence here. While the sorceress may think she's in league with demonic forces, she is in fact accessing a specific layer of subspace to cast her spells. Whether that particular layer is the devil's domain or not is a question best left for the theologians."

"Whether we believe it or not, I'm sure *she* believes it," Myles rebutted. "That would explain her motivation."

"I don't care why she's doing it," Ron interrupted. "I just want to know how to stop her."

Nora paused as she studied the screens. As the silence began to grate on everyone, she finally replied, "That won't be easy, I'm afraid. Simple, perhaps, but not easy." She grew quiet again and stared at Ron with troubled eyes.

"Tell me what I've got to do," Ron said.

"We'll have to terminate the origin of the infection."

"You mean the sorceress? Just tell me how, and I'll be more than happy to oblige," Ron said.

"I don't mean the sorceress," Nora said. "It's not the caster who needs to die, but the person who was first infected by the mystic plague who must die."

"Huh?" Ron asked.

"Killing the initial victim, the carrier, will release an anti-magic counteragent," Myles explained.

"I've never heard of something so preposterous," Ron said, refusing to believe it.

"It's advanced spellcasting theory," Myles explained. "Sorcery is considered a dark art for a reason. To fight it, you often have to stoop to the sorcerer's level."

"You're saying I have to kill a man who's done nothing wrong?" Ron said.

"That all depends on who the initial carrier is," Nora replied. "The drone should provide some insight into that."

"I think I have a pretty good idea already," Ron said, piecing everything together. The warning that Ezekiel Wiley had given to Doliber echoed in his head, and it coalesced with the start of the chaos. *"Edison will be the harbinger of doom for those who've wronged me and mine."*

There was little room for interpretation. To end the plague, they'd have to kill Thomas Edison!

* * *

The house wasn't so quiet in the morning, as Joella made her way down for breakfast. A group of children were running around in the living room, making a lot of noise as she passed. Their faces were familiar, though she couldn't recall their names. There were six of them, ranging from three to thirteen. Did Doreen really have that many, or was someone else visiting?

Stepping into the dining room, Joella froze at the sight of three women. They were all here, the widows of Mactus Sellius. Hittie, Yuba, and Doreen sat, sipping tea in disparate emotional states. Doreen looked downright pleased, Hittie was moping, and Yuba appeared indifferent. Considering their husband had been shot yesterday, they were all in pretty good shape.

"Good morning, Jo," Doreen said pleasantly before Joella could duck and hide.

There was no avoiding the widow pack, so Joella took a seat at the table. "Mehitable, Yuba, I didn't expect to see you here. What brings you out so early in the morning?"

"The same thing that brought me," Doreen said, wearing an unashamed grin.

"All of you want to marry my father?" Joella asked, stunned.

"No," Hittie replied, sounding ready to cry. "We have to."

"Well, not exactly," Yuba corrected. "Any of us could choose Gregory, but Doreen's so set on claiming Widow's Rights against Errol, and we don't want to break up the family. The children should grow up together, under one roof."

"So we're all going to stay marriage sisters," Doreen said. "Isn't it wonderful?"

"Yeah, wonderful," Joella said, thinking it was anything but. The whole situation made her skin crawl, and she could only imagine how her parents were feeling about it. Errol and Sienna had been monogamous throughout their marriage. Suddenly having three new women imposing themselves like this had to be more than unsettling to such a long-standing married couple.

"Muh, uh, mom. My mom. Where's my mother?" Joella asked, nervous and uncomfortable.

"In the kitchen with your sister," Doreen answered.

"They insisted on preparing breakfast without any of us. I'm sure that won't last. Once Hittie is feeling up to it, just try and keep her away from the stove."

"Right," Joella said, getting up and heading into the kitchen. Dealing with the widows was too much for her to handle first thing in the morning.

The door swung open as Joella pushed on it. The thing was customarily propped open, but this was not an ordinary day. As soon as she entered the kitchen, she spotted her mother stirring a large pot of oatmeal on the stove, while Sara sat off in the corner.

"Hello, Joella," her mother greeted, sounding pleasant enough.

"Are you okay, mom?" Joella asked, stepping over to see how the food was doing.

"Why wouldn't I be?" Sienna asked calmly.

Joella didn't want to add salt to any open wounds, but she had to say it. "The Sellius widows are at our dinner table."

"Yes, I expect they will be from now on," Sienna said, detached.

"Doesn't that bother you?"

"Not really," Sienna said without emotion.

"It bothers me," Sara said from her corner. She got out of the chair and walked over to stand by Joella. "In fact, it's gross."

"Thanks for the support," Joella said.

"Talus in name, Talus in blood," Sara recited the family motto.

Sienna smacked the wooden spoon against edge of the pot, shaking off a bit of the sticky oatmeal before putting the utensil aside. "I understand how you girls feel, but you're just going to have to get used to it."

"How can you be so accepting of this?" Joella asked. "Dad is getting three more wives."

"Yes," Sienna said, then took a moment to breathe. "It would not be my choice, but it is going to happen. Your father and I have had thirty-three years together, alone, and for a chieftain's family that is unheard of. In all fairness, if not for several childhood deaths, your father would have had four other wives this whole time, and our lives would have been very different."

"But they're not," Joella persisted. "Those other girls died so you and dad could have this monogamous life together. Sara and I grew up under that family structure, and after thirty-three years you can't tell me it doesn't make you sick to think of dad with another woman."

Sienna cocked her head a little, as if she'd been slapped. "It is a bit... unsettling. But there are other things to consider."

"Like Clan Law," Joella said with resentment.

"Yes, and the prospects of having another family," Sienna said, sounding pleased all of a sudden.

"What?" Joella exclaimed.

"Sit down, please," Sienna said, taking her regular seat by the carving block.

Joella and Sara found chairs and brought them over to the cutting table to hear their mother's explanation.

"Your father and I always wanted a large family with many children, but sadly we could not. For whatever reason, I was only able to give your father the two of you. Customarily, someone as esteemed as your father would take additional wives, but our emotional attachment over the years has stopped him from searching. Now, three new wives have been provided. They come with their own children, and in time they'll likely provide your father with many more. I know, they'll never be *ours* the way you two are, but it will still be nice to be part of their lives—to have that family we always wanted."

Joella sat, dumbfounded by her mother's attitude, while Sara smiled with understanding.

"You may have rationalized this, even come to accept it, but you can't honestly like the idea," Joella countered.

"Not at first," Sienna admitted, "but I'm starting to."

Standing up, Joella headed for the living room door. "I can't. I'm sorry." She kept on walking, even as her mother called for her to stay.

* * *

Mid-morning saw five riders from the Talus farm coming into Ravenna-West. Ordinarily it wouldn't cause much of a stir, but after word of yesterday's gunfight everyone was bright and alert, eager to see what would happen next. All eyes were on the riders as they reached the outskirts of the bustling settlement.

Leading the line of horses was Errol Talus, followed by his eldest daughter and the three Sellius widows. The laborers and businessmen of the elven town dropped everything they were doing to cheer their arriving chieftain as he passed.

"What are they so happy about?" Joella asked rhetorically.

"Their chieftain is getting married again," Errol replied, sounding pleased all of a sudden. "They'll probably want to throw us a formal reception."

"They can celebrate all they want later," Doreen interjected, pulling her horse even with Errol's. "Just as soon as we've made it official."

"I don't see how you can be so excited," Joella chided. "This is wrong in so many ways."

Doreen scoffed at the comment. "You've been living among humans too long."

"Now, don't belittle our human counterparts," Errol interjected. "Many of them have similar marital practices."

"Yeah, Mormons," Joella grumbled.

"There is nothing wrong with the Mormon faith," Errol said. "They share many of our customs and traditions."

"All the bad ones," Joella persisted.

"Really?" Errol asked, sounding disappointed by her last comment.

Joella thought it over, and realized how ignorant she sounded. In all fairness, she didn't know many Mormons. She only knew of their more notable practices, and to be fair most of them weren't all that objectionable. Other than the scourge of polygamy, there was much to be admired about their faith, though Joella wasn't in an agreeable mood.

"Women deserve monogamy," Joella answered.

"Speak for yourself, cousin," Doreen said politely.

The rest of the ride was made in silence, and the horses didn't stop until they reached the large, stone temple complex in the center of town. Once there, Errol and the Sellius widows dismounted and prepared to enter the building, while Joella stayed in her saddle.

"You aren't coming in?" Errol asked before opening the front doors.

"No, you go ahead," Joella said, knowing she couldn't do it. She could not go inside and watch her father accept three new wives—the women he'd won in a gunfight. It was all she could do to keep a civil tongue and not make a scene.

Joella waited until the doors closed behind her father, and then rode away from the temple, feeling homesick for Selwood. She never thought she'd miss the scratchy straw mattress of the boarding house, but right now it seemed preferable to the soft cotton of her bed at the farm. That was no longer her home, and there was no denying it any longer.

Moving through the streets, heading for the southeast road, Joella passed the newspaper office where a paperboy was waving around copies of the latest edition. It had been a long time since she'd read the *Talus Times*, and she was tempted to stop and read the headlines.

"What's the good news," she asked the paperboy.

"Selwood's burning," the paperboy replied, holding up a copy for her to grab.

Leaning over and snatching the paper from his hand, she looked at the front page headline, which read exactly as the boy had said. The latest telegraph reports described the scenes of chaos, telling of the deadly riots and burning of buildings that had happened the previous evening, specifying that the conflict was generated by pro-magic and anti-magic extremists. How could things have gotten so out of hand? She'd only been gone three days!

Joella pried a nickel out of her pocket and dropped it to the paperboy before turning her horse around. She had to get back to Selwood in a hurry, but the ride there could take the better part of a week. The only way to get there in a timely fashion would be via a teleport, but her magic reserves were still tapped out. The only thing she could do was ask her father for a lift.

Riding up to the temple doors, Joella hesitated, wondering how she would ask for the favor at such a time. She didn't dare go inside and interrupt the proceedings. Not only would it be impolite, but she doubted her own nerves could take it. There was nothing to do but wait. In a few minutes, her father would emerge with his new brides, and then she could be off to Selwood.

The madness of a burning town was now preferable to the fires of home.

CHAPTER 12:
A SCORE TO SETTLE

Henry Currant woke up to rays of sunlight pelting his eyelids. Cracking his eyes open, he saw the light of midmorning shining through shutter slats of the window beside the bed. His head was throbbing, though he was feeling remarkably refreshed after a restful sleep. He'd been more fatigued the previous night than he'd realized, and he was in far better shape now, despite the blow that had initially put him under.

Sitting up, he found himself in a cramped bedroom, barely larger than the mattress itself. There was only one other person in the room with him, the stoic inventor that Henry had wanted to see last night.

"I never knew you could be such a bold fool," Thomas Edison said after sipping from his cup of coffee.

"How's that?" Henry asked, gently feeling the lump on the back of his head.

"Running around town, trying to bust up the violence with that leprechaun, and then trying to rush past my guard?" Edison didn't sound terribly amused.

"I thought you might be in trouble," Henry replied. "Either way, I wanted to make sure you were all right."

"Yes, well, when I told my men that I wanted to be left

alone, I neglected to give them a list of exceptions."

"So I noticed," Henry said, standing up. Glancing around the tiny bedroom, he added, "Where are we?"

"One of the girl's rooms, halfway down the hall," Edison replied.

"You've been here all along?"

"Since we escaped from the doctor's place."

"Then why was your man guarding the other room at the end of the hallway?"

"It seemed like a sensible precaution," Edison answered. "This town is overrun with madmen, many of whom would like nothing better than to see me dead. Do you think I should be easily found?"

"I suppose not," Henry said, recognizing the wisdom in the maneuver. Even with the elves on guard, there was no telling who might slip past them, and seek to put a bullet in the conspicuous innovator.

"I'm glad you survived," Edison said, taking the edge off his frosty demeanor.

"Thanks. Say, how are things going outside?"

After downing the last of his coffee, Edison replied, "Not very well, from what I hear. Half the town has burned down, and there are still a few angry mobs roaming about, itching for a fight. On the bright side, I expect they'll eliminate each other before nightfall. Then, maybe, we can get out of here."

"Perhaps you can, old friend," Henry said, reaching for the door knob. "As for me, I still have a job to do."

Henry twisted the knob and stepped outside into the hall, almost tripping over a pair of inconspicuous men who were sitting to either side of the opening. Giving them a more scrutinizing stare, Henry recognized them as two of Edison's employees. Staring down the hall, he saw the large guard still standing in front of the last door down, allowing himself to stand out amongst the huddled refugees—a lightning rod for anyone seeking the inventor.

Making his way down the stairs, Henry found the saloon quiet. It had been a long night, and most of the people were still asleep on the floor. He did his best not to step on too many fingers or toes as he made his way through the sea of slumbering bodies, and took a seat at the bar, where Solen was already fiddling about.

"Sorry, but we're out of breakfast," Solen said as Henry sat down. "Drinks are still half price, if you've reconsidered."

"No thanks. How's Flaherty doing? Has he regained consciousness?"

"I haven't heard," Solen replied. "Sandy Annie volunteered to look after him—took him up to her room last night. I think she has a soft spot for the little man." The elf shivered as his mind conjured voyeuristic images.

Henry got off the stool and made his way over to the windows to have a look outside. After maneuvering around the sleepers, he reached the tall stack of furniture that helped to barricade the windows. Peering through the clutter of tables and chairs, he saw the haze of morning. The air was filled with smoke, as nearby buildings considered to smolder, and through the gray dead bodies could be seen lying in the dirt. It was like a war zone out there, and Henry wondered how it would end.

Moving to the front doors, Henry unlatched the inner shutters and made his way out onto the front porch. A vigilant elf spotted him immediately and sent him a filthy look before resuming his perusal of the empty street.

Looking down the road, Henry saw the south end of town was untouched by fire. Most importantly, the telegraph office was still intact, and the wires looked to be undisturbed. He could get a message out!

It was over a hundred yards to the telegraph, and there was plenty of room for trouble along the way, but Henry was determined to try. Checking the pistol in his pocket, he found the cylinder fully loaded. He hadn't shot anyone yet, and he hoped it wouldn't come to that, even now, but it was best to be prepared.

Things seemed pretty quiet as Henry started toward the telegraph office. The only sounds that greeted him were the crunching and crackling of a nearby house fire, as the timbers turned to blackened ash. Remaining vigilant, his eyes scanned the horizon, and for the first time he realized how much more he could see. So many buildings were absent, and the skyline was

far too visible. At least it reduced the number of hiding places for anyone planning an ambush.

The telegraph office appeared unscathed as Henry marched up onto the small, covered porch. All the buildings on its side of the street had avoided the fires, though the other side was little more than a streak of charred rubble.

A flash of light caught Henry's eye before he could duck inside. Looking toward the edge of town, he spotted a horse and rider on approach, trotting at a moderate speed. It didn't take him long to identify the new arrival, and it allowed the telegrapher to breathe a sigh of relief.

"Deputy Talus," he greeted as Joella reigned her horse to a stop beside him.

"Where's Sheriff Doliber?" Joella asked, dismounting.

"I don't know," Henry replied. "I haven't seen him since yesterday afternoon, Grimes either. They were planning to hunt down the culprits behind this mind altering spell, but there's no telling what has happened to them."

"You say magic is behind this devastation?" Joella said, feeling out of the loop. "That wasn't reported in the newspaper."

"Paper?" Henry asked.

Joella tossed down a copy of the *Talus Times*, with the report on the front page. "Selwood's Burning, they said. That's why I hurried back."

Henry skimmed over the news account, and noticed intimate details that could only have been reported firsthand. Someone in Selwood had been sending telegrams, telling of the devastation as it happened.

"If there's mystical manipulation involved here, we'd better get the word out," Joella said. "Let people know the rest of the story."

"Agreed," Henry said.

Stepping into the telegraph office, Henry and Joella spotted the familiar face of the assistant telegrapher, standing vigil at the wire. Without hesitation, Henry rushed over to relieve him, though the man wouldn't move. He didn't smile or greet his superior in any way, but simply sat there, catatonic.

Reaching for the equipment, Henry got his hand shoved

away by the silent assistant. He tried again, only to meet greater resistance. The young assistant remained emotionless in his expression, but he clearly had control over his arms and wouldn't allow anyone else to get to the telegraph.

Henry was ready to tackle his assistant out of the way when a syrupy voice startled him.

"I wouldn't if I were you. He is not one to be disturbed at the moment."

Turning toward the source of the voice, Henry and Joella spotted a middle-aged lady sitting in the corner. Clothed in a dark, flowing dress, and seeming very at ease, she stared back without a care in the world, never mind the destruction outside.

"Who are you?" Henry asked with suspicion.

"Oh, dear me, we haven't been properly introduced." The lady stood up and offered her hand, as if she expected Henry to kiss it. "Elena Pelletier, Mistress of the Southern Wind, pleased to make your acquaintance, Mr. Currant."

Henry shied away from the hand. "You're the one responsible for all this madness, aren't you? You and that Wiley fellow!"

"Clever boy," Elena remarked, remaining pleasant.

"I'm over thirty, so I'm nobody's *boy*," Henry rebutted, taking issue with the condescending insult.

"Please, I'm a hundred and forty six years old. All of you are children to me," Elena answered with a belittling connotation.

"And how many souls did you have to sell to Satan to pay for that unnatural longevity?" Joella challenged.

"You impudent little elf!" Elena said, raising her voice. "Do not deign to insult what you don't understand."

Attempting to capitalize on Joella's distraction, Henry pulled the pistol out of his pocket and prepared to fire upon the sorceress. The weapon was one of Doliber's uniquely enchanted weapons, capable of disabling mysticism. The bullets could punch through a conjured forcefield, and their wounds could not be healed by ordinary magic.

Henry pulled the trigger, and the first bullet hit right between Elena's breasts. She barely flinched at the assault, and glanced down at the bleeding hole it had created. "It will take more than a warlock's tinkering to harm me," Elena said, rubbing the spot where the bullet had penetrated, and in moments the wound healed. Once the skin was restored, she fixed the hole in her dress, as well, leaving no trace of the shot on her whatsoever.

Before Henry could let off another round, he was grabbed by an invisible force. He felt his arm yanked upwards toward the ceiling, as if someone were pulling it by the wrist. By the time he was on his tip toes, Elena was glaring at him with fervent passion.

"I love it when you normals play rough," she said. "It gives me all the excuse I need to reciprocate."

Henry's heels hit the floor again, as his arm began to descend. Slowly and steadily, as if someone else's hands were twisting his arm, he found the appendage lowering, and his elbow bending. As his shoulder dropped, he saw his gun-wielding hand closing in on his chest, as the barrel slid toward his chin. It was obvious what was happening, and he struggled to regain control, but it was useless. His thumb slowly cocked the hammer on the pistol, as the barrel jammed into the soft flesh under his jaw.

"No, don't!" Joella cried as Henry struggled quietly in vain.

"He sought my death," Elena said. "It's only fair that I repay the favor."

Henry's finger pulled the trigger, the hammer dropped, and the gun only clicked.

Elena gazed in surprise, and the momentary distraction caused her to release her mystic grip on Henry's arm. The telegrapher looked just as startled as he redirected the pistol away from himself and examined it. Pulling it open, he saw one empty chamber in the cylinder, but he knew the gun had been fully loaded. He'd just checked it.

As both Elena and Henry pondered the mystery, Joella fell against the wall, fighting off a bout of dizziness. She struggled to maintain her equilibrium, even as she dug her left hand into a pouch at her belt.

Noticing Joella's peculiar behavior, Elena came to a conclusion. Stepping over to the ailing elf, she grabbed Joella's right hand and pried the fingers open to reveal the missing cartridge. Both ladies locked eyes, as the truth was revealed.

"Oh, my, aren't you full of surprises?" Elena said.

"More than you know," Joella answered, bringing her left hand up into the sorceress' face. A film of red dust streaked onto Elena's cheeks and lips, and the substance began to sparkle as it soaked into the skin.

Elena stumbled backwards, shaking her head as she yawned. Her eyes fluttered as the sleeping powder did its job, sending her body into slumber. Even the sorceress seemed to be at the mercy of elven alchemy.

As Elena collapsed, Joella slid to the floor, overwhelmed by the strain she'd just endured. Teleporting the cartridge from the gun had taken a lot of effort, and she'd already overexerted her mystical abilities in recent days. Her head was stabbing with pain, and she felt like passing out, but she refused to quit.

"Are you all right?" Henry asked, rushing over to check.

"I'll survive," Joella said, looking over at the limp figure of Elena Pelletier. "Is she really asleep?"

Henry moved over and cautiously prodded the sorceress. "Seems to be," he said, moving her head from side to side. He tickled her palm, and when she gave no response he felt certain she wasn't faking.

"What do we do with her?" Henry asked.

"Take her to jail," Joella suggested. "The magic-neutralizing cell might hold her a while."

"There's just one problem with that," Henry replied, looking worried.

"What, the Sheriff's Office burned, as well?" Joella said.

"It was one of the first," Henry said. "Jesse was on duty, so I assume one of the mobs killed him in the process."

"I'm sure he'll be up and about again before long," Joella mentioned, knowing the former outlaw's unnatural nature. "Right now, we've got to deal with her."

Henry looked at the sorceress again, and considered their options. They were few and fairly unpleasant.

A commotion outside broke Henry's concentration, and he looked out to see a strange carriage rolling toward town. Powered by neither horse nor beast, the vehicle raced faster than any animal could run, kicking up a cloud of brown dust in its wake. As it approached the edge of town, a steam whistle blared out from the carriage, revealing the source of its locomotion.

The noise of the steam carriage drew a few people outdoors as it rushed up the street and pulled to a stop outside the telegraph office.

Henry helped Joella up off the floor and stepped out onto the porch to get a look at the vehicle. It was something he could have barely imagined, even beyond what he and Thomas Edison had conceived during their late-night inventor talks. The smooth, metal panels, the black wheels, and the tinted glass windows made it look like something out of a Jules Verne novel, a glorious relic of the future, belching steam and coal smoke right in front of him. What manner of being could ride aboard such a fantastic thing?

The doors creaked open, giving him an answer.

Hopping out of the back seat, Ron Grimes hurried up the steps in front of the telegraph office and gave Henry a friendly nod, while Myles Ferguson came around the front of the vehicle, having exited from a door on the opposite side. Meanwhile, the driver's side window rolled down to reveal Nora Ferguson behind the wheel and adjusting controls on the dashboard.

"Deputy Grimes, who..." Henry started.

"I'll introduce you later," Ron replied, moving into telegraph office and planting his eyes on the unconscious sorceress. Myles jogged to catch up, keeping a hand on the hilt of his sword all the while.

Henry and Joella followed the men into the office and joined them in their perusal of the unconscious lady.

"Is Thomas Edison in there?" Nora asked from the carriage.

"No," Myles answered. "It's some woman."

"It's the sorceress!" Ron added, glaring down at the familiar foe. "Are you sure it's her?" he shouted in Nora's direction.

Nora held up a glowing tablet and tapped its screen a few times. "According to these readings, yes. She's the original carrier of the magic plague."

Ron shook his head and grinned, as he pulled a slender pistol out of his vest pocket. "And you're sure this gun of yours is magic-proof?"

"It's from my Earth," Nora said. "The gun and its bullets are constructed from matter that resonates at a far denser quantum wavelength than what you find in this reality. Mystical energy cannot alter such molecular structures, and even a minuscule number of molecules left within the wound..."

"In English?" Ron interrupted, bewildered by the complexity of her explanation.

"Yes, it's fully magic-proof," Nora reiterated.

Ron grabbed the top of the pistol and slid it back to chamber a round. Nora had shown him the mechanism and explained its workings the previous night, as they'd discussed what needed to be done. The gun was truly unlike anything he'd fired before, but at such close range he knew he wouldn't miss.

It seemed like such a simple solution. Whoever was the initial "carrier" of the mystic plague had to die, and then all the madness would be over. When Ron had suspected that person to be Thomas Edison, he'd had misgivings about doing the deed, but he'd still been willing to accept the responsibility. Now that the carrier turned out to be this sorceress, the same woman who had wronged him so greatly in the past, he found himself less reluctant, but still troubled. Yes, in his mind she certainly deserved to die, though it felt wrong to shoot her as she lay sleeping on the floor. It was dirty and dishonorable. He'd much prefer to look her in the eye when he pulled the trigger, but knew she'd never give him the chance. If she were awake, there was no telling what sort of sorcery she'd weave to save herself.

What fortune that he came upon her in such a vulnerable state.

Ron aimed the gun at Elena's head, certain of what must be done... yet, he hesitated.

"Do you need me to take the shot?" Myles asked as Ron stood there, struggling with his conscience.

Ron replied by pulling the trigger twice. Two bullets flew out of the gun barrel and turned Elena Pelletier's face into a horrific mess. The empty brass casings jingled as they hit the floorboards, further startling Henry and Joella.

Handing the pistol to Myles, Ron turned and walked out of the office. He had all the feel of a man who'd just put down a rabid dog. It was the only thing you could do, but it didn't mean you felt good about it.

The morose silence was suddenly broken by a shocked exclamation from the assistant telegrapher. "What in God's name?" The young man had his eyes planted on the dead body, and he looked as pale as a ghost.

"Donny, you're all right," Henry mentioned, walking over to him. "What's the last thing you remember?"

"Before this?" Donny asked nervously, motioning toward the dead woman. "I, uh, was sending out the first reports of the riots. Miss Silcox had just left, and I'd been at the wire since morning. I guess I must've dozed off."

"I guess so," Henry replied, feeling relieved. Donny's recovery was a good sign. Perhaps the rest of the town would be waking up from the madness this sorceress had induced.

Patting his assistant on the shoulder, Henry saw the light grow suddenly dim. All around the telegraph office, the sun was hidden, and a cloud of darkness was settling in. As the light vanished, a cold wind began to blow, and the building began to creak and crack.

Outside, the darkness extended beyond the telegraph office. Stretching over the entire town, the evil sheet of black created an eerie twilight at mid-morning, foretelling the presence of another great threat.

As the dark descended, Henry darted for the door, but there wasn't time. The roof of the telegraph office was coming down, threatening to crush everyone still within the building. The senior telegrapher hit the deck and covered his head with his arms as the timbers fell, forced down my magic. He was certain death would claim him, but as the snapping wood silenced and settled, he felt no weight upon his body. Picking his head up slightly, he saw a green glow in the center of the room, where Myles Ferguson was using his own magic to hold the shattered ceiling from coming down.

"I can't hold it forever," Myles said. "Get out, all of you!"

Henry scrambled to his feet, and followed Donny and Joella out into the street. Myles was right behind them, as the building came crashing down in his wake.

Stumbling out of the collapsing office, Myles watched in shock as he saw the steam carriage leave the ground, tossed up into the air against the pull of gravity. The magical force tossed the machine to the far side of the street, where it came crashing down into the ash-covered ground, rolling on its side like a tumbleweed for a hundred feet until it came to a dead stop in a battered heap.

"Nora!" Myles screamed, racing toward the wreck. Before he could even cross the street, he had the wind knocked out of him by an invisible barrier.

A puff of smoke materialized in the middle of the road, and in seconds the figure of Ezekiel Wiley was seen with a gun in his hand. "You lowly cowards," he cursed. "Murder a sleeping woman who can't defend herself! That is despicable."

"So, you're Ezekiel Wiley," Ron said.

"You can call me your executioner," Wiley replied, raising his pistol. He fired at Ron, and the dwarf barely had time to dart out of the way before the slug flew past.

Reaching for his Remington revolver, Ron prepared to send a response, but quickly realized the futility of the move. His pistol wasn't anything special, and its lead balls wouldn't defeat the magic at Wiley's command. He thought of drawing the small Smith and Wesson he also carried, but its enchanted rounds had proven ineffective against the might of Sorceress Elena. Clearly, they were no match for dark conjuring.

The mad sorcerer fired another shot, and this time the bullet skimmed the ground at Ron's feet. Considering Wiley's true power, it was strange that he was using such a conventional weapon to do his dirty work. Couldn't he cast a spell to extinguish the lives of his foes with ease?

A burst of magic wind blew a cloud of dust up into Ron's face, and it distracted him long enough for Wiley to get a direct shot. As the third shot sounded, a burning sensation penetrated Ron's left shoulder, sending him to his knees, clutching at the bleeding wound.

Joella and Henry rushed toward the wounded dwarf, but found themselves blocked by one of Wiley's ever popular forcefields.

"I'll deal with you both in a minute," Wiley said nonchalantly, walking over to Ron. Stopping in front of the bleeding dwarf, he cocked the hammer on his revolver, ready to fire again. "Two bullets in her face," the sorcerer remarked. "Right back at you!"

Ron looked up at Wiley, and could see the rifling in the pistol barrel that hung a foot above his head. He'd always suspected it would end like this, at the receiving end of another man's gun. So much death and violence he'd seen; it would be good to finally be at rest, or so he told himself as he came to terms with his own impending doom.

A shot echoed through the air, and Ron flinched as he thought it was the final sound of his life. Yet, what happened next caught him wholly by surprise. The gun dropped from Wiley's hand, and the sorcerer fell over backwards.

Struggling to get to his feet, Ron saw a bleeding hole in Wiley's chest, and looked up to see Myles stomping over with the semi-automatic pistol in his clutches. The true anti-magic bullets of the other-worldly weapon had proven to be most effective against the evil conjurer.

Myles to one side, Ron to the other, Ezekiel Wiley laughed most peculiarly.

"You find something funny?" Myles asked, pointing the semi-auto at Wiley's face.

Wiley's laugh turned into a cough, and he spit up a wad of blood before answering. "Dying's not something I had in mind today," he said, "but at least I'll have some satisfaction."

"How's that?" Ron asked, pushing pressure on his own wound to slow the bleeding.

"I'm the only one who knows where Doliber is. I trapped him in a magical Purgatory you'll never be able to find. There, he'll experience a living death for all eternity, thanks to you killing me."

Ron and Myles looked at each other questioningly, uncertain of what to make of the claim.

Wiley coughed furiously, as he struggled through his last moments of life. When the coughs ended, he struggled to say, "You will tell his father, won't you?" With the last statement past his lips, the sorcerer breathed his last, and relaxed as death overcame him.

With the sorcerer dead, Myles returned his attention to the vehicle that held his wife within its crumpled form. The forcefield that had blocked his way was gone, so he was able to cross the road and wade through a long pile of rubble and ash to reach the carriage. It was a total wreck, with the roof collapsed halfway down the windows, preventing an easy extraction. As he neared the crumpled wreck, a wave of heat stung at his face, foretelling another hazard. The engine compartment was ablaze, turning the sheet metal red hot. There was no time to waste. He had to get Nora out, no matter the cost!

Ripping off his jacket and using it to insulate him from the heat, he tried the door handle, only to find it unresponsive. Wasting no time, Myles drew his sword and jammed it into the door crack, seeking to pry the panel off. Summoning the magic at his command, a golden glow surrounded the blade as he slid it further along the seam, and leaning with all his might the crumpled door flung open, revealing the smoldering interior of the carriage and the limp figure of Nora Ferguson on the front seat. Much of her clothing had already burned off, and there was a bleeding gash on her forehead from a blunt impact.

Myles grabbed his wife and carried her away from the burning wreck, smelling the stench of burned flesh as he rushed back into the street. "We need a healer!" he shouted.

Henry led the way back to the Lucca Saloon, where Doctor Redgrave was tending to the wounded. Solen's personal bedroom had been turned into a makeshift medical ward, though there was little the physician could do for Nora. Her injuries were extensive, and his abilities were limited.

"I've seen a number of people in this shape," Redgrave said. "So many homes have burned and collapsed, it's hard to calculate the number of deaths."

"She wasn't hurt in a house fire," Myles rebutted, sounding insulted by the assumption.

"Then how?" the doctor asked.

"The sorcerer did it," Ron said, staggering into the room. "He didn't take too kindly to me shooting his mistress, and Nora there got caught in the crossfire. Look, Doc, you've got to save her."

"If a med-lock were available, maybe," Redgrave said, rubbing his slim mustache nervously. "I'm sorry, I don't have the power."

"Doctor," a weak voice called out from the corner bed.

Myles followed Doctor Redgrave over to answer the summons, and found Clarence Davison, the young man so bruised and battered he looked almost as bad as Nora. His arms were shivering as he dragged himself into a sitting position to face the approaching men.

"I'll help," Clarence said.

"No, son, you're barely alive, yourself," Redgrave said, moving to lower him back into bed.

"Don't," Clarence objected. "Let me do this."

As Doctor Redgrave released his grip, Clarence reached one arm out toward Nora's wounded body. Closing his eyes, the young preacher released a stream of white energy from his hand, and the light flowed over Nora's blackened and bloody skin, restoring it to a rosy pink. The glow persisted for almost a minute, as the magic did its work, and as the light faded back to normal, young Davison sank into bed and fell back to sleep.

Myles hurried Nora over to a spare bed, and lay her down for an examination. Doctor Redgrave checked her as best he could, but couldn't tell the extent of the healing. Her outward appearance was much improved, with only minor cuts and burns still present on the skin, and her eyes began to flutter, as she regained consciousness.

"That lad saved her," Myles remarked, feeling optimistic.

"What he did was dangerous," Redgrave mentioned, pulling a blanket over Nora's half-naked body. "He's only a low level amateur, and he's lucky to be alive as it is. I can't say what damage he may have done to himself with that stunt, and there's no way of knowing how much he really helped this girl."

"My wife!" Myles said sharply.

"Sorry, your wife," Redgrave reiterated. "What I mean is, while she may look better on the outside, there's no way to know."

As if in response to the doctor's misgivings, Nora stretched and opened her eyes, looking up at the men around her. She moved her glance from one face to another, with a neutral expression before saying, "Hello?"

"Nora, thank God!" Myles said, overwhelmed with joy. He leaned in to give her a hug, but she didn't move to hug him back. Pulling away, Myles asked, "What's wrong?"

Nora studied him for a lengthy moment. "Who are you?" She glanced over at the other people around her. "Who are you?"

Myles' elation quickly vanished, replaced with a renewed sense of dread. "You don't know?"

Nora shook her head. "Should I?"

Doctor Redgrave leaned forward and asked, "Do you know who *you* are?"

Nora shook her head, and tears began to form in her eyes.

Redgrave frowned and stepped back, unable to help her further.

Taking his wife's hand, Myles tried to console her. "It's okay, Nora. You've just had a little bump on the head that's let your memories slip for the moment. We'll be okay."

"How do you know?" Nora asked, looking at the muscular hand gripping her.

"I'm your husband. I know," Myles promised.

Nora smiled and tears rolled down her cheeks as she was comforted by her forgotten lover.

Henry patted Myles on the back. "With our hopes and prayers, I'm sure she'll recover."

Myles breathed deeply and kept his eyes planted on his weeping wife. "I know."

"Come on," Doctor Redgrave said, turning his attention to Ron. "Let's look at that shoulder of yours."

Ron followed the doctor over to an empty packing crate that served as a stool. As he sat down, a nurse came over with a pair of scissors, ready to cut off his shirt, but he refused. Good shirts cost money, and he wasn't about to let a little bullet hole be the end of this one. Fighting through the pain, he managed to remove it in one piece. As he set the clothing aside, more blood flowed from the wound.

"You shouldn't have done that," Doctor Redgrave said. "There is no way to know how much additional damage you could've done by rotating the shoulder like that." He stopped talking as he began poking and prodding the wound. "The bullet's not that deep, and it doesn't seem to have hit any bones. You're lucky."

"Get it out of there, Doc," Ron said through clenched teeth.

"Nurse, clear a bed," Redgrave ordered.

The young orderly went over and evicted a beating victim from one of the beds, which was little more than wooden planks covered with sheets. It was hard but solid, so it would serve for surgery.

Ron sat down, and the nurse handed him a flask.

"I'm afraid that's the only anesthetic we have at the moment," Redgrave said, grabbing a scalpel and forceps from a nearby tray. "This is going to hurt."

Ron took a nip from the flask and said, "Let's get this over with." He lay back, and as his head settled against the hard boards he felt the cold steel of the blade cut at the bullet hole, widening it so the forceps could extract the slug. The pain was unbearable, but Ron managed to set his mind to other matters that distracted him long enough for the bullet to come out.

As the operation ended and the pain subsided, Ron closed his eyes and thought of what the future would hold. The world around him was changing yet again, and not for the better. What dark shadow lurked over him that refused to grant him a peaceful existence?

CHAPTER THIRTEEN:
<u>THE DAMAGE DONE</u>

With the influence of sorcery extinguished, peace finally prevailed in Selwood, yet there was no denying the devastation. Hundreds dead, and over fifty buildings destroyed, including the Sheriff's Office and the Town Hall. One thing was certain, it would be a long healing process for the survivors, and a frightening wake-up call to the entire nation.

An hour after the death of Ezekiel Wiley, a military detachment rode into town. With the sorcery extinguished, the soldiers were not necessary to restore order, but they stuck around to lend aid to those in need, and to make sure any lingering troublemakers were kept in line.

Three days after the violence ended, the truth of the situation had gotten out, despite the telegraph being down. Riders had quickly gone to Yucca Junction to spread the word, and every major paper in America was reporting it. Ezekiel Wiley and Elena Pelletier were being immortalized for their evil deeds, and their magical mischief sent shockwaves throughout all levels of government. From local councils to the Congress itself, everyone was asking themselves how such a thing could happen, and what they could do to prevent such an abuse of power in the future.

The same could be said of the citizens of Selwood, as they picked up the pieces of their shattered lives.

Henry Currant was out in front of the telegraph office—rather, what was left of it. The pile of rubble hadn't been touched since Wiley had torn it apart with a magic tantrum, and work crews were finally picking through the remains. Selwood had to get the telegraph back up and running, and the wires were still intact along the line. Once the wreckage was clear, they could rebuild and reconnect with the outside world in a more permanent fashion.

"Be careful when you get to that back corner," he advised the workmen. "The body of Sorceress Elena is under there, and I imagine she's quite ripe by now."

"Don't worry, we've smelled worse in our time, *Mayor*," the chief replied, prying apart splintered beams with a crowbar.

Henry smiled, amused by the statement on several levels. He hadn't officially won the mayor's seat yet, but his victory was all but assured. In light or recent events, his competitors had withdrawn from the race, and thanks to Henry's valiant service during the chaos he was quickly becoming a local legend, which might have explained their reluctance to waste time and resources to challenge such an opponent.

'Whatever will Thomas Edison think of me now?' he wondered, still unable to take his pending political position seriously. Before Edison's departure, the inventor had assured Henry that the job offer was still open, and Henry wondered if that wouldn't be a more fitting career choice. He'd have some time to consider it, either way.

As Henry watched the workmen picking through the rubble, Joella walked over from the Saloon, carrying a hunk of crumpled paper in her fist. She wasn't looking very happy as she came up beside the telegrapher and stared at the same spot he was observing, seeming uncomfortable in his presence.

"Everything all right, Joella?" Henry asked eventually.

"No," Joella said, tossing the crumpled paper at Henry.

Smoothing out the sheet as best he could, Henry looked it over, spotting Ron's signature at the bottom before reading the rest of the letter. What he found caused him to reread the entire thing several times before finally looking back to Joella.

"Is he serious?" Henry asked.

"Always," Joella said, staring at the rubble pile.

"How could he leave at a time like this?" Henry asked, knowing the answer but reluctant to admit it. Ron had more than enough reasons to cut and run, though Henry had expected more from him. He skimmed over the letter of resignation one more time, and handed it back to Joella. "I guess this makes you Nye County's senior law officer."

"Only until Doliber gets back," Joella said, crumpling the letter again and shoving it into her pants pocket.

"You still think he's alive?" Henry said, feeling the warlock sheriff should have been back or sent some word of his whereabouts by now.

"He's out there," Joella said assuredly. "I just need a little time to figure out where."

The workmen were making short work of the wreckage, and had started picking through the back corner. In a few minutes, Henry expected them to come upon the festering body of Elena Pelletier, which would delay their cleanup efforts for at least a few minutes while they disposed of the remains.

"Any sign of Jesse James?" Henry asked.

"None," Joella said.

Henry nodded and looked thoughtful. "Do you think Flaherty's right, then?"

"I guess it's possible," Joella replied, sounding dubious.

"Only possible?" Henry asked. "I saw the Sheriff's Office burning. Nobody could survive that."

"But Jesse was no longer a man," Joella reminded him. "He was a shadowganger, cursed to exist in a magically contrived body until he repaid his mortal debts. If he died in that fire, he would have been resurrected by morning, which means he's hiding somewhere."

"I prefer Flaherty's explanation," Henry said. "The fire utterly consumed the shadowganger's form, dissipating the energy and releasing Jesse's soul to whatever afterlife he's destined to enter."

Joella shook her head and continued to observe the

workmen. "I guess we'll have to get along without him, either way."

"At least we've still got Flaherty," Henry mentioned. "He assures me that he'll be sticking around for the cleanup."

"However long that lasts," Joella said, stuck in a pessimistic mood. There would be no pleasing her today.

As the men dug deeper into the rubble, Henry began to wonder how long it would be before they hit flesh. They were in the right place, and moving at such a quick pace it was surprising they hadn't already. Moving closer to the worksite, he tried to see how far they had to go, and grew further amazed to see floorboards under their feet. They'd hit the bottom of the wreck, and were clearing off the deck... yet no body could be seen.

Clamoring over the stray hunks of rubble to reach the workers, Henry stood in what would have been the center of the telegraph office, seeking to get his bearings. With much of the clutter out of the way, he could picture the building as it had been, and stared at the spot where he had last seen Elena's body. There was nothing there but gray planks. Not even a speck of blood remained.

Joella walked up beside him and stared at the same spot, causing the workmen to pause in bewilderment.

"Do you think Wiley teleported the body away before he died?" Joella asked, taken aback by the mystery.

"I hope so," Henry said. "I'd hate to think of an alternative."

* * *

Pastor Matthew Jameson marched up the steps of the Lucca Saloon, an establishment he'd sworn he'd never enter. The den of debauchery and sin was not a place for a man of God, nor for anyone who cared about eternal salvation, in his opinion. Yet, so many of his own parishioners still visited this place from time to time—all for the good food, they assured him. Some were believable, others not so much. Still, it was not his place to judge, so he left that for his Heavenly Father.

Walking into the saloon, Jameson looked around at the empty barroom. The place appeared civilized enough, with tables arranged nicely and the fresh scent of baking bread wafting through the air to drown out the stink of spilled drinks.

"Haven't seen you in here before, Preacher," a condescending voice greeted.

Jameson shot his glance to the bar counter, where Solen was lurking. The prim and proper elf looked more appropriately dressed for a church service than waiting tables. "I'm here to see Clarence," the pastor said coldly.

"So soon?" Solen asked cynically.

Jameson wasn't amused, and headed for the stairs.

"Third door on the right," Solen said as the pastor headed up.

It was a peculiar and uncomfortable experience, climbing the stairs and knowing the sort of terse conversation he was destined to have with his former ward. That's why Jameson had put off the visit for days, spending all his time aiding the members of his flock instead. Everyone had been hit hard by the devastation, though most had survived. What material things they'd lost would be regained, their homes rebuilt, and by the grace of God they would prosper anew. Repairing their lives was a simple thing to face, when compared to the conflicting opinions he would be forced to share with young Davison.

Jameson found the third door on the right, and stood in front of it for several moments, trying to think of what he was going to say. So much had happened, and he wasn't sure how Clarence would feel about any of it. Would recent events give them a common ground to restore their friendship, or drive them further apart?

Deciding it was time to find out, Jameson opened the door and looked upon the small room to find an unexpected sight. The thin bed was shaking, and suggestive breathing left little doubt of what was taking place. Horribly embarrassed, the pastor turned to leave, though before he could the couple under the covers took notice.

"Ah, Pastor Matt, how good to see you again."

Jameson turned around to see Flaherty peeking out from under the covers, with the blonde prostitute known as Sandy Annie smiling beside him. They were certainly an odd couple, a tall lady and a little leprechaun, so it was difficult to picture the two of them in the throws of passion, yet there they were, as plain as day.

Uncertain of how to proceed under the circumstances, Jameson merely cleared his throat and averted his gaze.

"What can I do for you, sir?" Flaherty asked.

"I'm looking for Clarence," Jameson said, keeping his eyes aimed toward the wall. "The barkeeper said he was in here."

"Nah, he's across the hall," Flaherty corrected.

"Oh, thank you," Jameson said, turning to the door. "Forgive the intrusion."

"No trouble at all," Flaherty said amiably. "I expect that Solen may be playin' a joke on us both, but I'm sure 'tis nothin' you've nay seen before."

Jameson shivered as he made his way out, and Sandy Annie started laughing before he could shut the door.

'How utterly shameful!' Jameson thought. On any other day, he might have been inclined to lecture the pair about their fornication, but he had more pressing matters to address. Wasting no more time, he opened the door across the hall and found a more comforting sight.

Stepping into the room, Jameson saw Clarence sitting up in bed and reading the Bible. The young man smiled and set the book aside as his old mentor came over to sit beside him.

"You're looking better," Jameson said.

"Yes, I expect to be back on my feet in another day or two," Clarence said pleasantly. "How are things at the church?"

"Very well, considering all that's happened," Jameson said. "A number of us stood guard over the meeting hall, and doused the flames of nearby buildings during the chaos. Our people were not directly affected by the witchcraft, praise God."

"I'm glad," Clarence said. "I'd hate to think of any of them falling prey to such wickedness."

"Indeed," Jameson said with a serious look on his face. "I hope we can all learn a lesson from that dark experience."

"Agreed," Clarence said, growing thoughtful. "Only, what lesson would that be?"

"Surely, it is clear now. All that we have believed has been proven correct. Magic is the work of the devil, an evil force to lead men astray."

Clarence shook his head. "I cannot believe that. I'm sorry."

Jameson leaned back and his eyes grew wide. "How can you not? After everything that has happened, all the death and destruction, you still deny it?"

"I do not blame the magic," Clarence explained. "It is just a tool, no different than a shovel or a hammer. Either can be used to create or destroy. Do you blame the shovel for digging a grave, or the hammer for bludgeoning someone? Surely, no more than you'd accredit the hammer with building a barn, or a shovel for sowing crops. It must be the man behind these implements that determines their function, and whether they are used for good or evil."

Jameson sat silent, reflecting upon the words from his former apprentice. There was logic and wisdom behind the assertions Clarence made. The old preacher could no longer deny the manhood of his former ward, and knew he could no longer lecture him about their differing opinions.

Jameson set a hand upon Clarence's shoulder and said, "I'll pray for you."

"And I'll pray for you," Clarence replied.

Jameson smiled and stood up, proud that Clarence remembered. "Thereby, God will make up the difference. Be well."

With that, the old pastor departed, wondering if they would ever see eye to eye again. He had faith that God could change a willing heart, but which one of them would ever be willing to change?

* * *

It had been a hard ten miles, but Ron finally came upon Yucca Junction near lunchtime, his chest throbbing with each clomp of the horse's hooves. The doctor had warned him against traveling until his shoulder had more time to heal, but he couldn't stay in Selwood. It was too depressing, and left him yearning for more than the clothes on his back and a pistol at his side.

There had to be more to life.

He'd thought of heading back to Montana. The few years

he'd spent in that northern wilderness had been peaceful enough. It was a decent place to hunt and fish, and he had a few friends there. Still, before he headed back to the life he'd known before coming to this arid expanse, there was someone else he wanted to see, someone who might change his mind under the right circumstances.

Feeling in need of a rest, Ron brought his horse to a livery stable, and was planning to find a decent eatery when he spotted a familiar looking carriage. The vehicle was unmistakably the same one that Albert and Fiora Silcox had ridden to Selwood, complete with a golden "S" on the door. He thought they'd be back at the ranch by now.

Throwing down two bits for the horse's afternoon feeding, Ron asked the stable manager where the owners of the carriage were, and the young man was able to point him in the direction of a lavish hotel at the center of town.

Stepping through the revolving door of the Nexus Hotel, Ron felt very out of place. The expensive establishment was not the sort of place he was used to visiting, and his dusty clothes were hardly the kind that the regular clientele would be wearing. Fortunately, the lobby was empty as he made his way over to the front desk.

Catching the eye of the desk attendant on approach, Ron asked where he could find Albert Silcox, and he was quickly directed to the dining room. Entering the spacious eating area, he made his way past the many occupied tables until he spotted the people he was looking for.

Albert and Fiora were at a small table in the back, enjoying a quiet meal with the rest of the hotel guests. As Ron approached, Albert gave him a dejected look and stopped eating.

"Ah, Deputy, I've been expecting you," Albert said solemnly.

"Really?" Ron asked, caught off guard by the chilly greeting.

"You're here to arrest me, aren't you?" Albert said. "Don't worry, I'll go quietly."

Ron pulled up a chair and asked, "Why would I arrest you?"

"For the trouble I caused while under the influence of sorcery. I know, the law might not hold me culpable under the circumstances, but I suppose that'll be up to the jury to decide."

"No, it won't," Ron said, looking at the colorful vegetable dishes sitting in his vicinity. He hadn't eaten much more than jerky all day, and his stomach was grumbling. Somehow, he doubted he could afford anything on the menu.

"Oh, please, Ron," Fiora pleaded, grabbing his arm. "Do what you can for him. It wasn't his fault."

"What wasn't his fault?" Ron questioned, totally perplexed by the pair.

"The bellboy who was shot three nights ago," Albert said. "Isn't that why you're here?"

"What? No," Ron said. "You're saying you shot a bellboy at this hotel?"

"Not personally," Albert said solemnly, "but I feel I was responsible. You see, I came here while under the influence of that dark sorcery, the same plague that caused Selwood to tear itself apart. I fear I unwittingly spread it to a number of susceptible people here, and there were a few spats as a result. A young bellboy got himself shot trying to break up a brawl between the desk clerk and an anti-magic waiter. Once the malicious spell had run its course, I suddenly realized my own part in the affair, so I have remained here, awaiting the law to come."

"If that's the case, I guess you'll be waiting a while longer," Ron said. "I'm not in the arresting business anymore. I resigned from the Sheriff's Department."

"Resigned?" Fiora said loudly. "Whatever for?"

"A whole lot of reasons," Ron replied. "This latest bout of chaos was just the last straw in a whole stack of them. After seeing as much death as I have, it's time for a change of pace. In fact, I'd like to come work at your ranch, if there's an opening."

Fiora smiled and leaned over to give Ron a kiss. "Of course there is. Right, Grandfather?"

"Have you done much ranching, Mr. Grimes?" Albert asked, sounding more like his usual self again. The morbid worry was fading from him fast.

"I grew up on a farm and have done a bit of droving," Ron answered. "Of course, it may be a few weeks before I'm much good to you," he added, touching his wounded shoulder.

Albert reached over and gently pried off the bandage. "Just a flesh wound? I'm sure the hotel medic can take care of that before we leave."

"They have a med-lock on staff?" Ron asked, knowing he shouldn't be surprised, considering the extravagance of the establishment.

Albert nodded and stood up. "He doubles as the head chef. I'll introduce you."

"Much obliged," Ron said, following Albert as they crossed the room. He was curious about the kind of healer who would work as a cook. Did the man practice on the steaks and fillets, or stock the shelves with the bodies of his failures? What a twisted imagination he had grown.

Nearing the back of the dining room, Albert added, "I hope you won't mind escorting my granddaughter back to the ranch alone. I feel compelled to remain here until I'm certain things have blown over."

"Sure," Ron replied. "Though, I wouldn't stick around this hotel forever. You weren't to blame for the magic plague, so I doubt anyone's going to hold you responsible."

"We can certainly hope not," Fiora said, pressing against Ron in a comforting manner.

Passing through the kitchen door, Ron smiled beneath his beard, knowing he'd made the right decision in leaving Selwood. The future was looking more promising already.

* * *

It was cold and dark when Jesse James awoke. Picking his face up off the ground, the resurrected outlaw fought to get his bearings, and the pitch black didn't help. It took a minute for him to get to his feet and he started feeling his way around, unable to find a wall of any kind. There was plenty of space on all sides of him, leaving him to wonder where he had been delivered.

Could this be a prelude to the afterlife at last? He shuddered to think of spending all eternity in this vacant space, though knew it was the least he deserved. So many lives he'd ended, so many widows he'd made, all in the name of revenge and his own self-aggrandizement. He was loath to admit it, but there was truly nothing righteous about what he'd done, even when it was justified.

As he continued to ponder his circumstances, a faint twinkling caught his eye. The tiny fleck of light appeared in the distance, so far away he wasn't sure it was real at first. That tiny star amidst the curtain of absolute night twinkled so faintly but began to glow little by little as he studied it. As it got larger and brighter, it was obviously too close to the ground to be a celestial object, yet it advanced unlike anything material he had ever seen. The glow persisted, getting closer, until he could identify it as a humanoid form. There was a body within that shimmering light, though it was too bright to see more than the faint outlines of appendages.

When the being came near, Jesse had to shy his eyes away, until suddenly the light faded. Taking his arm away from his face and looking forward again, he saw a woman standing before him, dressed in a silver gown and still glowing, but at a far dimmer illumination. She was impressive to behold, as he imagined an angel would be. She smiled at him and reached out a hand for him to take.

"Am I dead?" Jesse asked, wary of the stranger.

"Oh, no, my dear," the lady said with a comforting accent. "You and I are very much alive. My name is Elena, and I am very pleased to make your acquaintance, Mr. James."

Won over by her cordial greeting, Jesse took the offered hand and kissed it. "Always a pleasure to meet a fine Southern Belle," he said with his roguish charm. "I take it you've heard of me, then?"

"Very much so," Elena said with a smirk. "In fact, I'd say we have very much in common." With a flick of her wrist, the sorceress ignited a series of torches that hung on the distant walls.

"Where are we?" Jesse asked, examining the vast cavern.

"An old hiding place," Elena replied. "Come, there is much for you to see."

Jesse followed Elena toward a distant crevice, feeling

perfectly at ease. It felt odd to be so at peace with himself, and he knew he ought to be suspicious of his apparent savior, though he couldn't bring himself to question her motives. A voice in the back of his head told him to be happy and content, and he had no means to resist it.

"I know you have many questions," Elena said, as her magic continued to address the nagging doubts that lurked in the back of Jesse's mind. With an iota of her influence, she augmented the spell and sent it sweeping over his consciousness. As the manipulative sorcery did its work, she assured him, "All will be revealed in good time, my young apprentice."

"Of course, Mistress," Jesse replied.

* * *

The void was growing dark.

Doliber couldn't tell how long he'd been hanging in nothingness, staring at the blank screen that Ezekiel Wiley had created shortly before his departure. Its faint outline was now fading into nothingness, just like everything else in this place.

The magic still swirled all around, though Doliber's ability to perceive it was fleeting. There was only so long he could maintain a "mystic eye," and there seemed to be little point. The presence of pure energy all around did not provide a solution to his predicament. He had no way to interact with this sort of mysticism, no way to break free.

The dark was almost comforting. After all, what was there to fear from nothing? Best to close his eyes and rest, he decided. What else could he do?

So, Doliber set his mind to sleep, waiting for a rescue that was destined to come.

THE END...

...BUT FOR HOW LONG?

BONUS:
CUT SCENE FROM CHAPTER 3

As I went over the first draft of "The Six-Gun Conjurer," I ran into a little snag concerning the two separate storylines that run parallel for much of the story. Though I wrote the whole thing in-sequence, it turned out that the part featuring Joella ended up running a day longer than the story that takes place in Selwood, and in order to synch up the timelines I had to move Joella's departure up a few hours. To bring her back into chronological alignment with the rest of the story, I rewrote it so she left in the afternoon, during the political speeches in chapter 2, rather than later that night.

Changing things also gave me the opportunity to explore the growing emotions between her and Doliber, showing that her unrequited love might not be a lost cause. The first hints of the sheriff softening up to her advances can be seen in the rewritten segment, though it still remains pretty ambiguous. The potential for a relationship is something that helps to set up the forthcoming fourth book in the series, which will feature Joella's mission to save the man she so admires.

One downside to changing this scene was that we lost an exchange between Joella and Ron. This little piece does a lot to illustrate their own feelings for one another (purely platonic), and it gives readers a good example of the camaraderie and respect that is shared between these two characters. Even though it no longer fits in the book, it's a good bonus for those of you who are philanthropic enough to purchase a copy of the published work.

When I originally wrote this scene, Joella stuck around until after Edison was shot, and sneaked off in the middle of the night in chapter 3. Here's the original scene, as I first wrote it in November 2011:

The Bormans' Boarding House was pretty quiet around midnight, as Joella made her way down the stairs. She didn't want a big send-off, not when she wasn't sure if she'd be coming back. All she owned was in the pack on her back and the saddlebags on her horse. It wasn't much to show for the past four months of upholding the law, but she wasn't in it for the money. Nobody ever got rich fighting crime, and she'd known plenty of wealthy crooks. Fighting for what was right had to be a reason all in itself.

As much as she'd come to enjoy being a deputy, there was another wrong she had to challenge. Her sister needed her, so she was off to save the day.

Doliber had given her permission to leave, and promised that her job would be waiting for her when she got back—if she wanted it. That had been before the shooting, and she hadn't checked in with him since, fearing he'd change his mind. Better to not give him the opportunity.

She was ready to go under cover of darkness, and take rest once she was a few miles out of town. The itchy straw bed of the boarding house wasn't much better than the ground, anyway, so it wouldn't be a great inconvenience. She still had the want of a decent mattress, but it was nothing that couldn't wait. Personal pampering was overrated.

Closing the door to the boarding house, Joella crossed the open porch and made for her horse that was tied to the hitching rail. She was ready to mount when a voice startled her.

"Not even a goodbye?"

Joella recognized the voice of Ron Grimes. That low, gruff tone was hard to miss, and she'd heard it plenty.

"Did Doliber send you to fetch me?" Joella asked, getting

on her horse.

"Nope," Ron said, walking over. There weren't any street lights at this end of town, so only the moon revealed his stout form. "We haven't talked much since the annulment. Figured I ought to at least see you off."

The annulment. Mention of it brought back a flurry of bad memories, and a bitter reminder of why she was in this mess in the first place. For a time, she'd trapped Ron into a sham marriage, to protect herself from the ambition of Mactus Sellius. If not for a meddling U.S. Marshal, the imitation might have worked, but fate had chosen to expose the truth of the matter. An elf and a dwarf were never meant to be together, and she decided that a proper shunning was more desirable than coupling with either Mactus or Ron. So, she remained single, and very much alone.

"Did Doliber tell you why I'm leaving?" Joella asked.

"Just said you had family business," Ron replied, stepping up onto the porch deck. It added a couple of feet, but Joella's mount left her taller still.

"Then you understand," Joella said.

Ron nodded, then said, "If you need a hand, I'm there for you."

Joella appreciated the sentiments, but couldn't accept. "I'll be fine on my own," she said, knowing it was something she had to face by herself. Ron was good with a gun, but she didn't expect there to be any shooting, though one never could tell. She was riding into a war of ideas, which meant anything was possible.

"Don't be gone long," Ron said, bidding her farewell. It was as close to a compliment as the gruff dwarf could muster, and Joella felt reassured. While she'd never felt love for Ron, she did have the utmost respect for him, and it was good to know the feeling was mutual.

Nudging her horse, Joella turned to head out of town. The road west was dry and rocky, but she'd traveled it before. With any luck, she'd be able to cut the trip short with a quick teleport, though she hadn't tested her limited mystical ability since straining herself in a harrowing feat to save Doliber's life.

That daring move had proven successful, but it could have killed her, and she wasn't eager meet the reaper.

Doliber assured her there was nothing wrong with her brain, or so his own warlock skills told him. Though she trusted his judgment, there remained a lingering doubt. She wasn't sure what would happen the next time she processed magic energy through her brain, but she'd have to find out sooner or later. She'd either work up the nerve in the morning, or end up spending a week on horseback, worrying about her sister.

The dark trail welcomed her like an old friend, and for a moment she let herself forget about the troubles ahead, basking in the comfort of the open range.

ABOUT THE AUTHOR:

Martin T. Ingham is the author of various Science Fiction & Fantasy works, and is currently the Senior Editor of Martinus Publishing. His more notable works include the *West of the Warlock* series, *The Guns of Mars*, and *The Rogue Investigations*. When he isn't writing, he likes to dabble in numismatics, horology, and antique auto restoration, among other hobbies. He currently resides in his hometown of Robbinston, Maine, with his wife, Jenna, and their four children, Sylvia, Wyatt, Kathryn, and Lois.

Learn more about Martin's works at his website:
http://www.martiningham.com

<u>Also by Martin T. Ingham:</u>

THE FIRST TWO VOLUMES IN
MARTIN T. INGHAM'S
WEST OF THE WARLOCK SERIES:
<u>A CONTINUING SAGA!</u>

A dwarven gunslinger, a warlock sheriff, an independent elvish widow, and a scandalous elvish barkeeper, along with a whole host of Wild West characters set the stage for thrilling Fantasy Western adventures.

Available in Print, Kindle, and Nook formats.

http://www.martinus.us/books.html#westwarlock
West of the Warlock ISBN#978-0-9887685-1-2
The Curse of Selwood ISBN#978-0-9887685-0-5

Also by Martin T. Ingham:

Available in Print or Kindle format

Join rogue investigators Zachary McCain and John Rage as they seek to uncover the truth behind the paranormal and the unexplained!

ISBN#978-1-5003143-0-9

Also Available from Martinus Publishing

Stories of the future wars, and the veterans who fight them. 17 tales of valor, of brave men and women standing their ground in the world beyond tomorrow!

Also Available from Martinus Publishing

Altered America:
21 "What If" Tales about America's past!

Also Available from Martinus Publishing

**21 Time Travel stories by 20 different authors.
Explore the distant past, the far future,
and everywhere in between!**

Order your copy today:
http://www.martinus.us/books.html#temporalelement

ISBN#978-0-9887685-3-6